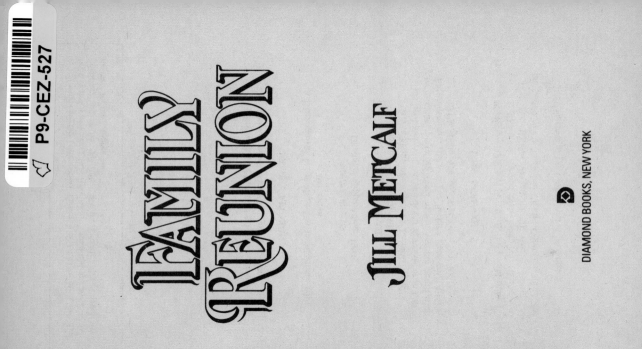

# FAMILY REUNION

## JILL METCALF

DIAMOND BOOKS, NEW YORK

This book is a Diamond original edition, and has never been previously published.

FAMILY REUNION

A Diamond Book / published by arrangement with the author

PRINTING HISTORY
Diamond edition / June 1994

ISBN: 0-7865-0011-5

Diamond Books are published by The Berkley Publishing Group, 200 Madison Avenue, New York, NY 10016.
DIAMOND and the "D" design are trademarks belonging to Charter Communications, Inc.

PRINTED IN THE UNITED STATES OF AMERICA

10  9  8  7  6  5  4  3  2  1

To Adele Leone and Carrie Feron,
super agent and editor extraordinaire

My sincerest thanks for your friendship and guidance

# PROLOGUE

Four powerful Clydesdales were harnessed and backed into the traces of the long cartage wagon. The animals stood patiently, with only a sporadic ripple of muscle or stomping of a feathered hoof, while the reinforced wagon bed was piled high with assorted goods, foodstuffs, and barrels of ale. When all was ready, the driver and his brother climbed up to the high seat and the horses were clicked into action. Slowly the heavily ladened vehicle rumbled forward, lumbering through Richmond's warehouse district, known as Shockoe Slip.

A few blocks away a man waved farewell to a friend and made his way toward Bank Street. His spirits were high, his step light this fine early spring day as he tipped his black bowler hat to passersby.

He had yet to reach his thirtieth year, but he had achieved much. Known as one of Richmond's brightest young lawyers, he had successfully defended an innocent young man accused of murdering two girls. The verdict had come down only the previous day, and he had been celebrating with high-placed friends most of the night. He was brilliant and everyone knew it. A man who was going places, and would-be rising stars, just starting out in the legal profession, were battling for the opportunity to latch on to his coattails and follow him on the way up.

He smiled at a particularly lovely young woman and tipped his hat again before he stepped out onto Bank Street.

Two playful boys were plaguing pedestrians at the intersection of Governor and Bank streets that day, begging pennies from everyone they encountered. Those failing to supply the funds were meted out a punishment of one well-aimed stone that usually struck the victim on the back or, if the boy's aim was particularly good, squarely on the rump. One stone missed its mark entirely.

The lead Clydesdale was startled when the stone struck his flank, and his cry of confusion prompted panic in his fellows. The wagon careened onto Bank Street, its load shifting, and almost instantaneously men were shouting and women screaming.

Distracted, the brilliant young lawyer smiled at a particularly lovely young woman and tipped his hat before he stepped out onto Bank Street.

His name was Chad Moran.

# CHAPTER
## ONE

Everything about Treemont Farm had flourished these ten years past.

Including Jennifer Downing.

Jennifer whirled through the steps of the waltz in the arms of Damon Lockyer, her flared skirt of yellow Tabby silk swirling around their ankles.

It was a local celebration. Her eighteenth birthday.

Young men, dressed in black, formal evening attire, flirted and teased young women, gowned and bejeweled. They were friends, all.

They had spent the day leisurely riding across the lush, rolling landscape of Treemont and were now wholly engaged in the spirit of the party.

"I think Jeremy will ask for Megan soon," Jennifer said to her dancing partner.

The dark-haired, stern-visaged Damon grunted. He preferred not to discuss such things, having only recently had his own suit refused by the woman in his arms.

"Don't you think?" she pressed.

"Luck to him," he muttered.

Jennifer raised her pale blue eyes, her frown now mirroring his. "I'm sorry, Damon," she said quietly. "But I thought we had an understanding."

"Oh, we do," he said nastily. "I understand completely that you don't want me."

3

With a weary sigh she shook her head. "Damon, we've been friends most of our lives. I'm just not . . ."

"In love with me?"

"I love you," she said softly, "but as my dearest friend."

"Friends don't make husbands or bedfellows, do they, Jen?" He thought about where they were and what he was doing to her as his eyes roamed over her pretty, unhappy face. Well, she could hardly expect him to be in a party mood. He, one of Virginia's most eligible sons, was not taking rejection lightly. In fact, it stuck in his throat and tasted damned sour.

Damon's hand pressed tightly against Jennifer's back before he turned them in a small, tight circle.

Jennifer held on to his shoulder and followed his lead. The silence between them had grown heavy and awkward, and she sought some diversion, some means of salvaging the remainder of the evening. She supposed the best way would be to avoid him for the rest of the night, but somehow she could not bring herself to do that. "I wonder when they'll bring Florence out of hiding?" she ventured.

Damon continued to appear disgruntled, but he responded to the change of topic.

"What makes you think Florence will be appearing?" smile. "She's my surprise, of course," Jennifer said, daring a I know Maggie and Hunter arranged for her to come." Her eldest sister, Maggie, had a way of knowing what would please Jennifer most, and Hunter, Maggie's husband, would see that it was arranged, if at all possible. There was only one small flaw in Jennifer's logic; it was a matter of whether or not Florence could tear herself away from her work.

"She's my surprise, of course," Jennifer said, daring a smile. "I'm not certain where they've been hiding her, but I know Maggie and Hunter arranged for her to come."

Jennifer's second eldest sister lived in New York City where she worked as a writer. And she was a damned good one in the eyes of her sisters. The competition was stiff, but Florence was slowly making a name for herself. Jennifer knew that Florence was making enemies amongst a clique of male journalists who had absolutely no use for a woman in their midst. Furthermore, Florence could little afford to ignore an opportunity for a story simply to make a trip home for her sister's party.

But Jennifer continued to hope.

The music stopped and Damon led Jennifer across the room.

"Denise and Tim have arrived," she said happily, dragging her escort toward the wide double doors of Treemont's front parlor.

Damon nodded a greeting to Dr. Tim Fletcher as the sisters embraced.

"Happy birthday, Jen," Denise said.

Jennifer stepped back, smiling warmly. "Where are the boys?"

Denise smiled triumphantly. "With Tim's parents for the night. God bless them. They've never taken all four of their grandsons at one time until tonight," she added lightly. "I hope the poor dears survive."

"So, have you got Florence?" Jennifer asked.

Denise arched a fair brow in surprise. "Florence? Jen, she was home not that long ago."

"Not since Christmas," the younger sister returned. "I know she's coming and someone's been hiding her."

Damon drifted away as he noticed the object of Jennifer's hopes slipping into the room from the dining area; he was not in the mood to participate in another family reunion.

Denise continued to hold Jennifer's attention while studiously avoiding looking over her younger sister's shoulder. Still, she was well aware that Jennifer's "surprise" was descending upon them.

"Happy birthday, Jen," Florence whispered.

Jennifer whirled, grinning. "I knew you would come,"

she cried, laughing as she threw her arms around her sister's neck. "Thank you for coming," she said softly. "I know you can little afford the trip." Although Hunter and Maggie provided Florence with a monthly stipend, living in New York was expensive, and Florence had little coin to squander.

Florence brushed off Jennifer's concern.

"Let's go somewhere where we can talk for a bit," Jennifer suggested, taking hold of her sister's hand.

The two young women crossed the room to make a discreet exit, but as Jennifer moved behind Hunter and Maggie, her attention was caught by the conversation that was being introduced by a distant neighbor.

"You've heard Chad Moran is back?" Charles Getty asked.

Maggie had not heard and said so.

"Half a man, mind you," Charles added with the relish of one who enjoys knowing news first.

Maggie started, frowning. "What on earth does that mean?"

Hunter, knowing Moran was an old and dear friend of his wife, sensed something unpleasant coming and tucked Maggie under his arm.

Getty dropped the bomb square in the middle of the small group of people. "No legs."

There were gasps of dismay all around him.

"Well, the legs are there," he explained further. "But they're useless."

Jennifer scowled at Charles. She remembered Chad Moran from her youth. She had once thought of him as tall as a giant and more handsome than any other prince of her dreams. "That hardly makes him half a man," she said hotly.

Maggie's eyes darted a warning to her sister. Jennifer refused to take heed. "What a terrible thing to say."

Getty did not care for any interference when he was the center of attention. "What would *you* call a man who can't walk?"

"A friend!" Jennifer retorted.

"Jen," Maggie said softly, placing a restraining hand on her sister's arm. Turning her attention to their guest, she explained. "Mr. Getty, your news is distressing to us," she said. "You must know that Chad Moran has been a close and cherished friend of the Downings for years. Our fathers were friends, if you'll recall."

Getty shot Jennifer a glance that clearly said he thought she was impertinent at the very least. He merely muttered an excuse and slinked away.

Maggie turned a worried frown in Hunter's direction.

"We'll visit Chad tomorrow."

Jennifer looked thoughtful.

But the four Downing sisters, escorted by Hunter Maguire, were turned away by Chad Moran's man the following afternoon.

"Perhaps Chad doesn't want anyone to see him the way he is now, Mag," Denise speculated.

Jennifer watched Maggie, her oldest sister, carefully.

Chad Moran and Maggie Downing had once been considered destined for marriage. But Chad had gone to Richmond to school when they were very young, and Maggie had suffered tragedy while he had been gone. Their lives had lost their previous complementary pattern and had turned around over the years.

And, more important, Hunter Maguire had happened upon Maggie Downing's life.

But Chad and Maggie had remained friends.

Jennifer stared slightlessly at the passing scenery as they returned to Treemont. She was miffed with Chad. How dare he snub Maggie. It was an embarrassment, actually, to be turned away from his door. His status as a friend had slipped a notch or two in her estimation. No, it was more than that. She had once fawned on his every word, admired him, and followed him around like a lost puppy. He had always teased her about her fat braids and tweaked her nose playfully. She had been too young to realize he had simply been treating her like any other child he knew. Jennifer tried to remember how old she had been when she first knew she was in love with Chad. Nine, perhaps? Ten? Well, she had gotten over her puppy love years ago. Still, there remained that ghostly feeling, that golden glow of first love that fades but never truly evaporates. That first love, the awakening of emotions, survives maturity and separation and other loves. There was a small but special corner of Jennifer Downing's heart that was reserved for Chad Moran and would always be there.

Simply put, Jennifer, like her eldest sister, cared what happened to him.

Obviously, someone needed to remind Chad of that fact.

It was late afternoon when a noise beyond the open doors of his library attracted his attention.

Chad Moran looked up from the book in his lap to see a woman bathed in light from an early summer sun.

Without invitation Jennifer stepped into the room and walked toward him.

She looked at him closely. He was not so different from the young man she remembered. He still possessed those dark brown eyes that were so intense they seemed to analyze a body on the spot. And his hair looked silky soft, the color reminding her of chestnuts. But a small touch of gray now accented the brown; unusual, she thought, for she knew he had yet to reach his thirtieth year. Still, it added dignity, softening the hard plains and high cheekbones of his face. It was a man's face, to be sure; gone was the boy she had adored as a child. "Do you remember me?" she asked softly.

With a weary sigh Chad closed the book and flung it onto a nearby table. How could he not remember? She was a woman now, all gracious curves and tall and slim, although the suggestion of youth stayed with her. Her hair was not as pale as Maggie's but was a darker shade of pale. The eyes spoke pure Downing, however—the palest of blue—and her complexion reminded him so of her older sister, his childhood friend. "I'm not receiving visitors, Jennifer."

Jennifer was careful to focus her attention on his face and not on the chair in which he sat. "I'm not a *visitor*," she said. "I'm a friend."

He laced his fingers together in his lap and gripped, hard. "Very well. I'm not receiving *friends*." "Why?"

Chad stared at her, incredulous.

"It doesn't appear as if I'm interrupting anything," she pointed out.

"You're violating my desire to be alone," he said firmly. "Does that suffice?"

"No," she said simply.

Chad could feel his temper rising. "You are here uninvited, Miss Downing," he said in an even tone. "That signifies trespassing. Please leave."

Jennifer looked to the left of his location and walked toward a straight-backed chair. "We were just informed of your return last evening," she said conversationally as she made herself as comfortable as possible. Taking the time to smooth her split skirt over her knees, she steeled her expression against the sight of the large wheels that bracketed his legs. "When we were turned away by your man earlier today, Maggie became very concerned that you might be ill."

"Perhaps you should leave now and assure your sister

that I am not ill," he said harshly.

Jennifer's gaze locked with his. "I know it must be difficult—"

"You don't know anything."

"Perhaps you could explain to me, then," she said firmly. "But try not to be too rude."

Infuriated, Chad pushed back on a wheel, turning his chair toward the open door. "Gerome!" he bellowed.

"Are you going to turn away all your friends?" she asked quietly.

Chad ignored her.

The large man Jennifer had seen earlier in the day stepped into the room. She had once seen pictures of a similarly muscular man somewhere before; that man had been a wrestler.

"Miss Downing is leaving."

Jennifer smiled up at the man who approached her chair. "No," she said, "Miss Downing is not."

Though Gerome was paid to carry out his employer's wishes, he appeared to hesitate at manhandling a pretty young woman.

Stymied, Chad frowned at his guest. "A polite young woman does not impose herself where she is not wanted," he snapped.

Jennifer's smile remained firmly in place. "This is 1892 and 'polite young women' have learned not to quake when snapped at by very rude men!"

Gerome watched silently.

"There is a cure for my rudeness," Chad informed her. "All you have to do is leave."

Jennifer frowned, shaking her head. "I can't do that, Chad," she said quietly.

"Why not, dammit?" he thundered.

"Because I care about you."

Chad stared at her for the space of several heartbeats and then his head fell forward, his eyes closing against some inner pain as his hands gripped the wheels of his chair. "If you truly cared, Jen, you would leave," he said quietly.

Jennifer shot Gerome White a pleading look, and the man, after a moment of indecision, glanced at the bowed head of Chad Moran before leaving them alone.

Jennifer watched the handsome man, so changed in temperament. She wished she knew the proper words to comfort him. "I'm surprised you recognized me," she said finally with feigned cheerfulness. "It's been years since you last visited Treemont."

Slowly, Chad raised his head, the palms of his hands moving down his face as if he could scrub all evidence of emotion away. "I'm not very good company, Jennifer," he said quietly.

"That's all right," she said brightly. "I've been surrounded by bores many a time."

His hands fell to his lap, and he looked at her as a hint of a smile curved his lips. "Have you?"

"Hmm."

He looked at her then; really looked. The braids and freckles were gone, replaced by a clear, porcelain complexion that boasted a hint of roses across high cheekbones. Her hair appeared abundant still, piled high upon her head and tightly curled in a crown. Her blue jacket was fashionably slim at the waist, sporting leg-o'-mutton sleeves and dark braid at the lapels and around the hem. Her matching split skirt deviated from the normal flare and was short, reaching only to the tops of her high-button black boots. She was slim and elegant and quite lovely. "You've grown up."

Jennifer laughed. "Children have a habit of doing that."

Chad watched her without speaking.

"Maggie and Hunter have another son," Jennifer informed him, attempting to fill the silence. "Were you aware of that?"

Sons? He didn't want to think about sons. For him there would be none.

In response to her question he shook his head. "Sons? Maggie had a girl . . . Courtney," he recalled.

"You *are* behind," she teased. "They've had two sons since Courtney."

Chad nodded before staring thoughtfully beyond the open patio doors, fixing his gaze momentarily on some spot outside. "How is Maggie?" he asked.

"Well. Happy," she added. "Still madly in love with Hunter and enchanted by her children."

His attention returned to Jennifer then. "That's good to know. Maggie deserves to be happy. I recall a time when she wasn't."

Jennifer's head tipped slightly to the side, her eyes questioning. "Do you know about that?"

Chad shook his head. "I remember only that there was a period in her life when she was very unhappy."

"I remember, too," she said. "But no one would ever tell me what had happened to make Maggie so miserable." Jennifer shook off the unpleasant thoughts of the past and told him about the lives of her other sisters.

He was most stunned to learn about Florence. "Shy little Florence?" he repeated a second time.

"I know," Jennifer said lightly. "No one ever thought Florence would leave the safety of Treemont, let alone enter a profession. It's hardly done, is it? A woman entering a man's world? But she's good, Chad," she added with pride and conviction. "She really is very good."

"And what about you?" he asked. "Are you surrounded by beaux vying for your attentions? Or are you madly in love with just one?"

Jennifer grinned. "I haven't been 'madly in love' since you," she said bluntly.

Chad blinked in surprise. "What?"

She nodded her head vigorously and laughed with just

a hint of discomfort over her confession. "I suffered a terrible crush, you know."

He felt suddenly very uneasy with the turn of their conversation. "I'm glad you got over it," he said bluntly.

But Jennifer was not entirely certain she had gotten over it. He had changed, it was true, but he was even more attractive. The boyish planes of his face had matured, had become ruggedly handsome. And he had not lost that air of magnetism that had pulled her toward him even as a girl. The difference now was, the magnetism seemed more potent. She wondered briefly if it could be pity that was moving her to suffer his curtness. Pity had never moved her to feeling her *body* did not. The attraction she thought had vanished when she had brushed out her braids forever was still there. Perhaps in smaller proportion, but it seemed to exist nonetheless.

Chad was the first to break eye contact and bellowed for Gerome.

Jennifer thought he was going to charge the poor man with a second attempt at evicting her, and she did not want to leave. Not yet. "Tea would be nice," she said hurriedly. "I assume you're calling him to serve some?"

Chad cast her a glance that could not exactly be described as warm. "Tea?"

"Tea," she repeated, smiling sweetly at Chad's man. She then proceeded to tuck one foot beneath her bottom, firmly ensconcing herself and letting Chad know she planned to remain.

"You're quite persistent." He turned back to her after Gerome had left them once again. "You'd make a good lawyer."

"We've faced each other, Chad," she said softly. "We've summed up the changes in each other. Now surely we can relax and continue catching up on all the missing years."

"One of us has changed more than the other."

Jennifer smiled. "True," she said quietly. "I don't recall you being quite so crusty."

"I don't care to be patronized, Miss Downing," he said tightly and turned his chair away from her, making his way toward a small table near the open French doors. His hands shook with agitation as he reached for a glass and the crystal decanter of brandy.

"I'm sorry you're in that chair," she said firmly. "But that does not give you license to be rude. Forgive me my human failings, but I can't seem to let go of someone I didn't come here out of curiosity, to gawk or pity or care about simply because of some damned accident. I embarrass you. I came here to remind you that there are people who love you and want to be supportive."

"Those are your needs, not mine." He took a healthy drink from his glass.

"Are they?" she asked softly.

"Gerome is all the help I need."

"You haven't quite driven me away yet, Mr. Moran."

He turned on her. "What will it take?"

"Why did you come back here if you didn't want to see any of us?" she asked calmly. "Did you really believe you could hide here at Stonehall?"

He had thought precisely that. He had come because he could not stand the piteous glances of his friends. He had come because he could not stand to see other men turn away to hide their sympathy and their relief that his plight was not theirs. He had come because his career was shattered, because he would never again command the attention of a jury with words, because he would never hold them spellbound and attentive to the importance of facts while they were preoccupied with his chair and speculations of how he came to be in it. He had returned to Stonehall to retire from the world. It was becoming increasingly apparent, however, that Jennifer Downing was not about to allow that to happen with any ease.

When he continued to ignore her, Jennifer rose to her feet. "Well, the least I can do is assure Maggie that she needn't anticipate attending your funeral in the near future," she said wryly.

Jennifer's gaze inspected the richly appointed room as she walked slowly toward the open French doors. It was a masculine room filled with overstuffed chairs upholstered in dark green. A huge rosewood desk filled one corner, and everywhere there were books. It was a cozy room for a man to choose as his prison.

She stopped beside his chair, looking down on the top of his bowed head. "I believed you were ten feet tall when I was a girl," she said softly.

Chad raised achingly expressive eyes, dark and brooding. "How tall could a man in a wheelchair be?"

"As tall as he chose," she said softly. "The funny thing is, the man I remember could be as tall as he chose to be and without having to stand on his feet."

# CHAPTER TWO

Jennifer did not tell Maggie about her visit to Stonehall. Certainly, she would have liked to assure her sister that Chad Moran was well, in relative terms. She was not at all certain about his state of mind, however. And for some reason she enjoyed her small secret.

Chad surprised Jennifer, however, by sending an invitation requesting that Maggie join him for tea.

After the earlier rejection, her husband was mystified.

"He has invited me, Hunter," Maggie said as she searched a drawer for a missing glove. "I can't refuse. And it's about time someone welcomed him back. Why shouldn't it be me?"

Hunter stood beside the dressing table, leaning back against the wall. He was nearing forty but was as straight and tall and as darkly beautiful as when Maggie had first met him. "Need I remind you that he refused you once?"

Maggie sighed wearily. "No, you need not. Perhaps he had his reasons. Perhaps we arrived at an inopportune moment."

"It's only going to upset you to see him like that, my love."

Maggie nodded her head. "Probably."

"I'm coming with you."

Maggie held up the matched gloves triumphantly. "Thank you, darling, but that's really not necessary. Jennifer will keep me company."

"And lend support?" Maggie stared up into the black eyes that mirrored his concern. "If need be."

"I *must*," she returned with a gentle smile of understanding; after almost nine years of marriage she knew his thoughts very well, and he was always protective.

"I'm coming along, regardless," he said firmly.

Maggie laughed and kissed his cheek.

Jennifer was already seated in the open carriage when Hunter gave his wife a hand up.

"What do we have here?" he teased as his eyes roamed quickly over her outfit. "Is that new?"

Jennifer shot him a disgusted look. "A gentleman would tell me I look lovely."

"You look lovely," he returned wryly.

In fact, she was lovely. Jennifer's hair was gathered back at the sides, falling loosely down her back. It was much darker than Maggie's almost white-blond hair, tending more to a light brown but highlighted with a softer shade. Her eyes were the pale blue of the Downings, and her complexion was clear and perfect. She was wearing a pert straw hat that barely protected her nose from the sun and a pale blue ruffled blouse with a darker blue skirt that was cinched at her small waist by a black belt.

Once the carriage moved off down Treemont's long lane, Maggie looked worried.

Secretly Jennifer shared some of her sister's concern, but only because she had kept her previous visit to Stonehall secret. She silently worried that this second visit could be a duplicate of the previous one. Or, if Chad were so inclined, this visit could be more impassioned than the last. Although, she reasoned, Chad *had* extended the invitation. Still . . . As a diversive tactic, to quell her own nervous tension, she filled the silence with good-natured goading. "Did you know that Maggie and Chad Moran were once considered a match?" she asked her brother-in-law.

Hunter had known that, of course. In fact, he had met Moran on one or two occasions. But he and Jennifer were known for their love of playful sparring. "Do tell."

Jennifer shifted and smoothed her skirt as she primed herself for the match. "Oh, yes," she said, "They were wildly, passionately in love."

"Jennifer!" Maggie laughed. "That's an outrageous—"

"And everyone hereabouts just knew that they were destined to marry."

"We were children together. Nothing more," her sister sniffed.

"Now don't fib, sister," Jennifer cajoled, smiling sweetly at her brother-in-law. "I know of the monumental love between you and Chad Moran when you were young."

A corner of Hunter's lips tipped upward ever so slightly. "Then, how is it *I* got the woman?"

"I'll never understand *that*," she muttered. She was not, however, able to convince them she was disappointed.

Hunter laughed.

With a sigh Maggie admonished, "I hope you two *children* will behave while we're at Stonehall."

As they neared their destination, an awkward silence fell.

As the carriage wound its way around the circular drive in front of the stone mansion, Maggie stared at the house she had known as a girl. "I don't think I've been here since Chad's father died," she said quietly. "That must be at least ten or more years."

"The place hasn't change much," Jennifer offered. Now that they were here, she worried about Chad's motives. He had been so adamant about not wanting to see his friends, about not needing anyone except that large bear he called Gerome.

Maggie shook her head, still trying to recollect the span of time. "It's a shame we've seen him on so very few occasions since Mr. Moran passed away. Chad was already enrolled in school in Richmond when that happened," she explained to her husband. "And his mother has been gone for years." In all the time she and Hunter had been married, Chad had ridden over to Treemont only twice. The driver pulled the carriage to a halt. "It's been so many years."

Jennifer looked at the stone facade, surprised that the house appeared so small. She had not noticed that the day Gerome had turned them away, and it looked so much larger when one approached from the back. "I remember the house as being larger," she said quietly.

Maggie smiled as Hunter helped her down to the cobbled drive. "You were much smaller when you were last here. Everything looks large to children."

Jennifer was careful not to correct Maggie. Somehow she felt that Maggie would be hurt to learn that Chad had to be persuaded—if that term could be applied to what she had done—to extend an invitation to his childhood friend.

The stone front of the house was exceptionally deceiving. Gordon Moran had added a substantial structure onto the original stone cottage in hopes that the numerous bedrooms would one day be filled with sons. Unfortunately, that dream was never to be realized, and Chad had remained an only child.

Once the two woman had righted the back, trainlike hems of their skirts, Hunter followed them across the flagstone patio that was flush to the drive. Unlike most homes in the area, Stonehall had no steps, no front porch or overhang, and no pillars, and so retained its cottagelike appearance.

Hunter dropped the black iron knocker against the door a time or two before stepping back with the two women.

Moments later a large muscular man appeared before them in the open doorway.

"We're the Maguires," Hunter explained, before turning briefly. "And Miss Jennifer Downing. I believe Mr. Moran is expecting us."

The man nodded abruptly and turned away.

"Jolly, isn't he?" Jennifer muttered.

Maggie shot her a dark glance.

"Mr. Gloom," Jennifer whispered.

"Stop that!" Maggie hissed.

Hunter grinned and shook his head.

Mr. *Gloom* returned quickly enough. "This way," he said.

Jennifer's eyes grew large and round as she followed Gerome inside; she had not remembered the entrance to the house being quite so impressive.

"Could you tell us if Mr. Moran is well?" Maggie asked softly. "How he's faring?"

Gerome graced her with unblinking eyes. "Well enough under the circumstances."

That gave Maggie pause. "Is there anything we can do for him?"

"No," the man said simply.

"*Rude*," Jennifer muttered under her breath as she followed her sister and Hunter.

Gerome showed them through the house and out to the patio.

A large table had been tastefully set there, and Chad was sitting beside it, looking decidedly uncomfortable.

Hunter and Jennifer hung back a step or two as a smiling Maggie walked toward her friend. "Hello, Chad," she said warmly.

Chad looked up and smiled a ghost of a smile, his coloring somewhat ashen. "Maggie."

"I'm glad you're home."

He laughed self-consciously. "Well, I'm not certain how *glad* I am. I never was much of a farm boy, you know."

Maggie nodded and moved a step to her right. "You remember my husband?"

"Of course," Chad said, holding out a steady hand. "Maguire."

"Moran," Hunter said, taking the offered hand.

"Why is it that men never use Christian names?" Jennifer pondered as she looked from one man to the other. "Maguire," she said in a simulated deep male voice, "Moran. It seems so formal."

Both men looked momentarily stunned, and then Chad laughed and presented his hand again. "Hunter."

"There! Are you happy?" Chad asked, looking up at her.

"At least that was *friendlier*," she said primly.

He looked closely at the young woman. She had done it again, he realized. She had broken down another barrier. He had thought about her last visit, long after Jennifer had left; for days afterward. One of the things he had realized about their first encounter was that Jennifer had somehow managed to convince him that he could see his dearest friends and possibly even survive the visit.

Jennifer held out her hand now. "It certainly is nice to see you after all these years," she said with a smile.

Chad stared at her in wonder for the moment their hands were joined. "Yes," he said wryly. "It certainly is . . . after *all* these years."

Curious though he was over her reasons for pretending they had not talked days earlier, he managed to nod his head before dragging his gaze away, turning his attention toward Maggie. She was a beautiful woman still. Looking at her he felt the stirrings of old emotions. Maggie brought back memories of his youth, of their childhood, of the warmth he felt in years past whenever he had come home to Stonehall and old friends. He hadn't remembered, hadn't felt that way with this homecoming. Until now. Seeing Maggie helped him remember he had returned to a safe haven, in spite of his anger and frustrations and unhappiness. Seeing these people seemed to help. Even though his parents were gone, seeing Maggie, most of all, gave him the sense that this was a reunion he should not have put off. "No hug for an old friend?" he dared to ask.

Maggie nodded and bent at the waist, putting her arms around his shoulders, pressing her cheek against his. "I'm sorry, Chad," she whispered.

He knew exactly what she meant. "Me, too," he said. "I'm alive, at least."

She pulled away from him then, turning as the moment grew awkward.

Hunter looked out across the open fields, his hands in the pockets of his trousers. "The farm looks to be in good shape, Chad. Do you still have Tandy as manager?"

"Yes." Thankful for any topic of conversation, Chad pulled back on the left wheel of his chair, turning to face the same direction as Hunter. "Charles has been managing this place from the time I was a boy. I wouldn't trust anyone else to look after my affairs here."

Jennifer looked thoughtful as she moved to a chair and smoothed the back of her skirts before sitting; she recalled the name, Charles Tandy, but she was having difficulty mentally matching a face to it. Well, if this Charles Tandy was the one responsible for keeping the Stonehall pond well stocked with trout, he had done a fine job; she'd been poaching from it for years.

They all settled around the table as tea and sandwiches were laid out by a prim little woman.

"Are you planning to stay on for the summer, Chad?" Maggie asked as she selected a dainty triangle sandwich.

"I've planned to stay on *permanently*," he said. Maggie appeared surprised by that. "Really?"

Jennifer peered at him suspiciously.

"You're going to practice law locally, then?" Hunter asked.

Jennifer's eyes narrowed as she continued to stare; Chad was refusing to look directly at any of them now.

"I've given up law," he said evenly.

"Well, that's a waste," Jennifer said.

He did look at Jennifer then. "It was my choice to make."

"It's still a waste."

"Jen . . ." Maggie started to interrupt, but Hunter shook his head.

"I can hardly work now, can I?" he asked the younger woman. Actually, it sounded more like an accusation than a question.

"I don't see why not," Jennifer said. "It seems to me a lawyer needs a clever mind and the power of speech. Don't you still possess those traits?"

"Has anyone ever told you you're an exasperating woman?"

Jennifer sighed wearily. "Several times."

They stared each other down for a painful moment, and it was Chad who first looked away. "Let's change the subject, shall we?"

"All right," Jennifer agreed as she reached for a sandwich. "How's the stock in that old trout pond of yours?"

Chad turned his head in her direction again, staring at her in disbelief. "I have no idea," he said, wondering now if the woman possessed one ounce of sense in that pretty head of hers.

Jennifer grinned at him as she nibbled a corner of bread. "Want to find out?"

The conversation became easier after that, and they

spent the following hour catching up on old times.

Eventually Hunter suggested that they should be leaving. "Surely the children are old enough to be left with others now?" Chad queried.

Maggie's complexion warmed as she explained quietly. "There is one I can't leave for too long, Chad. I suppose you aren't aware that we have an infant?"

He was aware, of course. Jennifer had told him. But for some strange reason he had decided he would respect Jennifer's reason, or reasons, for not disclosing her previous visit. So he asked, "Have you, Maggie?"

She nodded her head and stood when Hunter moved behind her chair. "A boy."

Although the earlier moments of the visit had been shaky, Chad now found he was reluctant to see these people go. Well, perhaps Jennifer was the exception; she was like a burr under the saddle. He shook Hunter's hand in farewell, but before Maggie could turn away, he touched her arm briefly. "Come again, will you? And bring the little fellow, if you like."

And then he was reaching for Jennifer's hand, and his brown eyes sparkled with a suggestion of life that had not been there before their coming. He squeezed her slim fingers lightly as he teased, "Wonderful to have seen you after *all these years*. You must call again. For tea," he added dryly.

Jennifer laughed lightly, pleased. She was not at all convinced that his invitation was sincere, but that bothered her little. She would return at any rate. Obviously he felt reasonably comfortable with her family, and that was a good beginning. Unconsciously Jennifer had taken on a personal challenge: to bring Chad Moran back to *life*.

"Take care, Chad Moran," she said with a smile. "We'll be back."

Chad did not doubt that for a moment. He was, however, concerned about Jennifer's intentions.

# CHAPTER THREE

Actually, Jennifer was the first to return to Stonehall.

It was Sunday morning, more than a week after their afternoon tea, when Chad looked up from his book and saw her standing on the lawn. He'd been growing drowsy with the warmth of the sun, and suddenly a female in male breeches was standing on the edge of his patio with two poles in one hand and a food basket in the other. He closed the book, resigned to the fact that Jennifer would not leave until she was good and ready. "An urchin?"

Jennifer nodded her head and sighed as she walked toward him. "Now you can see the real me."

He looked her over very carefully. "I don't know," he drawled. "I suppose that outfit has some merit."

She laughed. "When you determine what that might be, explain it to Maggie, would you?" she asked before plopping down on a chair and setting the basket at her feet.

He could hardly do *that*. Her sister would not have approved of the very appreciative male thought that had flashed briefly through his mind. But then the thought needed to be brief; it was useless, and painful, dwelling on things that could never be. "I was thinking it must be more comfortable than skirts and petticoats," he lied.

Jennifer nodded. "That's precisely why I love my breeches."

"I assume you're off for a day of fishing?"

27

"Came to poach from your pond," she confessed. "Want to try your luck?"

He shook his head. "No, I don't think so."

"Why not? I brought an extra pole in case you didn't have one."

"How did you get here?" He looked beyond the patio area.

"I came on my bicycle. Not an easy trip with all of this paraphernalia. And don't change the subject."

He could see she was winding up to pressure him again.

"Jen, think about what you're asking."

She hesitated. Very briefly. "I'm asking you to come fishing; I even brought along some food."

"Jen . . ."

"I didn't make it," she said hurriedly. "You needn't be afraid of that."

"Jen, how can I go fishing?"

"And wine," she said, before she realized what he had said. "You mean *getting there*?" she asked in confusion.

He nodded, clearly annoyed; he hated having his short-comings crop up, and it seemed to happen every time he turned around.

"Well, Chad, why do you pay Mr. . . . oh, what's his name . . . Gerome?"

What he saw as single-mindness in her caused him to lose control. "Do you think I'm going to have you watch him carry me?" he snapped.

Jennifer had not considered that, and it took a few seconds to get her thoughts in order. "If that's what it takes, then, yes," she said quietly. "If that's what must be done so that we can spend an afternoon enjoying ourselves, then, yes."

Chad rubbed his forehead wearily with the tips of unsteady fingers. "Dammit, you're persistent."

"Another fault," she said quietly.

"You don't understand what it's like for a man to be . . ."

He hesitated and Jennifer filled in the gap.

"No, I don't," she said. "I can try to imagine, but I really can't feel the things you're feeling. Not all of it, at least."

Chad attempted to replace his feelings of self-pity, but all he could muster was growing frustration. "I don't need you coming around here thinking I have to be entertained, or whatever it is that brings you."

She shrugged. "I was wanting to spend a sunny afternoon out by that pretty pond and needed some company," she said simply. "And I knew you'd just be sitting around."

That brought his head up. He stared at her and opened his mouth to speak. Instead, he was moved to laughter because of her temerity. "Who the devil raised you?"

Jennifer grinned ruefully. "I don't know what happened to me along the way," she conceded. "But, from what I've been told about my mother, the poor woman is probably turning in her grave."

He nodded his head in agreement. "Undoubtedly," he said quietly.

She continued to smile. "Well?" she asked hopefully.

Chad did not know why he was even contemplating her suggestion other than the fact that sitting beside the pond, surrounded by the peace of nature while listening to her chatter would be preferable to his own company. He nodded, hesitantly. "Ask Gerome to have the carriage readied, will you?"

Jennifer hid a secret, triumphant smile as she walked toward the library door. She turned back once, noting that he was wheeling across the patio in her wake. She noted the alterations that had been made to the wooden threshold; he could manage this much on his own.

Jennifer tactfully delayed leaving the house while Gerome lifted Chad to the carriage seat. When she saw that he was settled, she walked toward the conveyance with the basket and the fishing poles in hand.

"It's going to be a great day," she said enthusiastically. "You'll see."

Chad was not at all certain about that. In fact, he was already regretting having agreed to the excursion. This would be his first venture out into the world since returning to Stonehall. But he had never been a coward.

Gerome stopped close to the spot that Jennifer indicated, and she jumped down, making herself busy by spreading the carriage blanket on the ground close to a tree. Unfortunately, she could not avoid seeing the large man carrying Chad toward the place she had prepared. Her heart lurched, but she smiled as she hurried past them toward the carriage to retrieve her basket and their poles.

Maggie had been right; it was awful seeing anyone subjected to a life such as Chad would now lead. And Maggie had cried for him. Jennifer wished she could cry. Now, for the first time, she thought she understood some of his discomfort. But Jennifer had always been practical, and Chad's accident could not be undone. The sooner Chad accepted that, the sooner he could get on with life.

Gerome met her halfway between Chad and the carriage. "I'll wait with the horses," he said.

Jennifer smiled at him and shook her head. "We'll be fine, if you have other things to do. You could come back for us in a few hours."

He looked doubtful.

"If he needs you, I can run and fetch you. It isn't far."

That much was true. "All right," he agreed. "I'll be back in a few hours."

Chad had not reckoned on Gerome leaving. "Where is he going?" he asked when she dropped to her knees beside him.

"He's got things to do."

"At your suggestion?"

Jennifer was rummaging around in her basket. "I merely said we would be fine and he could come back in a few hours, if he chose."

"No one asked me about my preference."

She stopped searching, settling back on her heels as she stared at him in dismay. He was a man, not a child. And she and Gerome had unwittingly taken his authority away, as if he had not been there at all. "I'm sorry, Chad," she said. "I'm sorry. I'll fetch him back."

But he shook his head and stopped her departure with a steely grip on her arm. "It doesn't matter," he said. "Forget it."

"Sometimes I just don't think," she said in a small voice.

Now she was feeling badly, and he had not intended that. "Well, at other times you do," he said simply before looking hopefully toward the basket. "You said you'd brought wine?"

Jennifer nodded, much subdued by her own stupidity, and reached into the basket. First, she removed a jar wrapped in a white cloth and set it aside.

Curious, Chad frowned. "What's that?"

"Worms."

"Worms!" he asked in horror. "You put worms in the same basket as the food?"

"I wiped the jar," she said reasonably and handed him the bottle of wine. She failed to see his grin of amusement as she turned to search for the wineglasses. She held the glasses while he poured.

"Worms," he muttered lightly.

Jennifer took a sip of wine and then set her glass aside before unwinding the line from around one of the poles. "When was the last time you came out here for an afternoon?" she asked as she readied one of the fishing poles.

Chad shook his head and reached for the other pole. "Not for years. Since long before I moved to Richmond, at any rate."

Jennifer looked around at the clear water of the pond, the vibrant green of the grass and trees, the clear blue of the sky. "You prefer the city to all of this?" she asked after a moment.

"I was never much for the farm life," he admitted.

"Did you love my sister?" she asked bluntly.

He flashed her a startled look as he took the worm jar she offered. "What brought that up?"

"I don't know," she said with a casual shrug. "I've heard scads of stories about you two, I suppose."

"We were very young, and I went away to school when I was seventeen."

"Before Maggie's accident," she murmured as she attended to the baiting of the hook.

Chad gave her his undivided attention then. "Whatever happened to Maggie, Jen? I never knew."

"Even now no one will talk about it," she told him. "But Hunter came back for Maggie, and whatever it was hasn't seemed to matter since then. At least not to Maggie."

Chad smiled. "Hunter made everything right?"

"As I said before, he has certainly made her happy."

"Yes," he said softly with just a touch of envy in his voice. "Even I can see that."

Jennifer nodded. Everyone could see Maggie's happiness. She took both poles and walked toward the edge of the water. After throwing the lines toward the center of the pond, Jennifer returned to sit beside him, reaching for her wine. "Now we just wait for some nibbles," she said with a smile.

Chad took a firm grip on his fishing pole and rested his head against the tree at his back. "It really is quite pretty here, isn't it? Peaceful."

Jennifer nodded her agreement once again and managed a quick sip of wine before the tip of Chad's pole moved. "Oh, my God," she breathed. "You've got a bite." She moved onto her knees, blessing him with a delighted grin before returning her attention to the end of the pole.

Chad felt a rush of anticipation he had not felt in years and placed his glass aside to devote both hands to the task ahead.

The end of the pole bent again, sharply but briefly downward.

"Oh," she crowed softly. "I think you've got a good one!"

"You're right!" He laughed and pulled the end of the pole upward slowly.

"Ssh, ssh, ssh," she whispered. "Easy."

When he pulled the pole high, a good-size, lively trout arched and flapped near the bank. Jennifer ran forward and pulled the line in, holding the wiggling fish up for his inspection.

Chad nodded. The fish was indeed a good size, but he would need two or three for *his* supper alone. And Gerome might be partial to trout. He found his mouth was primed for the meal, simply by thinking about it.

Carefully Jennifer held the fish and eased the hook from its mouth. Then she turned and threw it back into the water.

"Why the devil did you do that?" he howled.

"Well, you don't *keep* them," she explained.

"*You* don't," he huffed mightily. "That was my supper."

"You don't *eat* them," she threw back.

"Stop telling me what I don't do!" he said, but he was laughing again. "Jen, you are the most exasperating creature."

Jennifer shrugged, looking sheepish, and returned to her place on the blanket. "I won't throw the next one back," she said.

"Thank you," he returned ruefully.

"Provided there is a *next* one."

Chad shook his head and reached for his wine.

He barked another short, disbelieving laugh and took a sip of wine. Then he rolled his head on the tree trunk and grinned at her.

"What?" she asked as she watched him. "Are you hungry?"

"No. I'm wondering what the devil you're doing here with *me*?"

"Why would you say '*me*' like that?" she countered with a frown. "I'm here with you because I want to be."

"But you're young and pretty and full of life. You must have an abundance of friends your own age."

Remaining silent, somewhat thoughtful, Jennifer reached for the bottle.

"So, why aren't you with them?"

Jennifer appeared tired of his questioning and sighed heavily before responding. "Most of them are religious folk and are in church at this moment."

"And you're not religious?"

"The Lord moves in mysterious ways," she said frankly.

"And I don't like some of His *movements*."

"That's sacrilegious," he pointed out.

"I can't help the way I feel."

"What caused you to feel this way?"

"Are you hungry?" she returned, blatantly changing the topic.

"No," he said. "And so far you've failed to answer two of my questions."

Jennifer frowned. "What was the other one?"

"Why are you here with me?"

"Oh, that?" she said as she removed a paper-wrapped bundle from the basket. She sat back on her heels, staring at him, thinking about possible answers to his question. Why? Because friendship was like her old breeches? Comfortable, so she just kept putting them on? No. They were not at all that comfortable together. Well, Jennifer thought she might be more comfortable than Chad. He snapped at her a lot, but she knew that was to cover a lot of anger and resentment. Still, she enjoyed being with him for those times when he was more gentle. The old allure was there as if her childish dream of him had not been buried with her youth but had matured along with her and had lain dormant all these years. He still managed to make her heart beat a little faster, though she knew he never would believe her. "Just because," she said at last.

He grunted a brief laugh at the short response. "*Because?*"

"I like you," she admitted with a grin and plopped a sandwich into his hand.

Chad frowned, as if confused, and laid the sandwich on a corner of the waxed paper. "You like me? It seems to me you barely know me, and I'm snapping at you most of the time we're together."

Jennifer shrugged and chewed thoughtfully on her sandwich. Once she had swallowed, she addressed his comment. "I believe that's just your way of getting rid of your frustrations."

"And you don't mind?"

"I would mind if you were snapping because you were angry with *me*," she explained.

"Is that why you take my . . . barking . . . so casually?"

Jennifer stared at him intently for a moment. "I don't take you *casually* at all."

Now it was his turn to stare. He just could *not* figure her out. "Most women would run from a miserable sod like me," he remarked.

"I am not most women, and you are *not* a sod," she said sharply. "Miserable or otherwise."

For a moment he was startled. She was not the playful, clever little tease, as she sometimes thought of her. Nor was she merely the noble neighbor. Jennifer Downing was far more complex than that, and he was beginning to understand. "Run from me, Jen," he said softly.

Surprised, her blue-eyed gaze locked with his. "Run? From what?"

"You'll be hurt," he said cautiously.

She took a moment to try and evaluate the comment. Eventually she gave up and laughed uncomfortably. "What are you talking about? We're friends, aren't we? How could I be hurt?"

"This is not the world of little girls and puppy love," he said softly.

Jennifer studiously avoided eye contact with him, fearing that, in her confusion over her own feelings, Chad had read and understood something about her that she did not. "I'm not a little girl," she murmured as she laid out a wedge of cheese and went searching in the basket for a knife.

"That's what makes this all so dangerous," he said firmly.

Jennifer eyed him with a front of casual bravado. "That's true," she said. "You're a man. Just a man. With all the frailties and shortcomings of the rest of we humans. You see? I understand that, Chad. I am *not* a child and I do know my own mind."

Chad began to wonder if his imagination had run rampant without his realizing. No woman he had ever met could possibly have been *this* naive. Unless she did not truly understand her own actions?

Jennifer felt unsettled. She got to her feet. Taking a deep breath, she returned to kneel beside him. "Why are we suddenly at odds, Chad?" she asked quietly.

"This isn't wise, Jen," he said sharply. "It isn't a good thing. Certainly not for you."

"I don't understand," she said, staring directly into brown eyes that displayed too many emotions to count. "What's wrong with being companions? What's wrong with friends sharing a picnic lunch and sitting talking beside a pond?"

"It's wrong because I think you're on a bloody *crusade*," he ground out.

"No," she whispered, but it was a forceful denial.

"Well, then," he said cruelly, "are you about to tell me you've loved me since you were ten or twelve or whatever bloody age you say you were? Are you about to tell me you still do?"

Jennifer took exception to his snarling. "That was a child's dream. If I hadn't gotten over it years ago, you would have shattered the dream quite easily the past few times we've been together."

He stared at her for a long, thoughtful moment. "I think you're romanticizing," he said unkindly.

"What?" Now she was truly confused.

"It isn't noble or romantic or even propitious to be with a cripple. Far from it."

Jennifer's mouth dropped open in unadulterated shock. "What a ridiculous thing to say!"

"Is it?" he asked, one brow arching severely.

"I think you're full of yourself," she snapped. "That's what *I* think!" She began slamming food back into the basket, occasionally slanting him a narrow-eyed glare.

Chad considered that perhaps his judgment was not the best right now as he watched her angry movements. "Why else would you be here?" he asked quietly.

"We've already discussed that."

"Why else would you be with me, then?"

With a weary sigh and deep breath, Jennifer sat back on her heels. "I'm beginning to wonder why," she muttered.

He stared at her.

Jennifer shook her head, confounded. "I still think you're mightily full of yourself, Chad Moran."

# CHAPTER FOUR

Jennifer stepped back for a time after that and examined her feelings and her actions; she was curious, now that Chad had forced her to think about what she had been doing. She did not think it was *pity* forcing her to seek him out. She hated seeing Chad without the use of his legs, that was true. But there was a lot more to the man than his legs. She liked being with him. Unlike at home, he treated her like an adult. And Jennifer was willing to help him in any way she could because she was convinced he was a splendid man underneath it all.

As to romantic inclinations . . . Jennifer knew there would never be anything more serious than friendship between them. Chad was pretty old, after all. At least ten years her senior.

No, Jennifer thought she would continue as she was for a time, having one great passion: the horses. Some of the finest riding and breeding stock in the country could be found at Treemont, thanks to Hunter, and it was exciting being a part of the world he had built.

"What are you thinking about?" Courtney asked after a long silence.

Jennifer smiled, pulling her mount back to a slower pace so that her niece's tiny mare could keep abreast. "I was just thinking what a fine day this is."

"Sure took you a long time to work that out," she teased.

Jennifer enjoyed Courtney more and more of late. Almost eight now, the girl was interesting and a good companion. "I'm not telling you all my secret thoughts."

Courtney's face lit up with new interest. "Do you have a secret, Jen?"

Jennifer grinned and shook her head. "Not really. I was just working some things out in my head."

The girl looked disappointed. "Ah, I thought it might be something important."

Jennifer laughed. "Perhaps it was!"

"But not a true secret that we could share?" she asked hopefully.

Jennifer had been about to respond when Courtney's little mare squealed and bolted forward. "Gather her in, Courtney!" Jennifer ordered as she kicked Sequoyah into action. The strong stallion raced forward, quickly coming abreast of the mare although Jennifer's stronger hand was not needed.

Courtney was willow thin but tall and relatively strong for her age, and she managed to bring the mare to a stand. "What spooked her, Jen?" she asked as her hand smoothed the silky neck of the animal while she looked around.

Jennifer turned her stallion back, and she, too, began searching the trees that lined both sides of the road. And it was *her* eyes that saw the culprit first.

He was a lad a year or two past the age of ten with eyes that said he was much older in terms of life. He was wearing a worn brown coat and a cocky grin, and his hair was long and shaggy.

And he stood his ground brazenly when Jennifer approached.

"Did you see what happened to the little mare?" she asked.

"Pears like the kid can't ride," he said insolent-ly.

"My *niece*," she said heatedly, "rides extremely well. What did *you* do?"

The boy jerked his shoulders upward with indignation. "Me? Why does it have to be *me*?"

Jennifer's blue eyes narrowed. "I don't see anyone else here, do you? I assume you threw something at the mare?"

"You shouldn't go around accusin' people, lady," he said.

He was brazen and brusque and Jennifer suspected he was not about to admit anything. "Perhaps your father and I should talk," she said.

The boy's grin broadened. "Right," he drawled. "You do that, lady."

Jennifer could feel her temper getting the better of her and struggled against the idea of warming this boy's backside with the palm of her hand. "Where will I find him?"

"I don't know which way to direct ya, lady!" the boy shouted as he began to laugh.

Courtney pulled up beside her aunt and frowned, first at Jennifer and then at the strange boy.

"He's dead!" he hooted.

Courtney gasped.

"Where do you live?" Jennifer asked in a clipped tone.

There was no response. Only continuing laughter.

"I think you'd better tell her," Courtney warned.

"*You* gonna make me?" he asked insolently.

That did it!

Jennifer jumped down from her horse and grabbed the boy by the scruff of his neck. "*I'll* make you," she said and pushed him up the road, still holding onto the back of his shirt.

The boy's arms hung out from his body as Jennifer pulled up on the shirt. "Le'go!" he shouted.

"We're close to Stonehall," she said over her shoulder to Courtney. "We'll see if anyone there knows who he is."

The expression on Gerome White's face when he opened the door to them almost fractured Jennifer's mien of command. "Do you know this boy?" she asked.

"Oh, we know him," Gerome rumbled.

"I suspect he threw something at my niece's mare. Fortunately, Courtney was not unseated, but it's a dangerous practice."

"Indeed," Gerome murmured and stepped back from the open doorway. "I think you had better speak with Mr. Moran."

Jennifer looked over her shoulder and saw that Courtney was dismounting, before she nudged the boy into the house. "What's his name?" she demanded.

"I can tell ya my own name," the boy grumbled. "Ya didn't bother to ask me that. It's Silas."

"Mind your tongue," Gerome warned as he turned and led the trio through the house to the library.

Chad frowned when he looked up from the papers on his desk and saw Jennifer marching Silas across the room. "What's he done now?" he asked with a sigh of resignation.

Jennifer could not get over the fact that Chad actually knew the young ruffian. "He belongs to one of your workers?"

Chad shook his head, looking anything but happy. "He belongs to me."

Jennifer's body snapped almost to attention, so great was her incredulity. "What?"

Chad noticed that she had released her hold on the boy's shirt, and he frowned at Silas. "I want you to sit there," he ordered, pointing to a settee against one wall.

"She started accusin' me—" Silas tried to explain.

"He threw something at my horse," Courtney put in.

Now Chad's attention was directed to the girl. "I don't believe we've met," he said.

"This is my niece Courtney," Jennifer explained. "She's Maggie's eldest, Chad."

Something in his expression softened as he returned his attention to the pretty blond child. "I should have known," he said. "You're as pretty as your mother."

Courtney blushed at the praise.

"Crap," Silas muttered.

Chad turned his head slowly, his eyes narrowed in disgust. "That's quite enough," he growled. "And I told you to sit."

"I don't take orders," Silas snapped.

Chad rolled back the wheels of his chair and then moved around the desk. "And I don't like to give them," he told the boy as he moved in. "But you will learn to respect my *requests* during your stay here, if you learn nothing else."

Jennifer and Courtney looked on as man and boy stared each other down. But it was Silas who turned away first.

Chad indicated the chairs grouped near the settee and that Jennifer and Courtney should sit.

Courtney could not help but watch Chad maneuver his chair. Seeing a man in a wheelchair was a new experience for her.

He positioned himself so that he was facing Silas. "Shall we discuss what happened?" he asked of all three.

Silas crossed his arms over his thin chest and turned his face away, indicating he had nothing to say.

Jennifer explained, in a quiet, controlled voice.

Chad turned his head. "You just never learn, do you, Silas?" he asked quietly.

His dark eyes hooded, Silas turned his attention on Chad. "You're takin' her word over mine?"

"You were throwing stones," Chad said with quiet, but intense, conviction.

"Well, you done made up your own mind," Silas snapped.

"Throwing stones at horses," Chad said simply.

"Again."

"So what if I was!"

"You could have caused an injury to Courtney," Chad returned harshly. "Is that your aim in life, Silas? To cripple as many people as you meet?"

Courtney sat silently, her eyes large and round in concern.

Jennifer was clearly confused. "He's done this before?" Chad nodded and turned troubled eyes her way. "This is one of the boys who caused the accident that left me paralyzed."

Jennifer's mouth dropped open before she slumped back in her chair. "Oh, my God," she whispered.

"Precisely," he said wryly. "The Richmond court has appointed me official guardian to Silas Hughes."

Jennifer covered her frown with her fingertips as a number of thoughts whirled around in her head.

Gerome entered with a tray of coffee, lemonade, and cakes and set the lot on the low table in the middle of the foursome. "Thought some refreshments might be in order," he said.

"Take Silas to his room, please, Gerome," Chad said. "I'll deal with him later."

Silas clearly did not want to be assisted by Gerome; he jumped to his feet and was out the door before any of them could take their next breath.

Chad stared thoughtfully, and sightlessly, at the tray for a brief interval before smiling at Courtney. "Would you like to help yourself to a drink and a sweet?"

The girl nodded and slid forward on her chair.

Continuing to smile, he watched her pour lemonade into a slim glass. "You're a bit darker in coloring," he said softly. "But you are very much like your mother."

"My father says I'm Mama's image."

With a little bit of Hunter's Cherokee blood thrown in, Chad thought. "And I'd wager you're the sun in your father's sky."

Unfeigned and honest to the core, Courtney nodded with a smile.

"Choose a cake or two," Chad coaxed.

"Enough!" Jennifer burst in. "Enough of this chitchat. I want to know how on earth you came to be guardian to that boy?"

He smiled wearily. "Pour us some coffee, would you, Jen?"

"This is absolutely absurd," she murmured as she did as he had asked. "Isn't sending that boy here a bit like putting the hare in with the fox?"

"That's chickens," Chad informed her as he accepted a cup.

About to reach for another cup, Jennifer rested her elbow on her knee and stared at him curiously.

"I think you mean 'setting the fox to guard the chickens,'" he said.

"Oh, for heaven's sake," she muttered, reaching for the cup. "Who cares what I mean! I'm interested only in an explanation."

Chad refused cake but sipped his coffee twice before he spoke. "Judge Herbert Lang is an old friend and a very wise man. At least I had thought he was wise, until recently." He shrugged then, gracing Jennifer with a lopsided smile. "Perhaps he is. Time will tell."

"Chad . . ."

"I'll get to what you want to hear," he said patiently before leaning forward to set his cup on the table. "Silas is an orphan and had been in trouble before this last incident. In fact, the boy has appeared before Judge Lang on three previous occasions. The judge had tended to be lenient with Silas because of the boy's youth. But on their next-to-last meeting, Herbert had told Silas he would go to jail should he ever appear in court again."

Again, Courtney gasped and Chad looked at her, assessing whether or not the child was too delicate to hear such a story. But Courtney met his perusal frankly and without wilting, and he decided to continue.

"Herbert Lang did sentence Silas Hughes to a term in jail, but the judge was plagued with guilt over having a child reside in such a place and in the company of hardened criminals. Herbert waited until he heard news of my return here before contacting me with his suggestion. He felt that Silas would benefit more from residing in the same house with the man he had injured than he would from spending years in jail. Judge Lang is of the opinion that the boy will come to understand the destruction of his actions better if he has a daily reminder of what he has caused. Silas is to be punished by having to look at me day after day for the next year."

"A year!" Jennifer squealed. "That's all well and good, but what about you? It cannot be good for you having the boy here as a reminder."

Chad smiled ruefully and nodded his head. "I think Herbert's theory is that having Silas here will be a catharsis for me. I'm not certain, mind you, but I have to believe he saw this arrangement as having some benefit to both the boy and myself. And I did agree, after much persuading. Although I've doubted my own reasons for having done so a thousand times, and Silas has been here only a week. I think, originally, my purposes in having the boy here were not so pure and generous as I would like to think."

Jennifer saw the arrangement more as cruel and unnatural punishment for her friend. "I simply cannot understand

Judge Lang's reasoning to have suggested such a thing."

Chad shrugged and stared thoughtfully at the material pattern of the settee. "Silas was not alone that day. There was an older boy who appeared to be the leader, according to witnesses. I suspect Herbert saw some hope of saving this younger child, and perhaps he is right. Given a chance, and taken out of the environment he was in, Silas may mend his ways." He looked at his legs briefly and then smiled sadly at her. "And seeing the results of his actions, on a regular basis, should have some impact."

"Well, I think you must possess a remarkably magnanimous nature to go along with this."

Chad laughed, although there was little humor in the sound. "Don't paint me as a white knight just yet," he said. "The boy can be shipped back the moment I give up on him, and his fate, should that happen, will not be pleasant." He seemed to ask a question of himself then. "Perhaps that is why I agreed," he said quietly. "Perhaps I wanted to hold his fate in my hand."

Jennifer smiled at Courtney, giving permission to the girl's silent request for a second cake. "Go ahead, darling," she said.

Chad's attention turned from Jennifer to Courtney, and he watched her select a treat as he wondered what the relationship between aunt and niece must be like. "Are you close?" he asked of Jennifer after a moment. "Are you close to Maggie's children?"

Courtney looked puzzled and wrinkled her nose at her aunt.

Jennifer shot the girl a teasing grin. "Well, we live in the same house!" she said, laughing. "But, yes, we are close. I love Maggie's children, and Courtney and I spend quite a bit of time together when she's not in school. I suppose she's a pretty good girl," she added lovingly.

Courtney had a question of her own, now that Jennifer had raised the topic. "Will Silas be attending my school, Mr. Moran?"

Chad smiled at the girl and nodded. "When the new term starts in September, I will see that he's registered. You'll soon be out for the summer now, I suppose?"

"One more week," she said.

He wondered then why Courtney had asked the question. "I'm very sorry for what happened today," he said. "Will it bother you, having a boy like Silas in your school?"

Courtney firmly shook her head. "He's not so tough," she said bluntly. "He probably likes to shock people by behaving badly. We have another boy at school who acts up all the time, and our teacher says it's just his way of getting attention."

Chad smiled with admiration for the girl. "Lord, you've probably hit that right, Courtney," he said. She just might have produced the key. Chad admitted to himself then that he had given little thought as to why Silas behaved as he did, other than the obvious fact that Silas had been running with a bad crowd. He and the boy had spent their first week silently pondering each other's motives and faults. So far, nothing productive had come from their relationship.

"Courtney may be right," Jennifer added thoughtfully. "Showering Silas with the right kind of attention just might help."

Chad thought about her comment for a moment and then smiled. "I don't suppose you'd be willing to assist with the *downpouring*?"

Jennifer looked momentarily stunned, and then she suddenly had some insight into Judge Land's decision and the reasoning behind it: The man had given Chad a campaign to launch. He would now find long moments of reprieve from troubled thoughts about himself while he concentrated his efforts into rehabilitating an under-privileged child. Perhaps Herbert Lang's scheme did hold some merit. "Where would you like to start?" she asked.

They started the following morning, a Monday.

Silas was caught up in a whirlwind.

"You need clothes," Chad explained as they waited for Gerome to bring the carriage around to the front of the house.

"What I got is fine," the boy said contrarily.

"You've outgrown your trousers, Silas," Jennifer said reasonably. The boy looked down, viewed his bare ankles, and then pursed his lips as he crossed his arms over his chest.

"They'll soon be *short pants*," she quipped.

"They're fine," he said again.

"Well, you can't go to Courtney's party looking the way you do now."

He slanted her a suspicious, narrow-eyed gaze. "What party?"

"My niece is having her eighth birthday party in a few weeks, and we would like you to join in the fun."

"Goin' to a *girl's* party won't be fun," he mumbled.

"There will be other boys there, too," she explained.

"I ain't goin'," he said firmly.

Chad and Jennifer shared a meaningful look as the carriage arrived.

Jennifer held back as Gerome pushed Chad's chair across the stone patio and lifted him to the carriage seat. She watched as Silas looked away from the procedure and wondered what the boy might be thinking about all of this. "There's a problem we have to solve," she said softly, placing her hand on his shoulder. "Mr. Moran will have to wait in the carriage while we shop," she added conversationally as she steered Silas around the back of the carriage. "There is no way to transport his chair, you see." She had the boy's attention, although grudgingly, as they looked at the carriage structure. "What would you think of adding a platform back here?"

Mockingly, he said, "It'd roll right off."

"It would have to be tied to the frame," she said patiently.

He shrugged his bony shoulders reluctantly and stared off into the distance. "Might work," he mumbled.

Jennifer smiled. "Let's go shopping."

Silas held his ground as Jennifer walked around to the side of the rig. And then Gerome wandered within sight and shot the boy a dark look. Silas arrived at Jennifer's side just in time to see Chad's hand reach out for hers to help her up.

"What were you two doing back there?" Chad asked as Jennifer settled herself opposite.

She smiled winningly as the boy sat beside her friend. "Silas has a wonderful plan," she said, "to add a platform to the back of the rig so that your chair can go wherever you go."

Silas wasn't about to admit to being a party to anything good. "It ain't *my* plan!"

"Well, you agreed it would work," she said.

"I changed my mind," he huffed.

Jennifer continued to smile, and Chad shook his head; he had the feeling this one boy would prove to be more trouble than either he or Jennifer had ever dreamed.

Arriving at the shops was a painful experience that none of them had considered.

Chad watched as Jennifer and Silas descended from the carriage and felt a whole volcano of emotions, of anger and resentment, well up inside him. It made him aware, once again, that he was restricted to being on the outside looking in; to being left behind because he could not follow; to being confined to a narrow world that denied him life's simple pleasures. He hated it, and his frown and dark, smoldering look said as much.

Jennifer felt the pain of his unhappiness as if she were the one directly affected, but she was careful to hide the feelings of misery she was experiencing in that moment. She smiled as she reached back into the carriage and touched his hand. "We shouldn't be long," she said softly. "Provided I get some measure of cooperation."

"I wouldn't count on that," he returned roughly. "You'd best take Gerome in with you," he growled. "In the event you need a *man* to assist you."

Jennifer was convinced that Chad was entitled to moments of doubt in himself, but his tone in reference to his manliness angered her. "We'll talk about this *attitude* of yours when we get home," she whispered fiercely and, with a swirl of her skirts, muttered a word or two to Gerome before ushering Silas into the nearest shop.

Chad stared thoughtfully at the door as she slammed it, closing herself and Silas off from him.

*So, I have an attitude, do I?* he mused. *Well, I'm entitled to any damned attitude I please.*

He looked about him, at people *walking* to and from their businesses and going about their errands. Few of them paid him much attention, but he had been away for years. The younger folk would not even recognize him, he assumed. An old friend of his father's did stop long enough to engage in a brief chat, but then Chad was left alone with his own reflections once again.

Tender reflections that turned to Jennifer. Reflections that seemed to haunt him more and more of late.

Eventually he became torn between wanting to be in that damned store and wanting to remain exactly where he sat. The thought of being carried in public, as if he were an infant, caused bile to rise up in the back of his throat, and he closed his eyes briefly in his battle against it. How could a man submit to such shame? He didn't think he could do it, and yet, he would remain on the periphery of life forever if he did not somehow effect a change.

And he had an *attitude*.

One that had obviously caused some sadness in Jennifer, his friend. And she *was* proving herself a true friend.

Suddenly it seemed important that Jennifer believe he had some backbone; that he was at least man enough not to abandon her to the task of dealing with an unwilling and unpleasant boy. The boy was *his* ward, after all.

Gerome stepped alongside one of the matched bays, catching Chad's attention.

"I thought you were going in there with her," he said.

Gerome was not certain how his next words would be received, but said, "Miss Downing told me to stay."

Frowning, Chad stroked his chin with a forefinger. "Oh, she *did?*"

Gerome nodded, walking to the carriage door.

"She takes a lot upon herself, doesn't she?" Chad asked.

The older man grinned. "Yes, sir. She appears to."

"Well, somebody needs to be in there with her," Chad muttered. "See if they have a chair for me in that shop, would you?"

Moments later Gerome was lowering Chad to a chair that had been placed amongst the counters piled high with ready-made clothes and bolts of yard goods.

Customers in the store had watched the procedure, first with puzzling stares and then turning away in their discomfort at the scene they had witnessed.

Chad spent a long moment paying attention to righting the line of his suit coat in an attempt to hide his mortification. He may not be able to walk, but he had just vaulted a very high hurdle. The problem was, it did not feel good.

Jennifer broke the disturbing moment with chatter. "I'm glad you decided to come in," she said as lightly as the moment would permit. She held out a pair of boy's trousers. "Silas has his own ideas about shopping with a woman."

"I ain't shuckin' my britches with no woman watchin'," the boy carped.

Chad was forced to grin at the indignant tone. "You will when you're older," he teased softly and held the jeans up by the waist. "Come here and we'll measure the length," he said.

Pouting, Silas stepped in front of the man.

Chad leaned to the side as he let the garment fall the length of Silas's leg. "These seem about right," he murmured and reached for the shirt Jennifer was clutching. "Do you like this shirt?" he asked the boy.

Jennifer stepped to Chad's side, viewing the shirt he held across the child's thin shoulders. "It seems right, too," she said quietly.

Chad nodded and gave the shirt and trousers to Silas. "You take these over to the corner," he said, pointing the direction. "You can go behind that curtain to try them on."

"This is crap," Silas grumpled.

Before he could step away, Chad took rough hold of the boy's upper arm and forced Silas to look at him, face to face, man to boy. "I won't hear that kind of language from you again. Nor will anyone else," Chad whispered harshly. "Do you understand?"

Silas looked into the man's dark, angry eyes and eventually nodded his head.

"Come back here when you've changed so I can see the fit," Chad said more gently. He watched the thin boy walk away, wondering how, in the name of all that was good and decent, he and the boy were ever going to survive. Apart, they both had their own burdens to bear.

Together, Chad feared they might just turn into some sort of destructive machine, feeding upon each other.

Jennifer also watched man and boy. And, more important, she *felt* the strain that went much deeper than putting these two individuals physically together. It had more to do with the aura of discomfort that had arrived in this place along with Chad Moran.

In a thoughtless moment Jennifer allowed her hand to rest on Chad's shoulder.

The tender touch nearly precipitated his undoing. With his head bowed forward, he whispered, "Don't do this, Jennifer."

"I'm sorry," she murmured, snatching her hand away.

"I can take anything," he said quietly, "except your pity."

"I told you once before, I'm not offering *pity*." She wandered away then, trying not to be hurt by his refusal to accept her demonstration of understanding. She berated herself with a humorless laugh as she poked about the shop. "It's better when he's angry," she murmured. "I can manage that."

During the time she was away from Chad and Silas, Jennifer made a small purchase of her own.

# CHAPTER FIVE

Jennifer walked into Chad's library after watching Silas climb the stairs to the second floor with his arms ladened with brown-paper-wrapped parcels.

"The only thing he enjoyed about that trip was the peppermint stick," she said, smiling as she removed her gloves.

Chad was silent and brooding as he wheeled his chair across the room and pulled open the French doors.

"Shall I fetch us something cool to drink?" she asked as she stared at his back.

"I think you should go," he said quietly.

Jennifer took a deep breath, as if preparing herself for a major contest. "I'll see what Cook has to offer," she said firmly and retreated from the room.

When she returned, Chad had made his way out onto the patio and was staring off across the open fields.

Jennifer gave the lemonade a second glance, set it on the desk, and walked toward a small table in a corner of the room. There she found several crystal decanters, which she tested by smell before choosing one. On a shelf below were a variety of glasses; she selected two. Tucking her wrapped package under her arm, she joined her friend outside. She flashed the decanter and grinned. "I'm not certain which one you prefer, but this one smells strongest."

Chad eyed the two glasses and frowned. "You just stay away from the stuff."

"I'm not a child," she said indignantly as she chose a chair beside him.

Lord, he *knew* that. The fact that she was, indeed, not a child was making his adjustment only that much more difficult; she reminded him of what women were all about in a number of ways. Her presence made the indignities that much more unbearable; he had found that out today.

"I've tasted spirits," Jennifer told him.

"White wine and sweet sherry, no doubt," he returned with mocking disdain. *"That* is cognac."

"Well, good," she said, pouring a glass.

When she reached for the second glass, Chad reached out and captured her hand. "Jennifer, what are you doing?"

"Pouring us a drink," she said slowly.

He sighed, shaking his head as he sat back. "I know you are not *that* obtuse," he muttered.

"All right," she said, proceeding to half-fill the second glass. "I'm going to sit here until you get a few things off your chest."

The look of misery in his eyes did not escape her before he looked away. "You might as well leave now," he said. "I have nothing to say."

"Yes, you do, Chad," she said. "I think you have enough unspoken words saved up that you could fill that silo across the way. I'm your friend, Chad. I've decided to stay and give you an opportunity to drain some of the silage."

His head snapped around and he glared at her. "Why are you doing this?" he stormed. "What do you hope to gain?"

"Why must I be seeking to *gain* something?" she countered.

"Isn't that why people form relationships?"

Her questioning blue eyes looked directly into his; they were dark and unhappy, almost brooding. "I wouldn't have thought of you as a cynic," she said quietly.

He wasn't. At least he had not been before his life had been shattered. He'd had relationships with women in the past, although, admittedly, he would not have classed those as *friendships*. They were alliances, to be sure, but not of the platonic variety. He had never maintained such a relationship with a beautiful woman—other than Maggie, of course, and they had been children back then. Chad was not at all certain that such a relationship could be possible. Then again, as he considered his altered circumstances, platonic relationships with women might very well be his only option.

But Jennifer was waiting for him to deny that he was a cynic, as she had accused. She was staring at him with those pale blue eyes that seemed to reach inside him and demand too much. She was particularly beautiful today in a green striped day dress with its high collar framing a face that was too close to perfection to be believed. He liked her better in breeches or her biking costume; in anything that did not present her as so damned feminine.

When he did not speak, Jennifer smiled sorrowfully. "It's all very simple, Chad," she said quietly. "I hope to gain a friend who will never again suggest there is any question about his being a *man*."

Chad stared in open-mouthed astonishment before throwing his head back and laughing bitterly.

She was confused by this reaction from him. "Well, it seems to me you have some doubt."

He shook his head and pinched the bridge of his nose with thumb and forefinger. "You don't know what you're saying," he managed roughly.

But it dawned on her eventually. It took several moments of watching him before Jennifer realized that she had said too much and said it badly. She had not even *considered* his male abilities in the sense that Chad apparently was thinking. She had been referring to the state of his male mind and *not* his male body. She closed her eyes as a rosy flush stole across her cheeks. "Stupid," she admonished in a whisper. "Witless."

Chad regained some semblance of control and reached for his brandy while pretending he had not noticed the heated condition of her complexion. "I suspect you have stumbled into unfamiliar territory, my dear," he said ruefully.

Jennifer faced him squarely, in spite of her heated condition. "I was thinking more about your insecurities," she said primly.

"Well, you have unwittingly uncovered another," he murmured. And, in spite of his heartache, he turned an understanding expression her way. "You see, Jennifer, there are far more complex elements to all of this than you had imagined."

"My intentions are good," she said.

Chad thought that this young woman's good intentions just might bring about the demise of his weakened spirit.

"Yes, I know."

"I saw how difficult it was for you today—"

Chad held up a hand to stop her in midsentence. "Please don't," he said, not unkindly. "You have to realize that you are asking me to face a number of things I'm not ready to face, Jen. I haven't had time to . . . there is more to reckon with beyond what you think you've seen in me," he finished wretchedly. "You must realize that now."

She nodded unhappily and reached for the gift she had purchased for him. "When Florence was a girl," she suffered terribly because of her shyness. We had a housekeeper when I was very young who took to abusing my sister. And because Florence appeared weak, the abuse continued for some time," she said as her fingers fumbled with the string around the parcel. "I had witnessed an incident or two, but Florence always swore me to secrecy and I was too young to know any better. I maintained my silence and so did my sister. Many years later Florence told me she survived that time in her life because she wrote her fears and unhappiness in a diary. She said it was a catharsis to tell everything in writing as if she were speaking to a real person," she said with a small smile as she raised her head to look at him. "This is for you," she said quietly and left the partially wrapped parcel on the table as she stood to go.

Chad watched her walk toward the house, and he realized he was feeling more miserable than ever because he had made her unhappy. He was the *cause* of her unhappiness. He regretted having asked her to assist him with Silas, because it brought them too frequently together. He realized now it could be a dangerous thing, seeing Jennifer Downing on a daily basis. Dangerous for them both. While she concentrated on their friendship, Chad suspected that association could very easily change. And neither of them were ready for that. Unconsciously he reached out and pushed the brown paper aside, revealing her gift.

Of course, it was a diary.

Hunter was in the main barn when Jennifer walked Sequoyah toward his stall.

"How did it go?" he asked.

She had told them about Silas and how the boy had come to live with Chad. "The boy is having trouble accepting any kindness," she said as she turned the big black into his box stall.

"Perhaps he's afraid to," Hunter suggested as he leaned against the board wall, watching her.

"Perhaps he's not the only one," she returned wry-ly.

Hunter ducked his head, trying to see the expression she would not lift to him. "Jen, are you involved with Moran?"

Jennifer's head snapped up and she laughed. "What on earth do you mean by *involved?*"

Hunter shrugged and pushed away from the wall. "I think you're old enough to understand my question," he said.

"Well, don't worry about it, Hunter," she said bitterly as she walked away. "Chad Moran doesn't think he's *man* enough for me or anyone else."

Hunter Maguire frowned as he watched her go, wondering if his sister-in-law had made up her mind to prove that Chad Moran was, indeed, man enough.

# CHAPTER SIX

Jennifer could not honestly remember having met Charles Tandy, at least not formally. She recognized him vaguely when Chad introduced them, but that was all. Chad seemed to think highly of the man—there was little doubt about that. But Jennifer did not like Charles Tandy, and she had no idea why she should have that reaction to him. There was just *something* about his eyes and the way he looked at her.

She and Silas walked side by side along the spotless corridor of the large barn as Chad and his manager proceeded ahead of them.

Tandy appeared a much taller man than he actually was as he walked beside his employer's wheelchair. There was a startling contrast between the shadows of the two men as Jennifer watched them progress farther into the cool darkness of the barn. It proved a bitter pill that the older man, a man of at least fifty years or more, appeared so tall and strong and brawny. Jennifer wanted that for Chad, also. Oh, she saw him as strong and handsome and virile, increasingly so, there was no doubt about that. But she also knew that others did not see Chad Moran through her eyes, and that caused her pain for him.

Silas was a good example. "Damned cripple, dragging me out here," he mumbled.

Jennifer's gaze dropped downward and to her side. "What did you say?" she asked harshly. But she had picked up enough from his tone to make an assumption.

"Nothin'," the boy returned.

As much as she would like to torment this child about his role in Chad's disability, she knew she could not. Silas was an embittered child who had become hardened against life while he had fought just to survive. Reminding him of his role in Chad's life simply would not improve the relationship between man and boy. And she suspected Silas needed no reminding; he lived with the *reminder* every hour of every day. "You know, Silas, what we see very often depends on what we look for."

The boy slanted her an insolent frown. "Is that supposed to have some meanin'?"

Jennifer's gaze returned to Chad's back as they walked several paces behind him. "Mr. Moran is an exceptional man," she said quietly. "You could learn a great deal from him if you were a willing student."

"I know all I got to know," he drawled. "Besides, you only think he's Mr. Wonderful because you got the itch for him."

Jennifer drew in a shocked breath before she could repress the sound. She stopped walking and, gripping the boy's shoulder, turned him to face her. "Your filthy street language is not all that shocking, Silas, but I suggest you demonstrate some respect around women."

Silas did not feel threatened, however. In fact, he thought she looked damned *shocked*, and he was quite proud of that. Grinning, he said, "I *respect* the fact that you're all red in the face." He laughed shortly. "I guessed right, didn't I? You got a ruttin' *case* for the cripple."

Jennifer's hand fisted at her side as the fingers of her other hand dug into his shoulder while she briefly contemplated which painful insult to attack first: the one to herself or the one to Chad. As was becoming her habit, Chad won out over all other considerations. With a wicked smile and a quiet, harsh tone, she suggested, "One more reference to

Mr. Moran in such terms, Silas, and you and I are going to take a walk out back to the manure pile."

"You and whose army's gonna make me?" he asked contemptuously.

"Have you ever seen how we house-train bad puppies out here in the country?" she asked with mock sweetness. "If you don't change your ways, and soon, *your* training could be likened to that." She left the remainder to his imagination as she turned from him and walked toward Chad.

A gatelike stall door stood open, and Tandy was not in sight as she approached.

Chad turned his head and looked up, smiling, oblivious to what had taken place between Jennifer and Silas. "I think you'll like this little mare," he said quietly. "She's got real promise."

Jennifer took a deep breath and pushed her confrontation with Silas to the back of her mind. "This is her first foal?" she asked.

Chad nodded, pulling his attention away from Jennifer as Charles led the regal mare toward them.

Jennifer's critical eyes took in every nuance of the mare's exquisite frame, from the tips of the ears, raised to indicate attention, to the polished black of a rear hoof and the delicate white stocking above it. "A single stocking," she murmured as her hand reached out to stroke the silk muzzle. "That's good."

Chad moved his chair toward the animal, and the mare's head tilted in alarm. "Hold her steady," Chad directed of his man. "She's not familiar with this contraption. Easy, little mother," he murmured as he reached out and stroked her neck. He eased his chair along her length with one hand while he continued to stroke the horse and talk softly to her. "I just want to feel what you've got here for us," he said.

The mare made to dance sideways in her nervousness, away from him, and Tandy reached along the animal's side, giving her a firm pat.

Jennifer frowned as she watched Chad ease forward until his legs were half under the mare's belly; if the animal should panic, he would not be able to get out of her way.

"Easy," Chad said again, stroking the roan's silky coat as he pressed the upper part of his body against her. "You're good and fat," he said, placing one arm beneath her belly. He turned his head after a brief contact and smiled at Jennifer. "I think we've got a good, strong foal here," he said. "Come feel." He rolled the wheels of his chair back, giving her space.

Jennifer's hand traced along the same route as Chad's had until she was standing facing the mare's rounded middle. She touched low on the belly with both hands and then leaned forward, pressing her upper body against the animal as Chad had done. Concentrating, remaining perfectly still and silent, she was rewarded by the movement of the foal within. "It's like magic every time I feel it," she murmured, turning her head to smile at Chad. "And I've felt it a hundred times or more."

Chad nodded and looked around for Silas, who had remained well back. "Come here, boy," he said. "I'll wager you've never experienced anything like this."

When Silas refused to move, Charles Tandy taunted, "You're not afraid of a little animal, are you, boy?"

Jennifer wasn't certain she liked that approach with Silas, but it did spur the child into action. After he shot Tandy a withering glare, he marched right up beside her.

"You have to wrap your arms underneath her," she said, directing him with both hands on his shoulders.

Silas leaned into the mare and waited. He, too, felt the stirrings of life and, after a brief moment, stepped back, glaring once again at Charles Tandy. "So she's got one in the oven," he snipped. "So what?" He turned and walked slowly toward the double doors then, his hands buried deep in the pockets of his jeans. Fact was, his heart was pounding fit to pop out of his chest, but he wasn't about to let any of *them* see his fear; he liked horses best when he could stand well back and fire stones at them. It was also a fact that he had been affected by the movement he had felt in the huge belly; it had not only been a new experience, it had been a curious thing.

"I don't know what keeps that boy from running off," Tandy observed as the three adults watched the child step outside. "He certainly seems miserable enough here."

"He'd be considerably more *miserable* where he could end up if he leaves," Chad pointed out dismally.

Jennifer was discussing with Chad and Gerome the possibility of installing an elevating device by expanding the cavity created by the dumbwaiter, when Silas slipped out of the house after supper that night.

"Dumb woman's always got some stupid idea," he muttered, scuffing the toes of his new boots along the route that led to the main barn. It seemed stupid to him that somebody should go to all that effort just to give a cripple access to more rooms than he needed. The parlor had been converted into sleeping quarters, and Silas could not understand why Moran couldn't be content with that. It was a big room, after all. To a boy who'd shared such a room with a dozen other boys, when he'd had a roof over his head at all, it seemed a waste.

He stopped briefly, rubbed his eyes with fisted hands, and continued. He was tired tonight and pretty fed up with everybody trying to turn him into something he was not. Moran and that Jennifer were now forcing him into learning to read, and one of them always seemed to be after him. Then Jennifer came up with another one of her brilliant ideas and wanted to teach him to ride a horse in the coming days. "Not bloody likely," he muttered and shoved his hands deeply into his pockets.

Silas looked up in time to dance away from the open barn doors as a young man led Jennifer Downing's big black horse past. "Sendin' her on her way, are ya?" he said smartly to the older boy. "About bloody time," he added more softly as he bent forward and peered into the barn to be sure the coast was clear. "Maybe I'll get lucky and she won't be back," he said aloud. He turned his head from side to side, suspiciously eyeing the horses that stared at him as he walked past. Without conscious thought, Silas stopped walking when he reached the stall of the pregnant mare. Her head appeared over the half door, and he was greeted by a soft nickering sound as her large brown eyes watched him. Boy and animal stared at each other for long moments before Silas grinned. "So, how do you get shuck of a horse-size baby?" he asked and then laughed lightly as if he had told a good one. His grin slowly disappeared, however, as he continued to stare at the stately animal with the soft brown eyes. "Bet that would be somethin' to see," he whispered.

Moments later Silas stood in the open doorway of the library, staring at Chad until the man sensed his presence. Chad looked up from the book he was reading and waited.

Silas sauntered boldly into the room and plopped into a chair opposite his guardian. "You sure read a lot," he observed.

Chad nodded, closed the book, and set it on the table beside him. "I've always enjoyed reading," he said as his fingers closed around his pipe and pouch.

"Never had much use myself," the boy muttered as he looked around the room.

Chad dipped the pipe into the open pouch and tamped tobacco into the bowl with an index finger as he waited to see what the boy had on his mind; it was unusual for Silas to seek anyone's company, let alone *his*.

Silas searched his mind for a trade-off for what he was about to ask. That's the way it was done in his world; no one got anything for nothing. "Ya want some brandy with your smoke?" he asked.

Chad barely hid his misgivings about the boy's civilized behavior, but eventually he nodded. "Yes. Thank you."

"Easier for me to get it than you," Silas said, as if that justified his offering. He moved quickly to the corner table and reached for the crystal decanter that held the dark amber liquid.

Chad watched silently and with growing curiosity. He just knew in his gut that Silas had either committed a misdeed or was after something. They had lived together for less than a month and had, as yet, failed to share any kind of civil conversation. He knew that had something to do with the fact that they had little in common and had a *lot* to do with what they did have in common: namely their separate involvements in that unfortunate accident months ago in Richmond.

Silas placed the well-filled snifter on the table near Chad's elbow and then returned to slump into the chair again. "Guess Jennifer's gone home," he said.

Chad nodded as he reached for the brandy, frowning over the quantity. "I don't like her to stay too late."

"Guess it isn't safe for a woman to ride alone after dark."

"I wouldn't allow that," Chad said simply as he raised the glass to his lips.

"So, what are you goin' to do about her?" he asked wisely. "She's got the itch for you, ya know."

Chad choked, barely refraining from spewing brandy across his lap. "That is no way to talk about a lady!"

Indignant now because Chad had raised his voice while *he* had unbent enough to even spend a little time talking, Silas bolted upright in his chair. "Well, she has!" he said. "She got all red in the face when I asked her!"

Chad put his glass aside and hung his head for a moment as he feared the worst and gathered the courage to ask. "You *asked* her?" he queried, raising narrowed eyes.

"Well, she's hangin' around here lots," Silas said defensively.

"*That* is none of your affair," he said dangerously.

"The last girl I seen followin' a man around like that got the humpin' of her life," the boy threw back defiantly.

"I watched."

"And you're proud of that, are you?" Chad asked with renewed control. Twelve years old and he had *watched*? Chad supposed, in that moment, that the old eyes in that young face had already seen too much of the hard side of life.

Silas shrugged casually. He felt cocky and confident, to be sure. "Doin' it's better than watchin'," he said.

Chad had realized, before now, that growing angry and *demanding* that Silas alter his behavior did not work; the boy was a product of his past environment after all, and could not be expected to change his ways overnight. But how did one deal with a twelve-year-old blustering braggart who was probably a fraud to boot? He reached for a match and touched flame to tobacco as he sorted through his thoughts. "A man of any consequence does not speak of such things with a lady," he said quietly as smoke billowed around his head.

"They do where I come from," Silas informed him.

Chad nodded his understanding as he drew deeply on the stem of his pipe. "What kind of *girls* are we talking about here, Silas?"

"Girls love men to talk dirty to 'em."

He thought about that for a moment and then shrugged as he slouched farther down in the chair. "All kinds, I guess."

"You're wrong," Chad told him quietly. "You think about Jennifer . . . and Courtney."

"So?"

"You think about growing up and becoming a man and earning the disdain of women like them if you continue as you are. And you will earn it, my boy, believe me."

Silas became defensive again, resenting Chad's remarks. "What's so all fired *hot* about them!"

"You think about them and you think about the *girls* you've known, Silas," he said quietly. "And you think about which type of woman you'll want when you become a man."

"So, what's to becomin' a *man*!" he sputtered. "I'm tougher'n you now."

Chad ignored his boasting. "You're going to learn a number of things while you're here," he said.

"And if I don't, you'll chuck me out?" he asked, getting to his feet.

That one comment told Chad a great deal. "Silas?"

The boy stopped halfway between Chad and the door.

"First, I think I would like to see you learn to be a *boy*."

Silas had no comment and turned to stomp angrily from the room. Nothing he ever did seemed right, and somebody was always nagging at him. Now he couldn't even brag about how worldly he was without someone looking down on him. Well, let them look, he thought as he climbed the stairs and marched toward the room that had been given him. It wasn't until he was pulling his nightshift over his head that he realized he had not even expressed his desire to watch the red mare birth her foal. "Be stupid and gory anyway," he muttered.

* * *

Had Silas but known of his accomplishments that day, he would have been gloriously smug for a month; his crudity had set two hearts and two intelligent minds into veritable chaos.

Jennifer lay in her lonely bed that night and wondered if Silas's suggestion could possibly be anywhere near the truth.

She continually explained to Maggie that her frequent attendance at Stonehall was due to the ward and not the guardian. That she had agreed to help Chad until Silas settled in. She also knew that was all a lie, a farce, a sham.

She was becoming more attracted to Chad Moran each and every time she saw him.

"Chad Moran is a charmer," Maggie had said late that evening after Hunter had gone up to bed. "I remember being attracted to whatever it is he possesses. He's attractive and bright, but, Jen, he doesn't even know what he's going to do with his life now."

"It isn't as if he doesn't have several options, Maggie," she had said quietly.

"Don't get involved, Jen," her sister warned. "I think you would just be asking for heartache."

"Because his legs won't support him?" she snapped.

"Jennifer, I just don't want to see you hurt."

"I think the difference between us is that I see the *man*, Maggie," she whispered harshly. "You see a wheelchair."

Jennifer had left her sister alone to think about that and had sought her own bed. But sleep was not about to provide her any relief from her confused thoughts.

Chad had accused her rightly from the beginning and pity had drawn her in; but that had changed. She saw something in Chad Moran that went beyond his virile good looks and, certainly, something far superior to that offered by young men of her acquaintance. And what she saw was with her every moment of every day. She saw his maturity and his youth. In her mind's eye she saw his smile and his frown, his laughter and his sadness. And she saw his darkness, so much darkness. But more vivid than all of these, she saw intelligence and kindness and a man now needing to *prove* that he was a *man*.

All Chad Moran needed was a strong woman behind him, and Jennifer Downing knew she wanted that woman to be herself.

Silas, with his youthful, too-wise eyes, had seen it all. She wanted to be near Chad for a number of reasons, all of them right. And lately, he had even haunted her dreams. "I suspect you have stumbled into unfamiliar territory, my dear," he had said. And she remembered. Jennifer rolled onto her side and pressed her legs together against the recently all too frequent ache as she remembered. She wondered again if what he had suggested that day had been spoken with absolute knowledge.

Chad Moran also lay awake that night, wondering if he should somehow try to apologize to Jennifer for the crudeness of young Silas or if he should just let it lie. It was a delicate subject, to be sure, and what the devil could he say? He could hardly be held responsible for the loose tongue of an ignorant boy. Still, it worried him. Jennifer Downing was young and innocent, and while he admired her fortitude in many ways, Chad suspected she must have been quite mortified over the accusation Silas had apparently made. But to talk with her about it would surely do only more damage and cause her more shame. No, he would leave it, he decided, knowing also he was taking the coward's way out. Because if Jennifer did, in fact, have desires toward him, Chad preferred not to know. It would serve no purpose and would cause only grief for them both. It was now impossible for him ever to have a natural, loving relationship with a woman.

And Jennifer Downing deserved all a man could offer.

She was young and full of life and would soon have a woman's needs, if she did not have them already. She was entitled to the physical as well as the emotional side of a relationship, although he suspected she was not fully aware of that as yet. But Chad feared he was no longer man enough to give it. Not to Jennifer. Not to anyone.

# CHAPTER SEVEN

Treemont's front lawn was overrun by at least a dozen squealing, laughing children when Gerome White brought the matched team to a halt in front of the main house.

Silas leaned back sullenly against the squabs in the open carriage, his arms folded across his chest as he flashed the throng of children a brief, disgusted glare. He wanted no part of a "*stupid girl's party*," and he and Chad had fought over coming here today.

Chad, however, was learning a great deal about Silas on a daily basis, and he suspected the boy had not wanted to come because of fear. This was a new world for Silas, and he did not, as yet, know how to walk around in it; at least not comfortably. So Chad had taken a patient line and promised Silas that if the party proved a bore, they could make their excuses and leave.

In fact, Chad had toyed with the idea of having Silas accompanied only by Gerome. He now had strong misgivings about being anywhere near Jennifer for any length of time, and spending an afternoon at Treemont, by invitation, was not something he had relished for several reasons. He knew he was right in trying to dissuade Jennifer's attentions in spite of the fact that he had not been effective in convincing her to stay away. And he knew he had not convinced her because he was suffering from a lack of conviction; deep down, he did not want her to stay away. The hell of it was, she had him scared

73

to death. He felt out of his element with her, just as he felt out of his element every single time he left his home. Stonehall had become a safe haven in which he moved around with confidence and relative ease, and his conscious mind could fool his subconscious, for brief periods, into forgetting that he would forever be physically challenged. Things there had been altered to suit and accommodate his needs. There was nowhere else that he had that advantage.

But Chad had recognized his unwillingness to remain within the safe confines of his home and knew he could not survive by hiding away. Somehow, at some point in the future, he had to make some decisions about what he was going to do with his life. He had the safety of Stonehall, to be sure. But he had also given up the work he loved when he had returned home to allow his body and his soul to heal. He wasn't at all certain he wanted to give up law forever, and if he were ever to return to a courtroom, he had to stop hiding away sometime. He had decided that this invitation to luncheon at Treemont was a jumping-off point. The decision, however, had not been accompanied by any appreciable level of comfort.

Jennifer was very aware of the arrival of the carriage but got the children involved in a new game before turning and walking sedately across the lawn. She forced herself to walk slowly, although, in her heart, she wanted to race across the newly trimmed grass and greet Chad with a joyous, triumphant hug. In spite of all her fears, he had come!

Jennifer had admitted quite frankly to Maggie that she would not have faulted Chad for staying away, because she had tried to put herself in his place and knew that every outing into the world was not easy for him. Yet, she had qualified. She understood and she hurt for him, but she had no doubt whatsoever that he would overcome his reluctance and learn to deal with the open stares, the flashes of pity, and the curiosity of others. Jennifer knew he had experienced all of these things whenever he had gone beyond the safety of Stonehall, and because of that knowledge, she admired him even more for his courage.

"Hello," she said brightly as she approached the carriage. "Hello, Silas," she added as she tore her gaze away from Chad.

Courtney had torn herself away from her friends and ran to Jennifer's side. "Hi, Silas," she said easily. "Want to come and meet my friends?"

The boy shook his head, frowning. "They're just a bunch of kids," he said disdainfully.

Chad frowned at the boy's rudeness and was about to express his feelings when Jennifer spoke.

"Well," she drawled, "the *old folk* are having lemonade on the porch. You can join us there if you'd rather."

Silas turned his head and scanned the occupants of the wide porch; a woman was holding a baby in her arms while a small boy leaned against her knee. And the most intimidating man Silas had ever seen was walking down the steps toward them. Staying with the oldsters would probably prove either boring or threatening. He immediately rethought Courtney's offer. "Let's go," he said and jumped down from the carriage.

Jennifer smiled triumphantly in Chad's direction. "That took care of *that*," she said easily.

He nodded and held out a pretty package tied in pink ribbon. "I don't suppose I will convince Silas to offer this, so I'll give it to you."

"Oh, what is it?" she asked, taking the soft package and squeezing it thoughtfully. Her brows rose as she stared at the thing, and when she raised it to her nose to sniff, Chad laughed.

"It's for Courtney, imp!"

"I know," she said, smiling at him. "I just like to guess."

Hunter dropped a hand onto her shoulder and reached forward with his free hand to welcome their guest. "Watch her," he warned. "She'll open a small corner to peek and then try to cover the deed."

"I will not!" Jennifer protested.

Chad nodded knowingly, but then the lighthearted atmosphere was dampened by the arrival of Gerome with the wheelchair.

Jennifer covered the procedure that followed, filling the silence with chatter. "You have a new chair," she said as Gerome's muscular forearm disappeared under Chad's legs. "Is it better without the arms?"

"The arms were a nuisance," he muttered as he was lowered onto the thing. "Had to sit too far away from my desk."

"And the supper table?" she quipped, smiling down at him.

He knew what she was doing, and he tried to be grateful. "I usually manage to get my fill when there's good food around," he said. "Regardless of the obstacles."

"Well, I hope you've brought your appetite," she said. "I've cooked up a feast."

Hunter laughed, moving behind the chair. "You did?" He winked at her before directing Gerome to where he could care for the horses.

"I *did*," she said with a feigned pout. "With a little help. I'm not very good in the kitchen," she admitted. "I take after Maggie in that."

Chad moved his chair back as Gerome drove the team forward. It was then he saw the wooden ramp to one side of the three steps that led to the porch. In silence he turned his face up to her.

Jennifer shrugged casually. "Well, come and say hello to Maggie and meet her brood," she said as she hastened forward.

Hunter pushed the high-backed chair toward the ramp.

"You didn't have to renovate your entire house," Chad said ungratefully.

Hunter smiled, even though Chad could not see. "According to Jennifer we did, and it was easy enough to construct. Besides, now you have no excuse for not coming to visit. Maggie enjoys the company of old friends."

Chad was beginning to wonder if there was some sort of conspiracy afoot.

Once the chair was on the flat surface of the porch, Hunter left Chad to his own devices and walked beside him.

Maggie smiled winningly. "I'm glad you came," she said.

Chad nodded, letting his chair come to rest beside her. "Thank you for inviting me."

There was a modest flurry of activity as Hunter determined everyone's choice of drink and Jennifer rearranged the remaining chairs while Maggie introduced Chad to her two sons.

Everett eyed the stranger warily before taking a cautious, curious step toward the wheelchair. "How come you got these?" he asked quietly, testing the feel of one wheel with a small hand.

Chad watched the boy and answered his question frankly. "I need the chair to get around, son."

The small boy looked Chad over slowly, and Maggie's heart took a painful twist as she contemplated calling her son away.

"Don't your legs work bery good?" Everett asked.

Chad shook his head, quietly enduring the moment, knowing two sets of female eyes were watching. "No, my legs don't work, Everett," he said quietly.

"Why?"

Maggie reached out a hand toward her son then. "Everett, come . . ."

But Chad was shaking his head. "Leave him, Maggie. I would rather have open curiosity over surreptitious glances." He returned his attention to the child and gave his knee a single pat. "I had an accident," he said bluntly.

"Do you want to sit up here?"

Everett nodded and raised his arms to be lifted. Once he was settled he smiled with pride at having a new friend and raised his innocent face to the man. "I could help you," he said.

Chad gave the small back beneath his palm a gentle, affectionate pat. "That would be nice. Thank you."

Jennifer suddenly found herself fighting to swallow against a lump in her throat and turned her attention toward the players on the lawn. "I'd best get a new game started," she muttered and darted away.

Maggie watched her go, surprised at her sister's cowardly retreat.

"It's not like her to run, is it?" Chad asked knowingly.

Maggie shook her head. "I wouldn't say she was—"

"She was," he interrupted. Everett wiggled forward, and Chad lifted the child down to allow him to scamper after his aunt. They were alone now except for the sleeping infant. "Your children are beautiful, Maggie," he said quietly.

"Thank you. I think so, too," she said with too much pride.

They both laughed and then the laughter drifted away, leaving discomfort.

Chad's attention was caught by Jennifer's laughter then, as she teased Courtney into trying a three-legged race with her. Her long hair fell forward, shining brightly in the summer sun, as she bent to tie a cloth around her own ankle and her niece's.

"She reminds me very much of you not all that long ago," he said quietly.

Maggie did not know how to respond and found herself wishing Hunter would arrive with their drinks and break this awful awkwardness.

And then, as he watched the activity on the lawn, smiling over the antics of the racers, he said, "I want you to warn her away."

Maggie wondered briefly if she should confess that she had already tried to do that very thing. She decided against it, fearing he would not understand her motives, and she did not want to hurt him. "I don't think that would do any good, Chad. In fact, it might have the opposite effect. Jennie can be stubborn."

He turned his head and frowned at her. "You're not denying that Jennifer is somehow attracted to me?"

She shook her head. "There's little use in denial. You obviously feel it, too."

"Doesn't that frighten you, Maggie? If you love your sister, aren't you afraid for her?"

Maggie stared directly into his dark, troubled eyes. "I don't want her to be hurt," she said quietly.

"And I don't want to hurt her," he confessed. "That's why I want her warned off."

That troubled Maggie more than anything else he could have said. She understood now that Chad cared for Jennifer; why else would he be afraid of hurting her? She also understood that he seemed not to have the fortitude to order her sister away.

Maggie Downing Maguire had the distinct impression that this conversation had come several weeks too late.

Jennifer laughed as she watched Hunter drive the hay wagon, topped high with hay and laughing children, down Treemont's long, tree-lined lane. "I remember you, along with a dozen other of Maggie's friends, going out on hayrides," she said lightly. She grinned and crossed her arms under her breasts. "I was always unhappy because I was too young to go along."

Maggie had gone inside to tend to Jason, leaving Jennifer and Chad alone to entertain themselves for the time being.

"I remember one occasion when you managed to turn up, however," he said ruefully.

She laughed as the memory returned. "Oh, Maggie was angry with me over that," she said. "The last thing she wanted was a little sister intruding when she was with her much more *sophisticated* friends."

"Well, you popped up out of the hay when she was kissing Darryl Rogers."

"I know!" she crowed.

Chad smiled at a memory. "I remember you as a perfect little pest," he said quietly.

"Maggie would agree, no doubt."

"And you're not at all abashed," he accused.

Jennifer tucked her hands into her skirts, between her knees, and shrugged. "That's what little sisters are for. To torment bigger sisters."

He looked at her, disbelieving, and laughed. "Well! If that isn't the most innocent little pose!"

Suddenly Jennifer wasn't laughing with him. "I'm not so very innocent," she said.

Chad was shocked sober. He stared at her for a very long time before his gaze fell away. "I believe you're wrong about that, Jen," he said.

Well, she had ventured into this conversation, having wanted to talk frankly with him for weeks. Weeks? The time could not possibly have been mere weeks; it seemed forever that she had been feeling this way. But now she had opened the dialogue, she did not know where to go with it. Her heart was beating fast and painfully as she turned her unseeing eyes to stare across the lush green of Treemont's lawn. "Somehow, along the way, I think I fell out of friendship and into love, Chad," she whispered honestly. "And I don't know what to do about that."

His head snapped around and he retorted angrily, "That is nonsense, and you know it."

"Why?" she asked softly as she watched him steadily. "Why is it nonsense?"

"You don't even know me," he threw back. "You've known me less than three months, Jennifer. Before that, you hadn't seen me in years."

"I feel as if I know you. I feel as if I know you as well as I know myself."

With a weary sigh Chad tipped his head back as if he were a man suffering a great deal of pain. "You should be with your friends," he said firmly when he looked at her again. "You should be having fun and going to parties with people your own age."

"Age has nothing to do with anything, and besides, you're not that much older than I," she said. "There is a greater difference in age between Hunter and Maggie than there is between you and me."

"Jennifer . . ."

"I don't think you want me to stay away."

"Well, you are quite incorrect in that, my dear," he said harshly. *And that,* he thought, *should be that!*

It hurt him to say those words, as much as it hurt Jennifer to hear them. He had given their relationship some serious thought, and he had managed to convince himself that she was suffering a powerful case of calf-love, and nothing more. In the next breath he admitted to himself that he would be quite lost without her visits to Stonehall. She was like a candle, bringing light and softness into his life. And selfishly he had enjoyed her. But he had already noticed the change in her in the past few weeks. Jennifer had taken a turn toward seriousness; she wasn't the laughing, teasing young woman she had been less than three months before, and Chad blamed himself for that.

For the first time in her young life, Jennifer Downing knew the painful wrench of loving and not being loved in return. She had been so certain that he held some fondness for her that she had dared to bare her soul and offer up her heart in a bold move that would have shocked most of the women she knew. And she was still not convinced that Chad did not care. She sensed that had his accident not occurred, things would have been far different between them, and yet, she did not know how to separate the wheat from the chaff so that he would forget his disability when he looked at her. She believed he was not being honest with himself, or with her, because she wanted to believe. Jennifer Downing saw a man of uncommon likeness, when she looked at Chad Moran. She saw a man who made her blood thunder through her veins when she looked at him sometimes. At other times she saw a quiet man of learning, a man of kindness, intelligence, and gentleness.

She spent her waking hours trying to determine how to reach him, how to make him see. And she spent her dream-hours laughing and loving him. But the wispy visions of loving extended only to resting within the shelter of his arms, because beyond that, she could only speculate. And beyond that, Chad had hinted there could be nothing more. At least for him.

Oddly, the lack of Chad's ability to perform what Jennifer surmised as "husbandly duties" did not have a negative effect on her. She assumed she would never miss what she had never had, and the thought of sleeping next to him, with his arms around her, seemed enough. It would mean no children, of course; she was not that unenlightened. But there was Silas and, no doubt, many children like him who could benefit from a good home. She could easily satisfy her maternal instincts by taking in orphans. She had already made up her mind on that score.

And she had made up her mind about a number of other things as well.

"If you could walk," she asked, "would you give me a second glance?"

Chad barked a humorless laugh. "My, God! You are something!"

"That doesn't answer my question," she said quietly.

"Your question doesn't deserve an answer," he returned harshly.

"I think it's the most important question I've ever asked in my life," she said with conviction.

"Don't you ever give up?" he countered.

"No. But you do, apparently."

He sighed and looked at her for the first time in several moments. "Jennifer, I'm growing weary of sparring with you."

"Then don't."

"Where the devil is Maggie?"

"Maggie's nursing Jason," she said easily. "And she can't save you from me."

"I don't believe anyone can," he muttered.

Jennifer dropped to her knees in front of him and reached for his hands. "You can, Chad," she said sincerely as she stared up at him. "If you truly want to be saved from me, all you have to do is say you do not care at all for me." Her fingers dug into his palms in her earnestness. "All you have to do is look directly at me and tell me you have no interest in me, that you do not ever want to see me again, and I will accept that. But you must tell me that as the man I *see* and admire and *not* as the man in the wheelchair."

"Dammit," he ground out.

"If that is too painfully honest for you, Chad, I'm sorry. I can be no less than direct with you, nor will I ever change."

"Direct!" he choked, shaking his head. "You *are* that."

"I'm only asking that you give a *fair* chance to whatever there might be between us."

"There can be nothing for us," he said. "Why prolong the agony?"

She took hope in the inference that the *agony* could include them both. "Then tell me you do not care," she whispered and held her breath, bracing herself for possible heartbreak; knowing he was worth the risk.

"I cannot tell you I love you," he said brusquely.

Jennifer smiled, a small smile, and shook her head. "I'm not asking that. I'm asking you to tell me you do not care."

Chad closed his eyes and raised his face toward the August sky as if he were praying to God. Obviously she did not understand the torment she was putting him through. He had not yet been able to settle his mind around the fact that he would never again get up out of a damned chair and walk like other men. Most of the time he did not even think of himself as a *man*.

He opened his eyes and lowered his head, staring at the exquisite features that stared back at him with hope in her eyes, and he found himself reaching out to gently touch her cheek.

So many thoughts had occupied his mind of late, and some were of a future that did not include a woman. He had come to the conclusion that he could not tolerate the thought of being a burden to anyone. As he stared at Jennie and touched her, he realized that he had lost precious moments of tender reflections that any other man would have enjoyed these past weeks. Moments when he should have been thinking about this beautiful creature and imagining himself virile and strong and in command of moments of passion between them. He wanted to devote his thoughts to her and not have dark fears intrude. He stared down at the slender hand that covered his own and traced the length of her index finger with his own. The doctors had told him that in time he would know whether or not he would be able to perform with a woman. His mind and his body had been reacting to her, to mere thoughts of her, for weeks. And he had actually lain in his solitary bed and cried with equal parts of joy and relief the first time he had experienced an erotic stirring. But how could he even think about testing his manhood with a virgin bride? And if he failed? This concern was something else that filled him with anger and resentment.

"Jennifer," he whispered. "If it should come to—"

"You can't tell me you do not care," she returned with badly disguised relief.

He looked down at her then, staring into the blue eyes that studied him so hopefully as he freed his hand from beneath hers and gently touched the softness of her cheek again. "No," he whispered. "Damn me for a selfish sod. I cannot tell you that."

Silently Jennifer rose to sit on his lap and wrap her arms around his neck. She curled up against him and nuzzled her nose and chin against his neck, sighing as she felt Chad's arms go hesitantly around her.

This was something Chad Moran had thought never to experience again; the softness of a woman as she pressed her breasts against his chest, the heat of her, the scent of her. It was a fact that the woman who was nurturing all his senses was a generous little feline who had brushed close to his heart just once too often. He could not deny her when she was playful, and he could not deny her when she was serious. And God help him when she discovered her sensuality. Still, he could not give it up, and tightening his arms around her, Chad pressed his cheek tenderly against hers. "Oh, Jen," he said, sighing. "What are we doing?"

"Don't be afraid, Chad," she whispered.

"But I am, Jen. I'm afraid for us both."

Maggie stepped out of the house with a tray of fresh drinks and stopped dead in her tracks. She stared in stunned muteness for a moment before whispering, "No, Jen."

The soft murmur was heard by Chad, and he pushed back on the left wheel, turning the chair in a small circle until he faced her. Looking as if he had been contemplating the theft of a national treasure, he said, "Maggie, old friend, I think perhaps I should have a chat with your husband."

# CHAPTER
## EIGHT

The party came to an early end after the hayride, and Courtney's guests were escorted home in carriages driven by Jeffrey Winter and Gerome White, who volunteered for the detail.

"I tell you, somethin' serious is up," Silas said wisely as they made their way toward the foaling barns.

David Winter had not taken to Silas and snorted, to avoid talking with him.

"The adults are talking," Courtney said wisely. "There's nothing strange in that."

Silas stopped walking and faced her, frowning. "Sure. First we gets kicked outta the parlor by the four o' them. Then the gents decides they need a room to themselves, so we gets ousted from the kitchen by the two women who want to *chat* with the cook. Since when do rich women want to talk with the *cook?*"

"That's my mother," David said defensively. "And Aunt Maggie is her friend."

Silas graced the younger boy with a brief frown. "All right. Don't get your knickers in a knot."

"They are friends," Courtney explained quietly. "They talk all the time about lots of things."

"If I thought old Moran could do it, I'd think Jennifer was cookin' one," he murmured as if the other children were not there.

Courtney wrinkled her brow. "What does that mean?"

87

Silas looked at her then as if she were a dimwit. "You know. Breedin'."

Courtney sucked in an offended breath before blurting, "What?"

Poor David, several weeks Courtney's senior, had not taken much note of such things in the past. He thought breeding was only for horses. He remained silent but curious.

Courtney had the advantage of having discussed her mother's last pregnancy with her parents. "Jennifer is not!" she returned hotly.

"Well, I bettcha Moran can't do it," Silas murmured. "So it must be somethin' else." And then the frowning, curious stares of his companions caught his attention. "I can see I'm goin' to have to teach you two *ignorants* a few things about life. Information is money, guys. Once you find out people's secrets, it's all in how you handle the *information.*"

Jennifer and Marie-Louise sat at the corner worktable while Maggie paced the length of the kitchen.

Marie-Louise's frown deepened as she watched her friend. "So, they shared a hug on the front porch. That's not a disaster, Maggie. Calm down."

Maggie whirled and faced her friend. "No, it's not a disaster. It isn't even the point."

Jennifer chose to remain silent; she would speak when the time was right.

"All right," drawled Maggie's friend. "What is the point?"

"The point is, I told her not to get involved."

Marie-Louise nodded wisely. "I see. *You* told her."

Maggie stopped pacing and frowned at the woman. "I told her that with the best intentions."

"Good intentions can trip you up, Mag."

"I love Jennifer," Maggie explained. "I want her to have a good life and every happiness."

"We all do," Marie-Louise said. "Maybe that means having Chad Moran. Who knows? Jennifer doesn't even know yet, Maggie. For heaven's sake, quit pacing. You're worse than a fox lookin' for a hole in the chicken wire."

Maggie ignored her friend's plea.

Jennifer blessed the cook and longtime friend with a grateful smile.

"I haven't seen her like this in a lot of years," Marie-Louise told the younger woman quietly.

Jennifer nodded and then turned her attention to her sister as Maggie dropped to her knees in front of her.

"Jen, I just want the best for you. Think about what you're doing. You're feeling sorry for Chad. We all are. But—"

Jennifer decided *now* was the time to speak. "You can't tell me how I'm feeling, Mag," she said quietly. "You don't know."

"I don't want to see you hurt," her sister explained.

"Does it follow that I'm going to be hurt because Chad has a disability?" she asked. "I could be hurt by any man, for all of that. I don't think you're being very honest about your objections to my having a relationship with him, Maggie."

Maggie didn't answer at first. "All right," she said, moving to a chair beside her sister. "You don't know about Chad's health."

"I don't know about my own health," Jen returned softly. "None of us knows what the future holds."

"You will face all manner of difficulties with him, Jen. I don't want life to be hard for you. And"—she paused, drawing in a slow, deep breath—"I'm afraid you're confusing love and pity."

"Chad has already accused me of that," she said. "He also accused me of being on some sort of crusade to show the world, and him, what a magnanimous person I am. We've moved past that, Maggie. At least I have." She smiled thoughtfully and looked from one woman to the other. "I'm not certain Chad is fully convinced as yet." Jennifer reached across the table and gripped her sister's hand. "I know what I'm feeling is not pity, Maggie. It's much more than that. Now we need time to discover just what there is between us. He's a wonderful man. You know that. You've known him forever."

Maggie shook her head. "I just have this terrible sense of foreboding," she said sadly.

Jennifer pulled her hand away and leaned back in her chair. "Well, you shouldn't," she said firmly. "And whether you object or not, Mag, I *will* see him."

Marie-Louise winced.

Hunter poured two liberal quantities of brandy and placed them on a table beside Chad Moran. He then offered his guest a cigar, which Chad declined in favor of his pipe.

"I take it this is the obligatory talk you would have had with Jennie's father had he been living?" he asked as he positioned a straight-back chair in front of the other man.

Chad nodded, waiting until Hunter was seated and had reached for his glass. "I'm seeking your permission to court Jennifer. Yes."

Hunter nodded and crossed his legs at the knee. "You have it."

Chad was stunned by the man's concurrence and showed it.

Hunter laughed lightly. "You were expecting objections, I take it?"

"Frankly, yes," Chad admitted and reached for his brandy; suddenly he *needed* this drink. It occurred to him, in that moment, that this was a very unlikely day.

He had accompanied Silas to a child's party. An innocent enough venture. And yet, somehow he was ending the day with a woman in his life.

Hunter shrugged away Chad's comment and took a sip of his drink before responding. "I can see nothing over which I should object," he said. "You have a home, a farm, and financial stability, I assume, whether or not you choose to return to your career in law. You have the material wherewithal to support Jennifer, should it come to that. I am also assuming you care for her and have no intention of causing her any hurt."

"You needn't assume," Chad told him, returning his glass to the nearby table.

"That's good," he said. "Because if you should hurt her, Moran, I'll shoot you."

Chad choked around the stem of his pipe, and there was a moment's stunned silence between them before he understood the small grin that played at the corners of Hunter's lips. He laughed, nervously, and shook his head. "I do care for her. It's taken me until today to admit that."

Hunter became thoughtful for a brief span of time, carefully considering whether he should give voice to his one concern. "Has Jen coerced you into this?"

Chad returned the older man's regard with a steady gaze. "She managed to elicit that which I would not concede," he said softly. "At least not openly."

"Well, as I see it, the decision is yours and Jennifer's and belongs to no one else."

Chad nodded and bit down on the stem of his pipe as he studied the Aubusson pattern of the French provincial settee to Hunter's right. "I tried to dissuade her, Maguire. I swear I did. For obvious reasons." He smiled crookedly at Hunter. "But Jennie is a fairly determined young woman."

Hunter nodded his head and grunted his complete agreement to that.

Chad looked away again, and Hunter sensed a sudden unease about the man. "I swear, whatever happens, it is not my intention to hurt her."

Jennifer found Chad awaiting her outside, just as Hunter had said. Her sister and brother-in-law were currently making use of the parlor.

"There are little conferences going on all over this house," she said lightly as she walked to his side.

Chad looked up and smiled uneasily. "I know. Sit down, Jen."

His tone made her frown. "Has Hunter upset you?" she asked as she smoothed her skirt and sat in the chair beside him.

"No," he said, shaking his head. "He feels the decision is ours alone."

She smiled winningly and raised her hand, palm up. "Well, there you go," she said lightly. "How do we proceed?"

He stared at her in confusion.

"Well, I've never been courted before, Chad. I don't know what we're supposed to do next."

He laughed briefly. "I think the idea is to get to know each other better."

"Oh, I don't need to know much more than I already do," she said blithely as she smiled at him with open admiration.

Chad stared at her, but he was not smiling. "Perhaps I'm not the man you think I am, Jen. Has that occurred to you?"

"Frankly, no. I trust my instincts."

He looked away then. "Instincts have been known to be wrong."

Jennifer's smile slowly disintegrated. "If you're trying to convince me you are not a good person, it won't work. And if you are trying to warn me off because you are experiencing some difficult moments still, that won't work, either. I expect you to feel angry and resentful and frustrated sometimes. I know I would feel that way. I've thought about this, you see," she said quietly. "You and me and *you*. I thought about all the arguments you might have presented, and I tried to place myself in your position. I've come to the conclusion there isn't anything we cannot overcome together."

He smiled sadly then and reached for her hand, gripping it lightly. "You would think that way," he said affectionately. "What do you know of relationships between men and women, my little innocent?" He tugged on her hand then, forcing her out of her chair and toward his lap. "Let's pick up where we were when your sister interrupted us, shall *we*?" he said softly. And when she was settled, he reached up and cupped the back of her neck with one hand. "We have some unfinished business, Jen," he whispered.

Her eyes were intense, as were Chad's, as he pulled her head down. Slowly, slowly, their lips narrowed the distance between them until, finally, he tilted his head to the side and pressed his lips tentatively against hers. He tasted and teased for a brief span, and then Jennifer wrapped her arms around his neck and his arms supported her back as the intensity of this kiss increased.

Jennifer was warmed by the heat of him, savored the scent of him, and concentrated on the texture of his lips against her own. But other, more intense things were going on inside her. She tore her lips away and blessed him with a tender kiss on his chin before pressing her cheek against his. "I feel so many things when I'm with you," she breathed. "I can't sort them all out, Chad."

He tightened his arms about her and just hung on, relishing the feel of her; she was soft and warm and gave him a sense that all could be right with the world. She was like a warmed blanket, a secure house, a resting place from the storm. She was all of these things, and yet, she took these peaceful feelings and somehow made them sensual deep inside him. And he had struggled against her, and himself, for too long.

Admittedly, he would be apprehensive about their first sexual encounter, but now he knew there would be an *encounter*. As he eased her head around and renewed the kiss, Chad Moran told himself he would love her and love her well. With Jennifer it would be all right. All of it.

"We shouldn't be doing this," Courtney whispered, pressing her back against the wall.

"Sshh!" Silas hissed as he peeked around the corner of the house. "They're talkin' real serious now. I can hardly hear."

"Well, you shouldn't be listening," she admonished.

He looked over his shoulder and grinned maliciously. "I don't see *you* runnin' off," he whispered.

"I'm not listening."

"Sure," he said skeptically and returned his attention to the couple on the porch. Criminy, old Moran was kissing Jennifer now.

He decided Courtney wouldn't understand what was being discussed and the kissing was probably getting her all in a tizzy. He could fill her in about a few things, but she was probably too prissy to stand and listen.

He watched the couple curiously; they seemed to be kind of timid with each other. Their kisses weren't rough with the kind of passion he'd witnessed in the back alleys of Richmond.

He wondered how much of a "man" Moran really was.

The following morning Silas laughingly shared his knowledge with a stable boy.

The stable boy was shocked and disgusted and told Charles Tandy he felt sorry for Chad Moran.

Charles Tandy wasn't sorry. He speculated that Jennifer would find herself a lover soon after she married Moran. One way or another, they all took lovers.

He thought about that for a time and then went in search of his woman.

# CHAPTER NINE

Diana Chester flopped backward across Jennifer's bed and stared at the canopied ceiling.

"Personally, I think you're out of your mind," she said.

Jennifer smiled wryly and continued her search. "You're entitled to your opinion."

Diana turned her head and gave a negative frown to the yellow gown. "Too insipid."

"Thanks," Jen said dryly and returned the gown to its place.

Rolling onto her side, Diana propped her head on her hand. "You could have any man you wanted, Jen. Why on earth would you choose Chad Moran?"

"Perhaps because I *want* Chad Moran," she returned, holding a vibrant blue dress high against her chest. "Well?"

"Better," her friend agreed. "Try the rose one." After a moment's thought, she said flatly, "He's old."

"He is not!" Jennifer laughed. "And watch how you say that around here. Chad is only a year older than Maggie. She'll scratch your eyes out if you infer that she's old."

"I can't believe you're allowing him to escort you to Megan and Jeremy's wedding. You won't be able to dance."

Jennifer graced her friend with a repugnant glance. "You can be so damned shallow, Diana. Honestly."

"Well, you love to dance," she said in her own defense.

"So, I'll dance with someone else if I feel like dancing," Jennifer said as she rehung the rose gown. She turned on the other woman in anger then. "And I am not *allowing* Chad to escort me. I'm honored that he's agreed to take me."

Now it was Diana's turn to be disgusted. "Lord, you're noble."

"I am *not!*" she returned in frustration. "What is the matter with you?"

Diana did not want to fight with Jennifer. In fact, she did not realize how they had become angry over this. They were lifetime friends, after all. "I'm sorry," she said softly, moving to a sitting position on the side of the bed. "I care about you and I want to see you happy, Jen. I just can't understand how you could do this."

Jennifer's expression softened somewhat as she realized Diana really could not understand. "Chad is a *man*, Diana. A wonderful man and I care for him. That's all there is to it."

"There's a wheelchair in there, too."

"If that is all you see when you look at him, that's your problem, not mine."

"How do you go about making love with a man who's legs are useless?" she countered.

"Well, for heaven's sake, Diana. How should I know? How do you go about making love with a man who has the use of his legs? I don't know the answer to that question, either!"

"I could tell you, if you like." Diana said quietly.

It took a moment for Jennifer's brain to absorb her friend's comment. "What?" she asked softly as she moved toward the bed. "Diana," she breathed.

"Oh, don't sound so scandalized," she muttered as a heated blush stole from her neck to her hairline.

Jennifer eased herself down slowly and sat beside her friend. "With one of the boys, Di?" she asked hesitantly.

"He's from around here," she admitted, unable to face her friend. "But he's a long way from being a *boy*."

Jennifer was so stunned by all of this, she was having difficulty forming any clear thoughts. "You must love him very much."

Diana laughed with obvious annoyance. "I don't love him at all," she confessed. "I was attracted to him—he is attractive, you see."

"You're not *attracted* anymore?"

Diana shook her head. "No."

"But you—"

Diana held up her hand abruptly. "Please don't judge me, Jen. I hadn't any intention of making love with him, but I was having fun and teasing him a bit, I suppose, and before I knew it . . . we were rolling around in some damned field."

"He shouldn't have forced you . . ."

Diana turned angry again, defensively so. "I was where I shouldn't have been, don't you see? What was I supposed to do? Cry rape?"

"Yes," Jennie said succinctly.

"After I had been leading the man on?"

"Yes."

"Oh, Jennifer!" Diana drawled with incredulity as she got up and began to pace. "You can be so naive. No one would believe me. In fact, if this story were to get out, everyone would say I got exactly what I deserve. Women don't recover their reputations when something like this happens, and you damned well know it."

Jennifer had to concede that point. "When did this happen?" she asked as she watched her petite friend stride around in agitation.

"A year ago."

At age seventeen.

"And it still upsets you," Jennifer said with understanding.

"Sometimes," she admitted, returning to sit beside her friend again. "Once in a while I get angry at my own stupidity all over again."

"I don't think you should, Di. If you said *no*, he should have respected that."

Diana Chester choked on something close to a laugh.

"By the time I said *no*, it was too late."

"Well, at least he didn't leave you with a baby," Jennifer said thoughtfully.

Diana did laugh at that. "He didn't leave me with anything else, either! How do I explain my lack of virginity to a future husband?"

Jennifer's brow crinkled while pondering that. "Would a man notice?"

"I think so," Diana said. "I'm not sure."

"Then you'd be best to tell *whomever* ahead of time."

Diana stared at Jennifer as if she had completely lost her mind. "How on earth could I do that?"

"Just talk about it," she said.

"Can you picture yourself having that kind of conversation with Chad?"

"Certainly," she said easily.

Diana gave that a brief thought. "I suppose it depends on the man," she murmured.

"I *suppose* you're not going to tell me who this lout is?" Jennifer said quietly.

"Lord, no!" Diana said rigidly, knowing Jennifer would run straight to Chad Moran with the name.

The name?

Charles Tandy.

# CHAPTER
## TEN

Later that day Jennifer dressed in her boy's breeches and rode over to Stonehall to lead Silas through his daily abuse of the English language. The difficulty was, of course, that the boy had no interest in reading. Still, she remained determined to teach him something.

She arrived shortly after the noon hour to find the house abandoned except for the cook. Apparently, there was a birthing going on!

Jennifer took a run at the back door of the house and increased her pace once she hit solid ground. She was breathless when she arrived in the barn, racing to a spot beside Silas.

She gave the vacant wheelchair a fleeting glance. "How's it going?" she asked the boy.

Silas was intent upon watching the activity inside the large box stall. "I think it must hurt the poor girl like hell," he mumbled.

"Watch your language," Jennifer reminded him as she, too, studied the movements of the men.

Gerome was standing close to the stall door, looking as if he wanted to stay out of harm's way.

But Chad was sitting on the straw-covered floor, facing the mare's hindquarters while Charles Tandy kneeled behind.

"I can feel the nose," Chad said with excitement. "Come on, girl," he coaxed as he leaned back, pulling against one of nature's obstinate idiosyncrasies and grimacing with the effort.

The mare raised her head and grunted with pain.

Jennifer rushed into the stall and dropped to her knees, stroking the animal's forelock as she smiled at Chad. "Need some help?" she asked lightly.

He grinned crookedly. "It's been a very long time since I've done this."

"Is that why you're doing it?" she asked quietly.

Chad nodded, grunting mightily as he leaned back again. He had felt a lessening of resistance against the foal. "He's coming!" he cried triumphantly.

Jennifer soothed the mare, talking softly and stroking the regal head.

Silas tipped forward, so intent upon seeing what was happening that he almost fell into the stall.

"Come here, boy," Chad called. "If you want to see something very special, now's the time."

Since he wasn't needed, Tandy moved away to allow room for Silas. He was just as content to watch Jennifer's slender hands soothing the weary mare.

Silas took up a place behind Chad and stared over the man's muscular left shoulder. What he saw made his eyes grow large and round. Two slender legs, then a nose, and then the remainder of the head appeared, all encased in a slimy membrane. "Awww!" he cried softly. "Gore!" But he couldn't drag himself away. "Wow," he sighed as the body of the foal slid onto the straw between Chad's spread legs.

There was a triumphant hoot from Chad as he snatched up a rag and began sponging away the membrane from the foal's nose and head. "A filly!" he crowed, as if he was personally responsible. "A fine one, too," he added.

The mare raised her head, suddenly intent upon getting to her feet.

"Keep her down, Jen," Chad said as he hurriedly dragged his lower body toward the corner. "All right. Let her see her baby."

Silas backed away and joined Chad in the corner as the mare struggled to her feet.

This first meeting between mother and newborn was something Chad would always cherish. The birthings were one part of farm life to be enjoyed by all. He raised his eyes and smiled at the intensity with which Silas was studying the scene in the stall. "Special," he told the boy. "Like I told you."

Silas nodded and was only vaguely aware that Jennifer had dropped to her knees on Chad's other side.

The filly raised her head tiredly, her sides heaving with the exhaustion brought about by her arrival.

The mare nosed her offspring, nudging the foal gently as if she were inspecting to ensure everything was in place; first a small hoof and coronet, a bent knee, a cheek.

"She's checkin' him out," Silas said softly.

"Her," Chad corrected as he wiped his arms with the dampened cloth Jennifer had brought him. "That's a little girl, Si. A filly."

Silas nodded, crossed his feet, and lowered his rump to the floor beside his guardian. "Sure was hard for her gettin' here," he observed. "She's breathin' awful hard."

Jennifer bent her knees and crossed her folded legs as she watched Silas with a sense of renewed hope; this was the first this child had displayed an interest in *anything*.

Chad watched from a different perspective; he was suprised, to say the least. Silas had always appeared the tough little monkey, wise to the ways of the streets and knowledgeable in a worldly way that went far beyond his years. The boy had, no doubt, seen far more than he should have for one so young, and yet, Silas was apparently awestruck over the birthing of a simple creature. A beautiful creature, to be sure. But Chad would not have believed Silas capable of caring one wit about a dumb animal, since he apparently cared not a jot for a single, living human being. "If we stay here another few minutes," he said quietly. "The filly will get herself up."

Silas nodded once to let the man know he had heard. Chad smiled, turning a sparkling expression in Jennifer's direction. "Hello," he said quietly.

She returned his smile. "Hello, yourself."

"This is sort of fun," he admitted. He felt a sense of accomplishment, having helped the mare. And now he had Jennifer to share it with him. He looked at Silas, who was eagerly taking everything in with big eyes, and amended his thought: he had Silas to share it with, also.

Jennifer laughed warmly. "Yes. It is."

Charles Tandy appeared repelled by the scene in the corner and quietly took his leave.

Gerome, a man born to the city, was rather enjoying himself; this was his first witnessing of a birthing, too.

Chad looked down at the rolled sleeves of his shirt, which were damp and grimy, and grimaced with distaste before pulling the thing over his head and tossing it out of the way. He alternated his attention between the filly and Silas then, as he rubbed his upper arms with the damp cloth.

"She's gonna get up," Silas declared.

"It may take her a try or two," Jennifer told him.

The boy looked quickly over his shoulder. "Should we help her?"

Chad shook his head. "She'll make it, son," he said quietly.

The term *son* was lost on Silas, but Jennifer had heard, and she felt a warm glow close in around her heart.

"There she goes," Silas whispered.

The filly was standing, shakily, with her four legs splayed at what appeared to be an awkward angle. And then she took a hesitant step, encouraged by the mare. As they watched, over the next few moments the filly worked her way around to her mother's side and nosed under the mare's belly.

"She's rooting for a teat," Chad explained.

"I knew that," Silas returned, clearly insulted that his guardian should think him so naive.

Chad managed to quash an impulse to laugh. "Sorry," he mumbled. He was having a good time. The most fun he'd had in months. In fact, he felt truly at ease for the first time in months. He grinned at Jennifer and, without consciously debating the matter, tucked her under his left arm. "He probably knows more than we do," he said lightly.

"Well, more than me, certainly, if we're thinking along the same lines," she returned.

Chad stared at her long and hard. Yes, she was an innocent. And, yes, he was happy she was that way. He just wondered for the thousandth time if he would be able to educate her the way he wanted to; slowly, gently, lovingly, and *completely*. He put those thoughts aside abruptly because they only caused him pain and he did not want to ruin this day. "Do you like that little filly?" he asked of Silas.

The boy nodded and flashed a smile over his shoulder. "She's a beauty, isn't she?"

"I think she's a good one, Si."

"It would be kinda fun to watch her get bigger," he said.

Chad watched the child's smile slowly disintegrate before Silas turned his head away, as if he had become doubtful of his residency. "That might be arranged," he said. "If you're interested."

Silas wasn't certain about that. After all, they put all sorts of restrictions on him here. Then again, the food was

good and he had a room to himself. A room? Having a
roof over his head was a big plus. Still, he just was not
certain he wanted to tow the mark for anyone. "Don't
know," he muttered.

Chad sighed with an equal mix of disappointment and
lack of surprise. "Well, regardless of what you decide,"
he said quietly, "you can still watch the filly grow up."

Silas looked over his shoulder again, clearly confused.

"She's yours," Chad said simply.

The only sound was that of Jennifer catching her
breath.

"What?" Silas asked after a moment.

"I said, she's yours. I'm making you a gift of the filly."

The boy's eyes narrowed suspiciously; folk just did not
give valuable things away. "Why?"

"Because you're twelve years old and it's time you had
something to care about. But I'll warn you now, if you
fail to look after that little girl, she becomes mine again."
Chad held out his hand, enticing the boy into the bargain.

"Agreed?" he asked.

There was a brief hesitation, a worried frown, and a
quick look in the filly's direction before Silas took the
offered hand. "Bargain," he said quietly.

"Good!" Chad said and tousled the boy's hair before
looking toward Gerome. "Would you tell Cook we'll
be needing some food once I've got myself cleaned
up? I'm starving!" He looked at his two companions;
Jennifer shook her head.

"I've eaten, but tea or coffee would be nice."

"Tea or coffee, it is!" he crowed expansively. "How
about you, Si?"

"I'm not very hungry," he said quietly. He was also,
suddenly, sorry he had told the stable boy that Chad
Moran couldn't get a hard-on.

Jennifer thought she understood. Silas may not be able
to demonstrate his pleasure, but she suspected he was

suffering a combination of emotions. He was probably thrilled with his gift, even while he was disbelieving of it. "Why don't we pack up a sandwich and maybe a cake and you could eat it here?"

Chad was very impressed by her insight and gave her shoulders an affectionate squeeze before he dragged himself toward the chair Gerome was holding in place for him.

Had Chad but known it, *he* had also scored high points for wisdom that afternoon.

"There you go," Jennifer said as she packed two apples into the small basket. "Two sandwiches, cookies, fruit, and milk. Will that fill the gap, do you think?"

Silas sat across the work counter from her and nodded.

Jennifer smiled, knowing the child did not know how to say thank you. Yet. "Then you're all set."

But Silas hesitated in picking up the basket she had pushed his way.

"What's wrong?" she asked kindly. "Would you like me to go with you?"

"No," he said, raising troubled eyes to her. "I don't need anybody holding my hand."

That little bit of defiance was slow to die.

Jennifer bent at the waist and propped her elbows on the counter. "What then?"

After several agonizing moments Silas confessed. "I don't know how to take care of that horse," he said miserably.

Jennifer smiled with relief. "Oh, that. You don't have to worry about that, Si. I'll be happy to teach you."

Again, he looked skeptical. "You will?"

"Certainly. But she won't need all that much care for a time yet. She'll need clean straw every day, and the mare will need feeding. But her mama will look after her needs for the next few months." She grinned as another thought occurred then. "She will need a name, though."

Silas blessed her with one of his rare smiles before he shot down from the high stool at the counter. "Bramble?" he said happily as he bolted for the door. "I want to call her Bramble!"

"Bramble?" Jennie muttered as she straightened up. "Bramble?" She walked toward the swinging door and the dining room then, wondering if Chad had returned from upstairs. "Bramble?" she muttered again as she stepped beyond the threshold. "Well, it's better than *Lucy*, I suppose."

"Lucy, who?" Chad asked from his place at the head of the table.

"Not who," she said as she moved toward the chair at his right. "What."

"What?"

"Mmm." She dropped a light kiss on his forehead and sat down. "It's that *prickly* boy," she said.

Chad laughed out of sheer confusion. "What the devil are you talking about?"

Jennifer grinned and braced her chin in the palm of her hand. *"Prickly,"* she said. "Silas wants to call the filly *Bramble."*

Chad shook his head, reaching for the silver coffeepot and pouring dark, steaming brew into two cups. He wasn't quite certain he understood her humor; not all of it, at least. "I think you're crazy," he said warmly.

"Mmm. I should have warned you about that."

"I wish you had," he returned with well-feigned mistrust.

"You were very clever out there today, Mr. Moran," she said softly.

Chad halted in the act of raising his sandwich to his mouth when he looked into blue eyes that were all soft and feminine. "Was I?"

"Mmm-hmm."

"Is this a new or shortened version of your vocabulary, Jen?"

She laughed and reached for his knife, cutting a wedge from half of his sandwich. "What a clever gander you are," she said conversationally. "Giving Silas a sense of responsibility is probably the best thing in the world for him."

Chad watched her munch on his sandwich with relish. "It's long past time the boy had something to call his own."

"But a horse, Chad? A fine filly like that? You're more than generous, I'd say."

Chad shrugged and took a bite of what remained of his food.

"Maybe Silas will learn to express some affection, too. Had you thought of that? He's as cold as a stone most of the time."

"I thought of that," he said simply as he watched her cut another generous portion of his sandwich.

"You don't have angry feelings toward Silas anymore, do you, Chad? You're coming to care for him."

He thought about that for a moment. "I suppose my feelings toward him have changed. Yes, that's true. As I see it, Silas is as much a victim of circumstance as I."

Jennifer smiled, and she would have expressed her pride over his reasoning had her mouth not been full.

"I understood you weren't hungry," he added wryly.

Jennifer looked at his plate in dismay and then covered her mouth with a delicate hand as she giggled around a mouthful of *his* food. "I'll fetch you another," she said and darted from the room.

Jennifer looked decidedly sheepish when she returned moments later. "I'm sorry," she murmured.

Chad reached out and captured her hand, bringing it briefly to his lips. "You're forgiven," he said as he accepted her offering. "I'm really quite willing to share with you," he added, "but we'd missed the noon meal so I was exceptionally hungry today."

"It doesn't drive you mad having someone's fingers picking food from your plate?"

"Not as long as they're *your* fingers," he said easily before biting into his newly built sandwich.

"Really?" she murmured and stored that bit of news away for future, private, consideration. She topped up their coffee cups with warm coffee as she contemplated discussing her morning conversation with Diana. Anonymously, of course. The entire situation that her friend had revealed had been plaguing her for hours now, and as close as she felt to Maggie and to Hunter, Jennifer felt that Chad was the only person on earth with whom she could discuss such a thing. "Could I talk with you about something?" she asked quietly.

Chad detected the hesitant note in her voice and turned his dark, brown eyes upon her. "Of course, Jen. What is it?"

"It's about a friend of mine," she explained. "It's rather a delicate subject."

Chad returned the last portion of his lunch to his plate and wiped his fingertips on a linen napkin. "I would hope there is nothing you feel you cannot discuss with me."

She smiled and allowed him to wrap his large hand around hers on top of the table. "Do you feel the same?" she asked quietly. "Do you feel you could discuss absolutely anything with me, Chad?"

He felt guilty over his response because there were some things, worries, that he was hiding from her, but he said, "Yes."

"Do you know you're easy for me to be with?" she whispered.

"Am I?" he asked with a smile.

Jennifer nodded, studying their joined hands.

"That pleases me, Jen," he said. "I think most people continue to feel uneasy around me. They don't know where to look most of the time."

"I expect friends and acquaintances will get over that eventually."

His wise little innocent, he thought as he waited for her to broach the subject that was obviously weighing heavily upon her mind. "Tell me about your friend," he said after a moment.

"I just found out today that a friend was . . . put upon," she said.

Chad's brows arched upward, causing a deep wrinkle across his brow. "Put upon?" he asked. "That's a very old-fashioned term."

"I call it rape," she said, looking directly into his eyes. "She won't call it that."

Chad had a sick, twisting feeling in his gut, and he squeezed her hand. Hard. "Who hurt you!" he demanded.

"No!" she said quickly, gripping his hand with both of hers. "Not me. I swear, Chad. It really is a friend."

"Jennifer . . ."

"I swear," she repeated. "I'm a virgin. I swear to you."

His eyes scanned her face, searching for truth. "It's not only your virginity," he said softly. "I just don't want to ever think that you've been—"

"I haven't", she said quickly.

He seemed to grow more calm as he searched her expression and became convinced of the truth. "Let's move into the other room," he said.

Jennifer followed him into the front room, taking their coffee and placing the cups on the low table in front of the settee as Chad transferred from his chair to the sofa.

"Come on," he said, patting the cushioned bench near his right hip. "Sit beside me."

Jennifer settled herself under his arm; it seemed so easy, so relaxed, so safe and warm. "I'm so glad I've got you," she murmured.

Chad hoped she would always feel that way. He dropped a light kiss against her temple. "Talk," he said softly.

She told him the entire story as it had been told to her, without hesitation or embarrassment; he liked that about her.

"Would you call it rape?" she asked when her tale was told.

Chad hesitated only briefly. "I would, but thousands wouldn't," he said.

"That's what my friend said."

"Do you know who this man is?" he asked.

Jennifer shook her head against his shoulder.

He didn't like the thought of such a man living within their community; not with Jennifer riding around the countryside without a care. "We never know what's lurking in the minds of our neighbors," he said thoughtfully.

His deep tone was so grim, it caused Jennifer to shiver.

Chad tightened his hold around her shoulders and ducked his head to speak. "I want you to have more of a care, Jen. Don't be riding across fields and through brush on your own."

Jennifer tried to laugh off his concern. "I've been riding on my own since I was a little girl, Chad."

"Well, you're a big girl now. That could make you more of a draw to such a man."

Jennifer frowned and her eyelashes fluttered as she looked up at him. "Only *could?*"

Chad did not respond to the bait she had cast him. "There are men who are attracted to *little* girls, Jen."

That was a repulsive thought. "Perhaps my friend did tease this man without realizing what she was doing," she speculated. "Perhaps the man does not have the kind of nature we're assuming he would have. I've not heard of any other . . . situations occurring in these parts."

Situations? It was unlike her to go round a word such as rape; or anything else for that matter. Chad also knew that news of that sort would have been kept away from tender ears such as hers. And he had been away so much of the time over the past years, he would not necessarily be privy to that sort of information.

Jennifer could see he had turned contemplative over the issue, but she had more questions. "Now my friend is worried that a future husband will know she is not a virgin," she said.

She had recaptured his attention, and he grinned at her. "Not a bashful bone in your body, is there?"

"Not with you," she returned frankly. "Does she have a valid concern?"

"Perhaps."

"Why only *perhaps*?"

Chad found that he could do nothing more than provide candid responses to her forthright questions; she was entitled to answers to any questions she asked of him, as far as he was concerned. "Most experienced men would know, Jen."

Her head tipped farther back on his shoulder so that she could see his expression more clearly. "Will you know, Chad?"

It was possibly the only thing he would *know* for certain, during their first experience at least. "I'll know," he said quietly, breathing deeply as her innocent, yet sensual, questioning stare caused a heated physical reaction in his body.

Jennifer lowered her head then and pressed heavily against his side. "I'm happy one of us will know what they're doing," she whispered. "I imagine myself clumsy and inept."

Now was the time, he thought.

"So you think about it, do you?" he asked and branded himself a coward for hedging.

Jennifer laughed. "Of course I do. Sometimes when I'm alone in my bed I dream about what it would be like to lie beside you and have you hold me."

"Is that as far as your night dreams take you?" he prompted.

Jennifer pulled out of his embrace and turned on the settee until she was facing him. Her gaze searched his, suspecting there was a deeper topic at hand. "You told me you didn't think you . . ."

Chad knew he could not back away from the conversation. Not now. "I know what I suggested, sweetheart," he said, taking her hand and holding tight. "That's because I haven't been with a woman since . . . Jen. I haven't been with a woman since my accident."

She thought about offering him sympathy and quickly decided against it; Chad did not cope well with sympathy. "Well, there you go!" she said cheerfully. "I won't have to be concerned about you being more experienced than I. We'll be testing the waters together!"

He stared at her in stunned surprise and then laughed. "You've just countered a previous statement, you adorable little twit."

That was true. "So, I'm fickle," she said. "I should have warned you about that, too."

"You are not fickle, Jen. I know that much about you, at least. As a matter of fact, I think you're wonderful."

Jennifer stared down at her bent knee where it rested against his hip, and then she raised questioning eyes to his. "Am I wonderful, Chad?"

He nodded.

"Is that just because I can be witty sometimes?"

"No," he said softly.

"Does *wonderful* mean you're attracted to me?"

"I think you're beautiful," he said.

"That's not much of a commitment, is it?" she countered. "I want to know if you think about *being* with me," she added boldly.

He knew exactly what she meant, and he did think about that. He certainly did. But she was not the kind of woman a man dallied with before being certain of his willingness to offer for her.

"Because if you do, I want you to know that I want whatever you want. And if that's too forward of me, then I'm sorry. But I feel I have to be brazen because I'm wondering if you're worried, and I don't want you to worry."

Worry had, indeed, played a role in the delayed development of their association, and he had thought about that. He had even suppressed his desire to show her any affection. Until recently.

He pulled her against his chest, forcing Jennifer to swivel until her legs straightened along the length of the settee.

"I'm not worried," he lied, whispering against her hair.

"Let's just go along, shall we, and see what comes of it?"

But Jennifer was becoming impatient with "just going along." She put her arms around his neck and held on tight, feeling he would coast forever and never discover what life held in store for them. He had been treating her more like a comfortable confidante than a potential lover, and she was determined that something should change, and soon. The progression from friends to lovers was simply moving too slowly. She was tired of feeling she was his buddy. Not that he did not treat her as a *woman*; he did. She just wanted to have more of a sense of being *his woman*.

The difficulty was, she was not at all certain how to go about affecting the change.

Her hands played across his shoulders, feeling the strong muscles tense beneath her fingers. "You're more taut than Marie-Louise's clothesline," she quipped as her fingers continued to stray to his upper arms.

"From pulling the filly out, no doubt," he murmured.

"Muscle strain."

That was a fabrication if she had ever heard one; he should be so well toned from pushing on the wheels of his chair that his muscles would never bunch up like this. Having suffered enough muscle strain from working with horses to know about such things, Jennifer made a quick decision. She scrambled up from the sofa and moved toward the dining room. "Take off your shirt," she said over her shoulder. "I'll be back."

She returned moments later, closing both sets of sliding doors that led to the front room. She approached him then, with a bottle in hand. "You haven't taken off your shirt," she said as she frowned down at him.

"What's that?" he asked, eyeing the bottle and ignoring her order.

"It's oil. It's about time you relaxed a little, Mr. Moran, and I'm going to see that you do."

"Really?" he asked suspiciously. "And how do you plan to do that?"

"A massage."

Chad shook his head. "No."

"Why not?"

"Because it's too intimate a thing to even consider," he said firmly.

"What are you afraid of?" she goaded lightly. And she was willing to play his game to get what she wanted. "I've had muscle strain, and a good massage does wonders."

"I don't need *wonders*," he muttered. What he needed was a miracle; this woman would not relent, and he needed more time.

"Perhaps those tense muscles aren't from strain at all," she said smoothly. "Perhaps it's something else and you're afraid to tell me."

Chad stared up at her mischievous grin with a jaundiced eye. "Perhaps I'm not fond of having a massage," he countered.

Jennifer laughed. "Fraud," she said affectionately. "Why would you be afraid of such a simple thing?"

For a thousand reasons. Because he knew where such a thing between a man and a woman could lead. Because he wasn't mentally ready to physically love her yet. Because when he did make love with her, he wanted everything to be perfect. *Perfect* did not include apprehension on the part of the experienced lover. And *perfect* did not cohabitate well with the obvious concerns about taking a virgin who should be a wife before she became a lover.

But even though he knew she was goading him, he would not allow her to see his cowardice; it was difficult enough secretly living with it himself. And he certainly did not want her to misinterpret his hesitation. "This may not prove to be such a simple thing as you would imagine," he said softly as he leaned forward at the hip and pulled his short-sleeved basque jersey over his head.

The rolled neck rumpled his hair, and Jennifer grinned as she reached out and finger-combed it back from his forehead. She set the bottle on the table near his elbow then and stooped to grasp his ankles. "Let's get your feet up so that you can roll onto your tummy," she said easily.

Chad, however, was not at all at ease. Still, he was determined to allow this.

Once he was settled on his stomach with his head resting on the back of his hands, Jennifer uncorked the bottle and straddled his hips, resting back on his buttocks.

Chad started when he felt evidence of her weight radiate to the small of his back.

"Am I hurting?" she questioned worriedly.

He shook his head. "No. But this is hardly seemly, Jen. If this should ever get out—"

"It won't," she returned with confidence and poured a bit of oil into her cupped palm.

He perceived her forward movement and saw her reach beyond his head to place the bottle back on the table. A moment later her warm, oiled hands gripped his shoulders and her fingers dug into his knotted muscles. It took only moments before his eyes drifted closed while he concentrated on the sheer pleasures of this experience. The movements of her hands caused a warm, fluid friction between his skin and hers, and the delicate scent of the oil drifted subtly around them. When her strong fingers dug deep into a particularly sensitive spot, Chad felt a tingling sensation along his arm to his fingers and, when her thumbs began a circular motion upward on either side of his neck, he turned his forehead onto his hands, groaning with pleasure as he gave her greater access.

"Feels good?" she asked softly.

"Yes," he whispered because a whisper was all he could manage.

"Have you been like this since the accident, Chad?"

"I hadn't thought about it," he muttered. In fact, now that he did think about it, he suspected he had only been in this condition since his feelings toward her had started to change.

"We're not going to let this happen again," she said softly, feeling some of the muscle knots loosen beneath her fingers.

She cupped one large, rounded shoulder with both hands and dug in with her fingers. His skin was supple and warm and smooth, but beneath it he was firm and bulging with a manly physique that was new and wondrous to her. He felt strong, solid, and dependable. Just the way she had always thought about him, long before she had ever touched him. In spite of the insecurities she considered he harbored, he was a man of substance and boldness and courage, and no accident could ever rob him of these qualities. The uncertainties would disappear in time.

Chad grunted as her fingers dug deeply into a sensitive spot.

Jennifer smiled.

"This is wonderful," he said quietly.

"All you need is a little of my womanly care," she said with license only the truly innocent could dispatch.

Chad choked back a tortured laugh.

Her thumbs worked in small circles down either side of his spine, her palms brushing lightly along his ribs, her fingers splayed. His shoulders and upper back were exceptionally wide but narrowed in beautiful proportion as she worked her way down to the small of his back, his narrow waist. He was more beautiful than she could ever have imagined, and she was savoring every moment: every sensation as she touched, every sight as she looked, every scent as she breathed, and every sound as *he* breathed.

It had never been this way with Damon. Granted, she had never touched Damon like this. Mainly because she had never had the inclination. He had simply never attracted her as this man attracted her. She felt a little guilty over that, knowing that when Damon Lockyer returned from a summer trip to the coast, he would expect to find the same old Jennifer. The girl everyone thought he would marry. The girl *Damon* thought he would marry. She had been trying to subtly put him off those kind of thoughts for over a year, and now Jennifer knew she would have to be a lot less subtle and a good deal more frank about their relationship. Yes, she knew that, when Damon returned, they would have to have it out.

Chad was totally aware of every movement of her hands and body. Every place she touched became a hotbed of tingling nerve endings, so sensitive was his upper torso.

He turned his head toward the back of the settee, as if he could hide his face and not betray what was happening. By the time Jennifer's hands reached his lower back, he found his heartbeat had begun to race and thunder. Jennifer had been right—her "womanly care" was working wonders. And if he were to flip over onto his back at that moment, she would be astounded by the "wonders" she had achieved. Astounded and perhaps a little startled.

Jennifer became concerned with his reactions, and she could feel the quick, solid thumping of his heart clear through to his back. She stilled her hands and leaned forward, peering over his shoulder as she tried to see his face. "Chad? Are you all right?" she whispered.

Alarmed when he failed to respond, Jennifer climbed down, wiping her hands on the thighs of her breeches as she dropped to her knees and placed a small hand on his shoulder. "Chad?" she questioned softly again.

He reached out and grasped her other hand as it rested on her thigh, but he would not look at her. "I'm all right, love," he whispered huskily.

Jennifer's frown deepened, and she pulled up on his shoulder, willing him to roll onto his side. "No, you're not," she insisted. "Look at me."

Not wanting to frighten her, he turned his head, reacting instantly when he saw her state of alarm. He raised her fingers and pressed them against his lips. "It's all right, Jen, I swear."

She stared into his eyes, trying to determine whether or not he was telling her the truth. "Then why do your eyes look the way they do?"

His smile was somewhat pained as he continued to hold her hand close to his lips. "Even for a courting couple we're having some very intimate conversations," he said softly. "Do you know that?"

"Why intimate?" she asked in confusion. "Perhaps a while ago when we were talking about . . ." She halted in midsentence, her eyes growing large and round.

She looked so adorably stunned that Chad could not hide a grin. "The look you see is pure male appetite running rampant," he said blithely.

Jennifer dropped back on to her heels even though he continued to hold on to her hand. She had wanted to stimulate some kind of a reaction in him, but she could not believe she had actually aroused him in the way he was suggesting.

"I did warn you," he said.

She nodded her head, looking decidedly doubtful. "I know, but—"

"Did you think you were rubbing down one of your horses, Jen?" he teased.

"Well, no, I just didn't think I would . . ."

It was the first time he had ever seen her speechless, and he was beginning to take pity. "Would what, sweetheart?" he asked, giving her hand an encouraging squeeze.

Exasperated with her lack of eloquence, Jennifer blurted out exactly what was on her mind. "Well, it was an experiment to see if I could get you to think of me differently, but I didn't actually believe it would work. I mean, I'm sitting here in breeches and a boy's shirt, for heaven's sake!"

"Clothes don't make the woman, Jen, and I don't think you want me to think differently of you. Trust me."

She moved a bit closer to him and wrapped her small hand around his hand; the one that continued to hold her. Her eyes sparkled with mischievous intent as she smoothed the fine hairs on the backs of his knuckles. "I want you to think of me as a sensual goddess," she whispered.

His bark of laughter startled her, but then his hand released hers and moved to the back of her neck. "You're a wanton," he said with delight as he pulled her close. "And you have no idea what you're doing," he added before he pressed a chaste kiss against her lips.

Jennifer grinned sheepishly. "I admit that. I've never really touched a man. Not in a familiar way, at least."

*Familiar* would not have been his choice of words.

"Does this mean it will be all right, Chad?" she asked hesitantly. "I mean, if we're going to . . ." To what? Marry? How could she ask him that when he'd given no indication that his regard for her went beyond affection? Although she admitted to suspecting he felt something more. And in that moment, Jennifer knew it would not matter if he did not marry her. As shocking as the thought may be, and knowing Maggie would never forgive her, she knew she would be with him no matter what he asked. She could deal with his hesitancy to wed as long as she believed that he loved her. She had never had such a scandalous thought, but somehow, with him, it did not matter. The only significant thing in her life was being with Chad. She wanted him to understand that. "I'm not very good at saying things in a delicate way," she admitted with firm resolve. "I'm trying to ask that you not worry. That we can be lovers whenever you choose."

He stared at her long and hard, and she met his gaze honestly and frankly. Neither looked away from the other's heated gaze as he rolled his hips and legs back a fraction.

"Don't be afraid," he said as he reached for her hand. She was doing her damnedest to appear confident, but he knew her boldness for what it was. Her sheer bravado touched his heart and so did the message she was successfully conveying. "I want you to understand what has happened," he said as he continued to stare at her with tender regard. "Don't be afraid," he said again as he pressed the palm of her hand against his erection.

Jennifer did not snatch her hand away, but her eyes grew large and round.

He watched her and smiled as she refused to tear her eyes away from his. "You did that," he said frankly.

"Should I be proud?" she asked hesitantly.

He laughed and nodded.

"I mean I know about ... well, I've seen the stallions, Chad, and I've guessed that men ..." She faltered again and hated herself for it. "I suppose this is the way it's supposed to be?" she asked in a strong tone that was meant to show confidence she did not feel.

He wanted to laugh with delight, but he didn't. "Did you mean what you said, Jen? Would you really become my lover?" he questioned with mild hesitation.

"Is that what you're asking of me?"

Chad shook his head firmly. "No," he said. "It's what I want, but it's not what I'm asking. Not now, Jen."

Jennifer frowned, not certain about his meaning. "Why not now?"

"Because I don't believe we're ready." *He* wasn't ready. But she touched a warm spot deep inside him with her willingness to make such a commitment. It told him a lot about how she was feeling.

"I *feel* ready," she whispered as she looked down at the place where their hands rested. "I haven't touched a man before," she confessed.

He should hope not! "That's all right, sweetheart. You can touch me."

She giggled as her fingers began to explore, lightly and tentatively, and a light blush covered her cheeks as she looked into his eyes again. "This is wicked, isn't it?"

"This is one of the happiest moments of my life, Jen," he said as he reached out and touched her cheek with his fingertips. "Share it with me." He could feel his breath catching in the back of his throat as he allowed her to explore. He gave her the freedom to do as she would even though she was causing his heartbeat to race again. He felt this intimacy between them was good; it was like schooling for them both. It would appease her curiosity, and it would, perhaps, banish his demons.

"Does this hurt you?" she asked, allowing herself another brief glimpse of the bulge she could feel through his trousers.

"No. It doesn't hurt," he said huskily.

"What do we do about this?"

"Nothing."

"It goes away on its own?" she queried, clearly puzzled by it all.

His smile was positively seductive. "It will. I promise."

She removed her hand and placed it on his upper arm as she frowned at him. "Aren't we being very clinical about this?"

He nodded his head. "I need it to be that way right now."

"I think you're more excited than you're letting on," she said sagaciously.

Chad felt an obstructive lump form in his throat, brought about by the tenderness of her tone. "I think you could be right," he managed to say.

Jennifer lowered her head, pressing her cheek against his, as she put her arms around his shoulders. "I know I shouldn't be so bold," she said softly. "It's not as if I wasn't raised to be proper. But it's difficult to be *proper* when I'm feeling this way, Chad." Because she was so overwhelmed with love for him and she didn't know how to say the words. Not yet. She wasn't certain he was ready to hear them.

Moments later Chad became aware of moisture falling on his shoulder as she clung to him. "Oh, Jen," he breathed.

Neither of them heard the whispering of wood as the doors leading to the dining room were gently pushed closed.

# CHAPTER ELEVEN

Jennifer and Chad were the first to arrive at the small church so that he could transfer from his chair to a rear-pew bench without the stares of curious eyes. Jen knew they would also be the last to leave. And that was fine. Whatever they had to do in order for Chad to feel less conspicuous was fine with her. Jennifer was wise enough to let Chad feel his way around, so to speak, when they were out in public. But she also knew there would come a time when he would care less about what people might think. He might never accept his restrictions, but he would adapt. And when that happened, she hoped they would be able to get on with their lives. Together.

The ceremony that joined Megan Fowler and Jeremy Hart as husband and wife was simple, yet moving. As the young couple turned toward each other and repeated their vows, Chad felt Jennifer's small hand work its way into his. He turned his head, seeing her eyes misting over, and smiled when she refused to look his way. His brave, sometimes outrageous little imp was a sentimental woman, after all. And he loved that about her, too.

He faced the front of the church again, appearing intent upon what was happening before the gathered crowd, while his thoughts turned to his life as he saw it now. Summer was almost at an end, and Silas would be starting school. The boy continued to be a thorn at times, but Chad was determined to keep him. Their relationship

127

was evolving slowly, and paying more attention to the little hooligan seemed to be paying off. It had come to the point where it was difficult for him to imagine Stonehall empty of thundering feet as Silas raced about.

And Jennifer? Chad was determined to keep her, too. He suspected that, with or without the use of his legs, Jennifer Downing was meant to be his. He had come to believe that she truly did see the man and not the wheelchair. While they would face difficulties in life that other couples might never have to deal with, he thought that they were strong enough and brave enough to present a united front and get on with being happy together. Jennifer was strong. He truly believed that. And himself? He was getting there. Slowly but surely, he was changing the way he thought every morning when he awoke to face another day.

He generously gave a lot of the credit for that to Jen. She would not allow him to think of Stonehall as the boundary of his world, and there were few places they did not attempt to go together. And the days he did not see her were long and dull, no matter how he filled them.

At night his dreams were erotically haunted by her—sensual imaginings that tortured him unlike anyone had since he had first discovered that a certain part of his anatomy was used for more than one function.

He had already talked with Hunter and Maggie and had their consent. Although Maggie's agreement had not been as jubilant as he might have hoped. Still, he understood that she loved her sister and might have some misgivings or doubts about Jennifer's future happiness. He was determined that Maggie's concerns should be quickly set aside.

He heard Jennifer sniff delicately and rotated on his buttocks until he could retrieve a linen kerchief he carried in his trousers pocket. He smiled when she took his offering, although she still refused to turn her head and allow him to see her tears. She was funny that way. She continued to be mortified by the fact that she had cried on his shoulder, not so many weeks ago. Jen did not understand why she had cried, but Chad knew. He also understood that she was becoming increasingly frustrated, sexually frustrated. The stolen moments that allowed them the privacy of passionate kisses and tentative caresses were taking their toll. Knowing she was in such a state heightened his own anticipation of the time to come when they would share a moment of release.

Jennifer touched a corner of the kerchief to the corners of her eyes. Stupid to cry, she thought. And yet, this ceremony moved her as no other she had attended. Perhaps because she found herself wishing it was she and Chad up there at the front of the church with the minister speaking directly to them. Words and vows that would wrap around them and secure their love for each other. In her heart Jennifer prayed it would not be long before Chad would ask for her. Their relationship was strengthening and they could barely stand to be apart. He was becoming more bold in his advances, and she was becoming more brazen in her responses. He made her feel things she had never expected a woman would feel, and she felt if something did not happen between them soon, she just might explode with pent-up emotion.

Jennifer held Chad's hand and devoted her complete attention to him as the wedding guests slowly filed past them and out of the church. "It was a lovely ceremony," she said, for want of something better to say.

Chad cast a doubtful look over her head and grinned at Hunter as that man tore his attention away from his wife.

Boldly Chad tipped his head to the side and whispered close to her ear. "Ours will be lovelier, I'm certain."

There was a moment of stunned silence before Jennifer turned questioning, anticipatory eyes upon him. "Ours?" she breathed.

He nodded. "If you'll have me."

Jennifer hauled back with a small fist and struck him on the shoulder.

Stunned, Chad covered the spot with his hand. "What was that for?"

"You had to ask me in a public place," she hissed, her frowning face very close to his. "How am I supposed to react here, of all places? I have to maintain some semblance of decorum."

He laughed. "Why don't I believe you?"

Knowing her sister and her brother-in-law were the only onlookers, Jennifer graced him with a sweet smile and a delicate squeal before throwing her arms around his neck. "It's about time," she breathed. "Of course I'll have you!"

Maggie and Hunter looked on. Both smiled, both maintained their own separate thoughts about what was to come.

"Well," Hunter drawled. "Are you going to tell us outright or not? We might have a few words to share."

Jennifer refused to let go, but Chad managed a smile. "She says she'll have me."

"As if you doubted," Maggie said softly. She reached out and touched her sister's shoulder affectionately.

Jennifer turned and was enfolded in Maggie's arms. "Be happy for me, Mag," she whispered. "I love him so much."

"I know, darling. I know you do."

Hunter pressed his chest against Maggie's back and reached around the two women to offer his hand. "Congratulations, Moran." Hunter had already told him he was getting one hell of a good lady. He did not feel he had to remind the younger man of that; Chad knew exactly what kind of woman he was about to marry.

As the two male hands unlocked, Maggie noticed the bloodstone ring Chad was wearing on his right hand. It was of heavy, hammered gold, and the large stone was held in place by four high-sitting claws. It was beautiful, a man's ring to be sure, and it was unusual.

The moment was broken when Jennifer pulled back and smiled at Hunter. "You're finally getting me off your hands," she said teasingly.

"Thank God!" he returned.

They all laughed, and Chad squeezed her shoulders.

"Well," Hunter said, getting to his feet and pulling Maggie up with him. "I'm for going on to the wedding feast. We can discuss the details of this engagement and hold our own celebration."

Jennifer slid across the pew as Gerome approached with Chad's chair. "It's going to be a great evening!" She laughed.

It was as far as Chad was concerned. He planned on seeing to it that this was a night she would never forget. She deserved something memorable.

Jennifer was filled with excitement and even kissed Gerome on his leathery cheek. "Brace yourself, my friend," she said. "You're going to see me more frequently from here on out."

That was not a problem. Gerome liked the young woman, and she did more for Chad than she would ever know.

"Congratulations are in order, I presume?"

"You presume correctly," Chad informed his man as he settled in his chair. "Let's go!" he said, smiling up at his future wife. "I'm starving."

The food and drink never seemed to stop that night as the celebration moved on past midnight. Hunter arranged for a small table to be set for them after the meal where they could watch the dancing and yet hold a private conversation.

"I want a small wedding," Jennifer said as she reached for Chad's hand and looked around the crowded room.

"Nothing this elaborate and certainly not this many people."

Chad frowned slightly at that but decided he could discuss the size of the wedding with her later. In private.

"You'll want to discuss a date," Maggie suggested.

"Just remember we need *time* to make all of the arrangements."

"The date will be soon," Jennifer said, looking hopefully at her future spouse. "Would you agree, Chad?"

He smiled. "Whenever you wish, love."

Hunter chuckled quietly.

"Next week," Jennifer said firmly.

"Jennifer!" Maggie breathed. "You can't do that."

"I don't see why not," the younger sister returned. "You married Hunter within a matter of days, as I recall."

"You don't remember anything about it," Maggie said.

"I do."

"Jen," Hunter put in quietly as he reached for Maggie's hand. "The circumstances were a bit different for us. I think your sister would like to plan a nice celebration for you."

Chad was silently curious about those *circumstances* to which Hunter referred.

Jennifer reluctantly agreed that the wedding would take place Saturday, November fifth. "It will seem like forever," she said unhappily.

"Jennifer, it is barely over two months away," Maggie pointed out. Barely a respectable period of time, as far as she was concerned. But then, Maggie remembered her own eagerness to be with Hunter, once she had come to the realization that she wanted him. Acknowledging her love for him had come much later. It was so much different for Jennifer. Jen knew she loved Chad and was confident in his love for her. They were impatient to be together. Maggie hadn't wanted to marry Hunter.

Maggie looked across the small table and watched Chad and her sister talking quietly. It was when he laid his right hand over Jen's on top of the table that Maggie noticed the ring once again. It was a beautiful piece of jewelry and she said as much.

Chad looked briefly at his hand before responding. "It was my father's," he said. "I'd forgotten about it, it's been so many years since I've seen it. I was searching through some of his private things when I found it." Actually, he had been about to throw the box of papers out, certain he had searched them years ago. It was luck that he had found the ring. Lucky and a bit puzzling. He kept all of his parent's gems in a felt-lined box in the master bedroom. He was still puzzled as to how his father's favorite ring had turned up in a box of old documents after all these years.

Hunter looked at Maggie with curiosity as she stared at Chad's right hand, frowning. "What?" he asked softly.

Maggie shook her head and took a deep breath before blessing him with a winning smile. "Nothing," she said lightly. "I could use a glass of punch."

Jennifer was distracted from the scene at her own table as she spotted Damon Lockyer walking their way. "Shoot," she muttered.

Chad looked in the same direction and saw a very dark, good-looking young man. "Is he a friend?" he asked quietly.

Jennifer nodded.

"You must dance, if he asks you, Jen."

She turned her attention toward him. "No."

"Yes," he said firmly.

"Perhaps I don't wish to dance with him."

"Won't that seem a bit odd?" he countered. "You must not feel you have to sit at my side the entire evening. I want you to enjoy yourself."

"I am enjoying myself," she pointed out. "I would rather be here with you."

"You can't do this, Jen," he said softly.

She understood what he meant, but if she couldn't dance with him, she knew how that would make Chad feel; he did not want her deprived of anything because of him.

Damon had eyes only for her when he arrived at their chosen place. "Jennifer," he said.

"Damon," she acknowledged, managing a smile. "I didn't know you had returned."

"Couldn't miss Hart's party," he said succinctly.

"How was the coast?" she asked for want of something better to discuss.

"Fine, as always. Gets one away from the cursed humidity."

Jennifer thought the small talk had gone on long enough, and Damon was obviously not going to acknowledge the presence of anyone else unless she forced him. "You know Maggie and Hunter," she said. "Have you met Chad Moran?"

Damon managed a brief glance and a curt nod in Chad's direction. "We met some years ago," he said. "Will you dance?" he asked.

Jennifer wanted desperately to tell him to go find a river and jump in it, but she smiled and conducted herself politely. For Chad's sake. "A dance would be nice." She stood, hoping Damon caught her meaning. A singular dance would be all she would give, and he didn't deserve that, considering his rudeness.

Damon swept Jennifer into his arms and gripped her waist firmly. "What are you doing with *him*?" he growled.

Jennifer tipped her head back and frowned up at him. "That's not a nice way to go on, Damon," she said severely.

"I asked you a question."

"And I'm about to shorten this experience," she returned.

He felt her intent to break away and tightened his hold on her waist and her hand. "I'm sorry," he said, although his sincerity was sadly lacking. "I arrived here less than an hour ago and have already been told by a dozen people that you've been spending a great deal of time with Moran."

"That's true," she agreed.

He frowned fiercely when he realized she was not about to deny what he said. Neither, apparently, was she about to make any excuses. "Jen, you and I—"

"Please don't, Damon," she said softly.

"It's understood that we are a match, Jen," he said harshly.

"Understood?" she asked, her frown deepening. "By whom?"

"By everyone, including us."

Jennifer shook her head and said as kindly as possible, "We're friends, Damon. I hope we can continue to be that."

"Does that mean you're passing me over for a cripple?"

Jennifer could feel the mounting anger inside him as it radiated to her hand on his shoulder. "Don't speak in that tone, Damon," she warned. "And don't call him a cripple."

"That's what he is," he said in a deceptively soft voice.

"What the devil are you going to do with a cripple, Jen?" he asked derisively.

"Stop."

"You need a man like me to love you."

"Damon . . ."

He whirled her around the floor with angry, impassioned movements that were drawing the attention of other dancers. "A cripple can't make love to you, Jen."

Her complexion tinted by her own mounting anger, Jennifer said in a low tone, "Let me go, Damon."

"Tell me what you're doing with that goddamned cripple!" he ordered.

"I'm going to marry him!" she snapped.

Damon came to a jolting stop and released her.

Jennifer managed to retain her balance and return his angry glare.

"Oh, Lord," Maggie breathed from the sidelines.

Everyone in the room was watching now as Damon and Jennifer seemed to square off in angry silence.

Hunter started to get to his feet, but Chad held up a halting hand. "It's my place," he said and pushed away from the table.

The dancers parted to make way for him as Chad progressed toward the center of the area that had been set aside for dancing.

When he reached the two young people who had become the center of attention, he said, "Perhaps this discussion could be carried on outside, where we won't interrupt the celebration." He turned his chair then and made his way toward the vestibule.

Jennifer followed, without question.

Damon held back a moment, saw the expectant faces surrounding him, and decided to join them. One way or another he had to get her back or lose face in front of his friends and neighbors.

Chad proceeded out to the front of the house, grateful there was no threshold to hinder his progress. Once he reached the wide, ceilinged porch, he turned and faced the two behind him.

"I'm sorry, Chad," Jennifer said softly.

"I know," he said. He looked up at Damon Lockyer then. "There seems to be a problem," he said, knowing he was understanding the issue.

"Jennifer is mine," Damon said bluntly.

Chad raised a dark brow. "I hadn't been aware of that."

Jennifer placed a firm hand on Damon's forearm. "That isn't true, Damon. We've been friends for years but nothing more."

He looked into her pale blue eyes, searching for something that would give him hope. He failed to find it. "I thought . . ."

"You don't love me, Damon," she said with conviction.

"Don't I?" he countered.

"You're simply used to me being around."

He continued to stare in silence.

Jennifer shook her head. "Go away and think about it, Damon. Please," she added kindly.

She was determined. He could see that. But once she got over this nonsense with Moran, she'd be back. And he would tell his friends as much. Perhaps then he wouldn't want her. As for now, this very moment—he could hardly be uncouth enough to physically take on a cripple. That would be bad sport, and he wasn't about to tarnish his standing in the community. Circumstances had defeated him and nothing more. "You're being a little fool," he whispered and turned away, entering the house once again.

Jennifer stood staring at the closed door for several moments until she felt Chad's hand capture hers.

"Did you love him?" he asked.

She smiled down at him and shook her head.

"He's half in love with you, I think."

"No, darling," she breathed and eased herself onto his lap. "Damon loves only himself. We've been nothing more than friends. I swear."

Chad liked the feel of her arms resting lightly on his shoulders and his hand smoothed the skirt over her thigh as he looked into her beautiful blue eyes. "Perhaps he felt you'd given him hope in the past," he speculated. Chad knew just how alluring she could be, but he also understood she wasn't aware of her natural sensuality.

"If I did, it wasn't intentional. And after tonight even friendship between us is doubtful. He's very arrogant, really."

Chad reached up and took her hand from his shoulder. He looked at the long, slender fingers as he eased his thumb along their length. "He upset you quite badly," he said, raising his eyes to look at hers again.

Jennifer was not about to lie. "He made me very angry."

"Because of me?"

"You saw him, Chad," she said, warning toward anger even as she thought of the tone Damon had used in calling this man a "cripple." "You heard him. He thinks he's jealous of you."

He smiled sadly, shaking his head slightly as if to deny what she was telling him. It was half-truth, for a certainty. But she would never speak the rest of whatever Lockyer had said. "People say and do stupid things, Jen, and often it isn't their intent to hurt. Perhaps with Lockyer there was intent. I don't know. But you can't take on the entire world because of me. You can't become angry every time ignorance causes me discomfort. You've heard voices dripping with pity when some talk to me. You've heard others raise their voices to me, as if I must be deaf because I'm in this chair. It's sadly funny, in a way. It can be irritating, and yes, I do feel anger and resentment on occasion. But not as frequently as I used to, love. I'm adapting and you must, too. I don't want you angered by every slight against me or taking on my defense over mere words. You're my lighthearted, witty girl. I want you to stay that way. I love you that way."

Frowning, Jen's eyes followed her fingertip as it traced his collar. "I love you," she said softly. "It's impossible for me not to come to your defense."

"And I love you for that, too. But ease up, darling," he said tenderly. "Go lightly, for your own sake."

Jennifer sighed heavily. "I'll try, Chad," she said.

He pressed a chaste kiss against her lips and then grinned. "Good," he said succinctly. He paused briefly and then attempted to lighten the moment. "I suppose now we don't have to plan an event to announce our engagement," he teased.

Jennifer blushed heatedly as she remembered the scene that had just taken place inside the house. Hiding her face against his neck, she muttered with dismay. "You're going to have to do something about my mouth, Chad."

He liked her mouth just the way it was, and he told her so with a long, passionate kiss.

"They shouldn't be going off on their own," Maggie said as Hunter handed her up into their carriage. "It looks bad of them."

"We're the only ones to know, my love," he said as he settled his bulk close beside her.

"I should have gone along as chaperon," she muttered petulantly.

Hunter laughed and tucked her under his arm. "Maggie, they're in love. Give them a little time together. And it isn't far to Treemont?"

She frowned up at him before dropping her head wearily onto his shoulder. "Time? They're alone in a closed carriage, Hunter. They have ample time to get into all sorts of mischief."

"Really?" he drawled, considering the rolled shades on the windows. "Do you truly think so, little one?" he questioned softly as he reached beyond her and pulled the first shade down. "Let's test it out, shall we?" he teased quietly and pulled the second and last shade. He turned toward her, sheltering her from the darkness which surrounded them, and smiled lasciviously. "What kind of *mischief* did you have in mind, Maggie?" he questioned in a deep seductive tone.

His hand found her breast, and as always when he touched her, Maggie caught her breath. "I don't know that I want to think about that," she said softly.

Hunter stared into her eyes, shook his head, and then moved his lips slowly toward hers. "I think we'll just create our own mischief," he said. "And not worry about them."

"Are you sleepy?" Chad asked before lightly kissing the top of Jennifer's silky hair.

Her head was resting comfortably on his shoulder, but sleep was a distant thing. "Tired but not sleepy," she said, snuggling closer to his side. "I'm glad we're away from all those people. I just want to enjoy being alone with you."

"Me, too, with you," he murmured as he placed his index finger under her chin and coaxed her head up. "We always seem to be surrounded by people. Have you noticed that?"

"We're alone now," he said suggestively.

Jennifer looked into the dark brown eyes she adored and smiled her understanding. "There are few places to which we can escape for privacy. It's true."

She laughed softly, briefly. "What did you have in mind, sir?"

"I thought I might beg a kiss," he said.

Jennifer became tenderly serious for just a moment. "My darling, you won't ever have to *beg* for anything you might want from me."

He searched her eyes for a moment, eyes that never looked away from his. "You mean that, don't you?"

"I do."

"Oh, Jen," he breathed. "I do love you."

"It took you long enough to say it," she teased, and then she threw herself at him, wrapping her arms around his neck as she pressed her forehead against his. "I love you, Chad. Sometimes I feel beside myself, I'm so filled up with love for you."

"I know. I feel the same," he admitted. He kissed her then, tilting his head to the side and pulling her up tight against his chest. The kiss was not innocent but demanded all they had to share. It was a kiss far more passionate than any they had permitted themselves, and Chad soon found his breathing hampered as his desire for her threatened to rage out of control. But he knew he couldn't take her. He would not. Not here and not yet. He also knew that he had best find a place for them to be secretly alone and comfortable; he suspected they were not about to survive without each other for another two months.

For tonight he would concentrate only on Jennifer's needs. He would teach her one of many ways a man could love his woman.

Jennifer groaned and tore her lips away from his. She showered lingering, heated kisses across his face before she pressed her cheek against his and breathed deeply. "I think, once you do more than kiss me, that I might die, Chad. It seems to intensify with no end," she whispered, pressing her lips against his neck.

He smiled and held her close. "What intensifies, love?" he whispered.

"It's making me frantic," she breathed and seemed to choke on a small, self-deprecating laugh. "I'm not certain I understand it."

"I do," he said simply. He turned her away from him and silently unfastened the buttons on the back of her gown.

"What are you doing?" she asked stupidly. But she sat perfectly still and allowed him to proceed.

"Trust me, Jen," he said.

"I do, but . . ."

He turned her back to face him and lifted her then, instructing her quietly to sit on his lap. And then he tipped her back until she was resting comfortably against his arm and the thickly padded squabs. He lowered his head, moving slowly toward her lips. "There's so much I want to share with you," he said softly.

And then her world burst into heated, breathtaking passion as Chad's kisses became more bold. He gently forced her lips apart and explored the depth of her mouth with his tongue.

Jennifer started momentarily, but the initial surprise did not last long, and she soon found herself returning the challenge and enjoying this most intimate attention from him. And as her mind concentrated on the sensations his exploration was fostering, she became aware of his free hand caressing; moving upward from her waist. She drew in her breath in anticipation of his touching higher.

Chad felt her go still and raised his head only far enough that he could watch her eyes as the palm of his hand pressed against her breast. He smiled softly as she looked up at him, trusting him, and he eased one shoulder of her gown down her arm. "I don't want you hidden under all this," he muttered as he proceeded to push the other sleeve down and away. A brief moment later her ample breasts were bared to his view. "Beautiful," he breathed.

Jennifer held her breath and watched his eyes as he stared at her. He touched and smoothed her flesh, and she closed her eyes briefly against the sweet agony of his caresses. Her nipples were painfully taut as the palm of his hand skimmed her heated flesh. "I wish they were high and pert," she muttered.

Chad raised his head and laughed. "Why?" he questioned, smiling at her curiously.

"Most of my friends say theirs are. I think it's favored."

"By whom?" he asked, amused once again by her cockeyed thinking. "Not by me. These are the breasts of a woman made to please a man," he explained as his palm cupped her breast. "A perfect fit. Do you see?" Her breasts were too heavy to be "high and pert," as she said, but they were beautifully rounded and firm beneath her silken flesh.

She looked down at herself and his hand, then smiled and nodded her understanding.

"You are beautifully made, Jen."

"Well," she whispered. "As long as you like them."

He laughed again, dropped a tender kiss on her lips, and then turned his head to capture a taut nipple.

She groaned, arching her shoulder forward while she raised her hand to the back of his head. His tongue caressed her, his movements slow and worshipful, and Jennifer felt a tense drawing sensation that was new to her. She pressed her legs together and bent her knees as she groaned again.

Chad turned his head and slanted his lips across hers, breathing heavily against her as his hand pressed between her upper thighs. "I know," he whispered on a harsh breath.

"Ohhh, God. I must be wicked," she whispered in return.

He raised her skirts hurriedly, and his hand caressed her thigh beneath the leg of her silk, lacy drawers. "Wicked . . . seductive," he murmured between lingering kisses. "Bewitching . . . enticing." The restrictions presented by her drawers became a bother, but Chad lost little time in finding the ribboned bow at her waist and tugging it free.

Jennifer started as his fingers began to explore, and she experienced a momentary, fleeting need to deny him. But then she was curling up against him, silent begging for release from this torture he was inducing.

He sensed her reflexive rejection of his intrusion. "Be easy, Jen," he whispered. "Relax."

Relax? When every nerve in her body was wound as tight as a watch spring? When the temperature inside the carriage had risen to such degrees, she worried they would both be consumed by flames?

His fingers were moving against her. Jennifer sensed something overwhelming flow through her entire body and wrapped both arms around his neck. The first shock was ghostlike, elusive, but then she was rocked by a continuous flow of spasms. "Aagh!" she breathed harshly against his ear.

Chad stilled his hand as his arm around her back drew her firmly against his chest. He turned his head, pressing his lips against her neck as he tenderly held her while she rocked against him.

Jennifer felt the tension drain from her, flowing like warm liquid through her body, leaving her deplete, as the quivering eased. "Ohhh," she sighed as she sagged against him.

Chad smiled his understanding. "All right, love?" he whispered.

Jennifer did not trust herself to speak but managed a slight nod of her head.

He was exceptionally uncomfortable with the state of his own affairs, but there was little he could do about that now. And he had accepted such would be the case when he initiated his petting of her.

Jennifer's eyes remained closed as her mind began to function, slowly but surely. She could feel the hardness of him even through their clothing, and she listened to his ragged, uneven breathing. "What can I do for you?" she asked softly.

Chad shook his head.

"There must be something," she insisted quietly as she eased her bottom away from his lower torso.

But Chad reached for her hand before she could touch his aching erection. "Not this time, darling," he said.

Jennifer stared into his eyes. "Tell me what to do."

Again, he shook his head. "We've got to get you home."

Home! Jennifer bolted upright, frantically looking toward the shaded window. "We must be . . ."

Chad grinned at her state of panic. "Gerome was asked to take us on a bit of a tour."

"Lord, I'll never be able to face the man," she muttered as she began fussing with her clothes.

"I told him we needed some time to talk," he said and laughed at her awkward attempts to right her attire. "Your drawers," he teasingly reminded her.

Jennifer blushed uncomfortably as she reached under her skirts. "I wasn't embarrassed when you undressed me," she muttered. "But somehow this is different."

Chad grinned and steadied her with a hand on her back. "You'll get used to it," he said.

Jennifer flashed him a shy smile. "Will I?"

"Mmm-hmm."

She kissed him soundly before slipping onto the bench beside him and presenting her back.

"Reach over and tap the forward wall, would you, darling?" he asked as he fastened the first button.

She did as he asked before questioning her actions. "Why did I do that?"

"Because I asked you to."

She laughed shortly. "All right! Why did you ask me?"

"It's the signal that we're ready to return to Treemont."

Jennifer suddenly had several fleeting thoughts of possible disasters and quickly checked the silk drawstring under her skirts. "I just envisioned stepping down from here and having my drawers fall about my ankles," she said laughingly.

Chad tipped his head and kissed her ear, happy that she was at ease with him again. "You're fastened," he said.

Jennifer eased back against his side as she fingercombed her hair over her ears. "Lord, I hope I don't meet up with Maggie," she muttered. "I must look a fright."

"You look beautiful," he said as he assisted her by tucking a wayward curl into place.

Hers eyes sparkled with delight as she smiled up at him. "I imagine I look *beautifully loved*."

"Thoroughly," he teased.

Jennifer became serious quite suddenly. "You mustn't be so selfless, Chad," she said, tucking her small hand in his. "I have some understanding and . . . well, you have needs, too."

"My time will come, Jen," he said quietly, smiling. "When the time is right, you'll know what to do. And what you don't know, I'll teach you."

"When?" she asked succinctly.

He laughed. "Soon."

"Two months is going to be a very long time if you're thinking of waiting until we're married," she pointed out.

He studied her hand, caressing her palm with his thumb as he raised his eyes to hers. "I've been thinking about finding us a place," he said. "I don't want us to wait. Not any longer, Jen." He pressed the palm of his hand against her cheek. "Are you willing to be with me?" he whispered.

She noted that he had not added *out of wedlock*, but there was no hesitation on her part. "Do you have to ask?"

He shook his head and his fingertips moved downward along her neck. "I don't have to ask," he said confidently. "We must be careful, however. I don't want to risk a scandal."

"There must be a place," she said softly.

But where?

Maggie was jolted out of sleep and bolted upward into a sitting position.

At her side, Hunter sensed her movements and reached for her, gripping her forearm. "What is it, Maggie?" he asked softly as he pressed his naked chest against her shoulder.

Maggie shook her head, denying the vision that had frightened her out of a sound sleep. "It feels like a nightmare," she said in confusion. She pressed her hand over her breast; her heart was thundering. "It's the ring," she added.

Hunter frowned in bewilderment. "What ring, little one?"

Maggie shook her head again, as if to clear her thoughts. "The bloodstone," she said.

It took a moment, but Hunter did remember. "Chad's ring?" he asked.

Maggie nodded her head, turning to look at him. "I saw it in my sleep. Isn't that ridiculous?"

Hunter was clearly baffled, more so because of her obvious concern. "What is it about the ring? You were staring at it earlier as if it meant something to you."

"It doesn't," she said firmly. "I'd never seen the thing before today."

He felt her quiver and pulled her back to lie beside him. "It's frightening you."

Maggie pressed herself more securely against his side and laughed with chagrin. "As I said . . . ridiculous."

# CHAPTER TWELVE

Chad sat near the corral gate, laughing as Silas and Jennifer squared off against Bramble.

Jennifer had her arms around the filly's neck. "Just slip it over her nose," she said.

The filly raised her nose high in the air as soon as Silas approached with the small leather halter, and Jennifer was almost swept off her feet.

Chad laughed softly.

"This isn't goin' to work," Silas grumbled.

"We'll do it," Jennifer said with obvious determination.

"Look, let her sniff the halter so she knows it won't hurt her. Then hide the thing behind your back and walk around to her side opposite me."

Silas did as she instructed.

"Now. Put one arm over her neck close to her ears."

He did that, too.

"Now. Bring the halter up from under her chin where she can't see it."

He tried that.

But Jennifer had been so intent upon giving instructions, and Silas had been so intent on following, that their attention was not directed to the foal's behavior, and she broke free.

"Shit!"

"Silas!" Jennifer scolded.

Chad shook his head, grinning over their failure.

"You're a fine pair," he called.

Jennifer turned on him in mock anger. "Let's see you do better!" she returned.

He nodded his agreement and held out his hand for the halter.

Silas stomped across the width of the paddock and handed it over. "She's stubborn and stupid," he said petulantly.

"She was smart enough to get away," Chad pointed out as he positioned the small halter across his knees. He then turned his attention to the filly, who now followed Silas around more like a puppy than a horse. "Come here, baby," he coaxed. The curious foal nosed his outstretched hand as Chad eased his arm back and his hand toward his lap. "That's a good girl," he crooned. When the animal began to nose about his legs, Chad reached up with one hand and scratched her ears. "You like that, baby?" he whispered.

Silas stood beside Chad's chair and watched, amazed. "Pretty baby," Chad said softly as he continued to scratch.

Jennifer thought, with disgust, that the dumb animal just might close her eyes and groan with pleasure.

With slow, subtle movements Chad continued to talk and scratch while he caught a halter strap in the palm of his free hand and began rubbing upward along the filly's nose, easing the halter up as he went.

"Damn," Silas whispered in awe. The man had a knack.

He had to give him that.

A moment later the filly was angrily backing away, shaking her head against the foreign thing that was loosely strapped in place.

"Ta-da!" Chad sang egotistically.

"Ta-da, yourself," Jennifer said in a well-feigned fractious tone.

Chad grinned at her and grabbed for her hand as she attempted to walk away. "You just don't like losing to a man in a chair."

"I don't like losing to a man. Period." But then she smiled easily as he continued to grin with pride. "I think you've got a very big ego, Mr. Moran," she teased.

"I'm surprised you haven't noticed before now."

"Oh, I've noticed," she said lightly.

Silas felt excluded when they talked to each other this way. And staring into each other's eyes the way they did was sort of sickening. "Aw, you two are always lovey," he accused.

Chad wrapped one arm around Jennifer's waist and smiled at the boy. "Pretty disgusting, huh?"

Silas nodded.

"Well, you'd best get used to it, son," he said. "Jennifer will be coming to live with us in a couple of months."

"Aw, shi——" He caught Chad's instant, disapproving frown and changed his mind. "Shoot," he said firmly and ambled away. "I suppose I'll be trippin' over 'em every time I turn around. Lovin' and carryin' on. Worse than livin' in the streets," he muttered.

Jennifer laughed as she watched until the boy disappeared into the barn. "I don't think he's going to take well to this."

"He will in time. As soon as he figures out that it's all right to feel something toward others, he'll learn to love you. Perhaps he'll even come to love us both," he said. And then he grinned rakishly. "We'll simple have to set him an example."

Jennifer laughed. "I think he's a bit young to learn *that* kind of love!"

"Not according to Silas," Chad explained in a more serious tone. "Claims he knows all about it. We'll have to show him there is more than one kind of love."

Jennifer frowned. "You're serious. You really believe he knows about physical loving?"

Chad turned his chair, and Jennifer silently stepped behind him to assist by pushing; it was hard going in the loose dirt of the yard, and it took their mutual strength.

"He's a kid from the streets, Jen," he reminded her. "We'd probably be shocked by some of the things he's seen and learned."

Jennifer did not doubt that for a moment. "We're going to keep him, aren't we, Chad?" She knew he had come to care for the boy, and she wanted him to know she felt the same.

Chad nodded his head as they reached the ramp that led to the raised patio. "He's a little rough around the edges, but I don't want to give up on him."

He extended his arms and gripped the newly installed, shoulder-high bars on either side of the ramp and easily pulled himself to the top.

Jennifer walked a few paces behind; she never impeded his independence and helped only when her help was needed. The bars had been another of her ideas. She had come to realize that pulling himself up to raised surfaces was easier for Chad than pushing on the wheels of his chair.

Gerome was walking across the patio carrying a tray of coffee and sweets as Jennifer dropped into a chair.

She smiled at the man she felt was a true friend. "Your timing is impeccable," she said lightly.

The older man nodded and smiled as he set the tray on the round table. "How did it go with the filly?" he asked.

Jennifer wrinkled her nose in disgust. "The task was taken over by a show-off."

Gerome twisted at the waist and looked at the decidedly innocent expression his employer was flaunting. Turning back to pour the coffee, he said quietly, "He tends to be that way at times."

Jennifer laughed as Chad's expression turned to that of a man betrayed.

"*You* can be replaced," Chad muttered.

"Humpf! Not likely," the older man returned and then walked toward the house.

"I'd say he knows you fairly well," she teased.

Chad smiled and reached for a cup, but Jennifer caught his hand in both of hers.

"You haven't kissed me today," she accused softly. "Does this mean you've fallen out of love?"

Now he laughed. "Not bloody likely," he muttered as he leaned forward.

Jennifer met him halfway and pressed her lips eagerly against his. But the kiss was chaste in the extreme due to their lack of privacy. It satisfied neither of them.

"This is awful," she said huskily, sitting back in her chair. "Sometimes I want so badly for you to touch me that I think I'll go mad." She reached for her coffee then, quickly gazing around to ensure that there was no one within hearing distance. "I have a confession to make," she said.

"What's that, love?" he asked as he studied her intently.

"I have actually thought about sneaking out of my room one night and riding over here to creep into your bedroom."

"Why haven't you?" he teased.

"Because directly on the heels of the thought, I feel as if I'm a debauchee."

Chad shook his head, smiling his understanding. "You're hardly that, sweetheart. You're a healthy young woman. No more, no less."

"I just love you so, Chad. It's torture not being with you every day. I think it's the hoot of the century that some of my friends are discussing the amount of time I spend here at Stonehall and are speculating about the intimacies we must surely share." She sighed heavily and set her cup aside. "With the exception of one brief carriage ride, we've never been alone long enough to be intimate."

He could not dispute the truth; there was seldom an occasion for them to be alone. But he thought he had found a solution and a place where they could be alone. "I've found a place," he said, setting his cup on the table before turning to look at her with a sheepish grin. "If we were in Richmond, I could rent a luxurious hideaway, but we don't have that freedom here. The place I've found will offer privacy and little else. A perfect trysting for secretive lovers."

"Where?" she asked eagerly.

Chad shook his head, barely believing what he was about to suggest. "There's an abandoned church back of my property. It's perfect because only the facade and part of one wall still stand. I can drive the tilbury right into the place." The light, single-horse, two-wheeled carriage offered Chad a number of advantages, and he used it often around the property. He could also pull himself onto the driver's seat without assistance. "I'd wish for better for you, though, Jen."

"I don't care," she said earnestly. "It won't matter where we are. Only that we'll be together."

Chad had been feeling a bit foolish about all of this; he wasn't a boy prowling after his first skirt, after all. But Jennifer was right—they could be together. Nothing else mattered.

"Tomorrow, if the weather is fine," she said. "I'll bring a picnic lunch!" she added happily.

"I don't need food, Jen," he said quietly. "I need you."

Silas had spent many a solitary afternoon exploring the farm that had become his home. For the most part, there was little of interest, but he had come to enjoy the freedom and openness of the land. Anything was better than the dirty, crowded corners of the city in which he had previously resided. And for the most part he liked Chad Moran. It had not been easy in the beginning, of course. Silas had expected Chad to be vengeful, but there had been nothing spiteful about the man. Silas had soon given up his resentment over being sent out to the godforsaken country. Now he was beginning to wonder if he would be allowed to stay. Perhaps the old judge in Richmond had served up a fitting punishment after all; it would be justice, indeed, if Silas had to return to his life in the city after having had a taste of something better.

The front of the old church could be seen a good distance away, and Silas decided he would explore the ruins. "Might find a gold cup or somethin'," he muttered as he waded through the long grasses of the pasture.

Before he could set foot in the place, however, Silas heard the unmistakable groans of a man and the softer, more delicate whimpers of a woman. "Tandy," he said softly. He would bet himself a gold coin, if he had a gold coin, that it was Charles Tandy at some poor girl again. Silas had caught the man roughing up his own woman in the hay one day. He figured Tandy had a more than active pecker.

Silas crept closer to the remaining partial wall of the church and peeked around the broken stones. It was Tandy, all right, and with some girl Silas had never seen before. She looked as if she wasn't enjoying it much, because her head kept rolling from side to side. But Silas knew that women did that when they were really hot. He'd actually seen it for himself a time or two when an older friend had chosen to indulge in a little bit of skirt in some back alley. This woman had a giant bruise on her face, too. But some of them liked the rough stuff.

He saw nothing surprising in what was going on, but he was beginning to note the effects of watching. Silently backing away, he decided he would go in search of a private place where he could *indulge* himself a little.

Jennifer took the long way around to reach the abandoned church the following day. She had raided the pantry, stuffing bread, cheese, and fruit into a sack, and at the last moment had filched a bottle of Hunter's favorite wine. They would have to drink from the bottle, but *sharing* the wine would be half the fun.

As she approached the ruins she removed her delicate gold watch from a pocket and checked the time. Early by ten minutes, and there was little she could do but wait. Anxiously.

Chad would bring a blanket, as it would not be so obvious a thing to carry in the tilbury. So she could not even pass the time by preparing a place for them.

"Just as well," she muttered. She had been awake the entire night in anticipation of this tryst, and if a blanket were handy, she might just lie down and fall asleep.

She searched for a place to tie her mount where he would be out of sight from the road. She removed Sequoyah's bridle and replaced it with a halter and tether so that he might graze. Once she had tied the end of the lead to a sturdy tree limb, she sauntered into the sheltered area of the remaining church walls.

In the near distance Jennifer could hear the approach of a carriage and prayed it was Chad's tilbury as she stared at the flattened, twisted grass and weeds in the vee formed by the church facade and the partial remaining wall.

Chad drove his vehicle into the wide expanse at the back of the church and pulled the bay mare to a halt as he stared at Jennifer's back. "Hello," he said softly.

Jennifer backed toward the tilbury in silence.

Frowning in confusion at this strange behavior, he questioned, "Jen?"

Jennifer's buttocks bumped against the side of the gig, and she reached back a hand for him. "I don't think I want to stay, Chad," she said softly.

He easily detected the anxiety in her tone and wrapped his much larger hand around hers. "What is it, love?" he asked anxiously. "Jen?" he said again, finally gaining her attention. When she turned her head toward him, Chad was staggered by the paleness of her. "Come up here," he said, tugging firmly on her hand.

Jennifer climbed up on the seat beside him, but her eyes returned to the corner of the ruined building. "Someone has been here before us," she whispered.

He looked then and saw a rumpled mound of white cotton. "What is that?" he asked as he continued to stare at the thing.

"Drawers," she said. "Women's drawers."

"Damn," he muttered, realizing their secret place was not so *secret* after all.

"There's blood, Chad," she said simply, quietly.

Surprised, Chad looked from the cotton drawers to his pale companion. "Don't jump to conclusions, Jen," he said, squeezing her hand in hopes of reassuring her.

She looked away from the corner of the church and stared at him, looking for answers.

Chad wrapped his other hand around hers and looked directly into her eyes. "When it's a woman's first time . . ."

"I know about that," she said. "But it seems . . ." Jennifer shook her head, shocked and dismayed.

She was not a woman given to hysteria, nor even commonplace fears. But this place and what she had found upset her. When it came right down to it, Chad did not feel good about the place, either. "Obviously, we can't remain. Where's your horse?" he asked.

"What are we going to do?"

"At the moment we're going to get you out of here," he said and reached for the reins, pulling back until the mare responded to his commands.

"I think something terrible happened here," she whispered.

"Darling, we have no proof that anything happened at all beyond a lovers' encounter." But the possibilities were nagging at him.

He waited while she rebridled her Sequoyah and then turned the mare toward the road. "Come back to Stonehall," he said. "We can talk and you can rest there until you feel better."

"I feel fine," she said as she mounted the tall horse. "I'm all right, Chad," she added when she was settled in the saddle. She simply wanted to return to Treemont alone with her thoughts. She wasn't some flighty female who would "jump to conclusions," and she wanted time to reason out the feelings the scene in the corner of the old church had aroused.

Chad granted Jennifer her own misgivings about what they had found because he was experiencing some foreboding himself. He needed time to think about what he should do, but foremost in his mind was ensuring that he protected Jennifer. Her reputation must remain intact at all costs.

He directed the tilbury toward Treemont and rode in silence beside her until they reached the long carriage path that would lead her to home. "I'm sorry, Jen," he said as she prepared to leave him.

Jennifer turned back and stared at him for a long moment before dismounting. Right there on the public road, she stepped up and sat beside him, putting her arms around his neck. "Kiss me," she ordered softly.

He did. Quite thoroughly.

"I'll come tomorrow," she said.

Chad squeezed her upper arm affectionately. "All right, love," he said before she turned away.

He sat and watched her ride up the long, tree-lined drive toward her home before he tugged on the right rein and turned the mare toward Stonehall.

Silas found Chad a silent, thoughtful companion at breakfast the following morning. There was something about sitting up to a meal, and not sharing any talk, that upset his digestion. "Suppose Jennifer's comin' over today?" he asked quietly as he reached for a third helping of ham.

Chad looked up from the letter he had been reading and watched the boy heap his plate with ham and grits. He had a healthy appetite, for certain, and he had even grown a little. "I expect she'll be over a bit later," he said.

"Guess I'll have to be readin' with her?" The reading was a struggle, no two ways about it. But he was trying.

"It's good of Jen to take the time with you," Chad said as he reached for the silver coffeepot. "You'll be starting school next week, and you're behind for your age."

Silas thought that sounded suspiciously like a talking down and opened his mouth to blurt out an angry retort.

Chad held up a hand. "I know you've done well, Silas, but the extra practice will help you catch up to the others."

That came as a surprise. "I have?" he questioned softly.

"Certainly," Chad said, noting the boy's astonishment. He realized then that he should have praised Silas before now. But the young devil had always spurned any accolades in the past. Perhaps things were changing. "You've worked hard and have come a long way with your reading. It has occurred to me that you're a very intelligent boy," he said.

Ordinarily, Silas would have taken exception to being called "boy." But he was so stunned by Chad's praise, he forgot to remind his guardian that he considered himself almost a man.

Chad managed to hide his smile over Silas's state of speechlessness as he picked up the letter that rested beside his plate. "I have a letter here from the judge," he said. "He's wanting to know how we're getting on."

Silas returned his attention to cutting a wedge of ham. "How are we getting on, Silas?" Chad asked quietly.

There was a moment of silence while Silas chewed.

"Right enough, I guess."

Chad settled back in his chair and studied his young companion. They were entering uncharted territory here, and they were both being cautious. Understandably. "Do you like living here?" he asked, considering the question a fairly bold move.

"Better'n jail."

"Have you considered staying on?" he probed.

"Food's good."

Tough little hooligan, Chad thought in frustration. "You're not going to help me out here, are you, boy?"

Silas propped both elbows on the table and glared at Chad. "You hold all the cards," he said, hiding well the fact that his heart was hammering away painfully in his chest.

Chad had a fleeting thought about teaching Silas a few manners. Starting at the table. "You're right," he said, having organized his thoughts. "I'm inviting you to stay on."

Silas sat back in his chair, staring hard, not quite trusting. "For how long?"

"As long as you want," Chad said, returning stare for stare.

"How does Jennifer feel about me stayin'?"

"Jennifer is fine with this. We've talked about it."

Silas looked away, trying not to betray his feelings, trying not to sag with relief. "Is that judge goin' to let me stay?" he ventured.

Chad wasn't fooled now, however. He thought he was reading the boy fairly well. "I believe I can persuade him, Silas. Don't worry about that."

Hoping he sounded reluctantly agreeable, Silas said, "I guess I could stay."

Chad hid a delighted smile behind his index finger. "There's one more thing. Jennifer and I will be marrying soon. I was wondering if you would be my best man?"

Silas turned startled eyes in Chad's direction. "Me?"

He nodded.

"You mean stand up with you?"

"So to speak," Chad said wryly.

Silas blushed with pleasure and was instantly embarrassed. Sliding off his chair, he backed toward the swinging door. "Well, shi . . . shoot," he muttered and disappeared.

Silas ambled on down toward the barn to say good morning to Bramble and noticed Charles Tandy walking that way from the opposite direction. Silas and Tandy had not come to any agreement about whether one trusted the other or not. In fact, they continued to give each other a wide berth. Consequently, when they met at the open double doors, they nodded rather than spoke and went about their separate business.

Bramble and her mother were not in the large box stall, so Silas retraced his steps and wandered over to the large paddock. Spying the filly and mare grazing contentedly, he climbed the fence and whistled. The mare raised her head and looked in his direction. Seeing nothing out of the ordinary, she returned to chomping grass. The filly, however, raced twice around her mother, kicking up her heels before trotting toward the boy.

"Hello there, baby," Silas said softly when the animal approached. "How about a good ear scratchin'?" he invited.

The filly nosed his hand, and Silas stroked the velvety softness. "You're gettin' big," he said. "Looks like I'll get to see ya grow bigger, too. I'm goin' to be stayin' on, Bramble," he whispered in awe as he rubbed her nose. Once he'd said the words aloud, Silas began to believe them. And if it weren't for the fact that *men didn't cry*, he would have.

Jennifer saw him in the near distance and waved as she rode Sequoyah toward the barn to be stabled.

Silas watched her disappear inside the barn and watched for her to emerge. "I don't know what it's goin' to be like havin' a woman around," he muttered to the foal. "Guess I'm goin' to find out, though."

Brief moments later Jennifer walked out of the barn and into the morning sunshine, smiling as she realized Silas was talking a blue streak to a horse!

He watched her walk to the fence and climb over. It was then Silas noticed Charles Tandy standing in a shadow of the barn. It was not the first time Silas had noticed Tandy watching Jennifer. "Horny old bugger," he muttered.

"Good morning!" Jennifer called as she approached. "How's she doing?"

Silas walked around beside the filly and dropped an arm over her neck. "She's gettin' big," he said.

Jennifer stepped up to the animal and began to finger-comb Bramble's forelock. "She getting there."

"Soon be able to ride her, I bet."

"Oh, not for a while, Silas," she said kindly and noted a flash of disappointment in the child's eyes. "If you ride her before she's two years, she could go sway-backed."

"Oh," he said thoughtfully. "I guess that's not good."

"Not good," Jennifer agreed with a smile as she rubbed the filly's forehead. "Perhaps we could talk to Chad about another horse for you to ride until Bramble is grown."

"I'm not much for ridin'," he said, shifting his weight to one foot.

"You could get yourself back and forth from school, if you had a horse," she pointed out.

Silas stared off thoughtfully toward the horizon. "Well, I guess I'm goin' to be goin' to that school for a while."

Jennifer smiled at his offhandedness. "Will you, Si?"

He nodded abruptly. "I told Chad I'd be stayin' around for a while."

"Did you?" she asked quietly. She wasn't fooled by his coolness, either.

Silas cast her a questioning glance, needing to be sure. "He said it was all right with you."

Jennifer's smile turned positively radiant. "It's *very* all right with me, Silas."

"Well," he drawled, looking away, uncomfortable with her soft tones. "I don't know if I can stand much o' you two bein' lovey, though."

"Try," she said before dropping a light kiss on his forehead. "Please." She turned and walked in the direction of the house.

"Aw, shoot," he muttered.

Jennifer found Chad in his study, behind his desk. "Morning," she said brightly.

Chad raised his head and smiled. Having her enter a room was like whisking away a window covering; the sunshine would suddenly pour in. "Good morning," he said as he pushed back from the desk.

Without hesitation Jennifer plopped onto his lap, wrapped her arms around him, and kissed him warmly. When she raised her head, he said, "I've always admired shy women."

Jennifer frowned. "You have?"

"From a distance," he murmured and pulled her back against his arm. He stared down at her, his lips moving slowly toward hers. "I like you better."

"Like?"

"Mmm-hmm."

"Because I'm *not* shy?"

"Correct."

"I don't think I'm being complimented," she said.

"You *are* a compliment," he murmured and slanted his lips across hers. He lingered as long as he dared, knowing how much they needed each other, knowing how easily they could be aroused. He had thought about their situation and had decided he would not start what he could not finish; it was simply becoming too difficult. Affection and teasing were tolerable. But the passion between them was running high, and there was no place or time for gratification. Only frustration.

He raised his head after a moment and smiled into limpid blue eyes. "Are you all right?" he asked softly.

"Couldn't be righter," she returned huskily.

He laughed. "Lord. Sit up, Jen," he ordered lightly and pulled her upward. "You're too damned tempting when you're reclining."

"You think my *sitting* will save you?" She propped her forearms on his shoulders and allowed her hands to hang limply behind his back.

"Am I really responsible for you're being this way?" he asked.

She feigned a moment's thought about that. "Actually—yes."

"Truly?"

"I've never been this way with anyone else, Chad Moran," she said firmly.

"I wasn't suggesting—"

"I should hope not."

He reached behind her neck and fingered the long, fair hair she had caught back with a ribbon. "No residual effects from yesterday, Jen?" he asked quietly.

Thoughtfully she smoothed the shoulder of his jersey.

"Disappointment," she said.

He smiled tenderly and stroked her arm. "Me, too, darling."

"I have to admit I thought about the other when I was finally alone last night, Chad. About what we found."

So had he. And he had remembered her friend.

"I decided I had jumped to conclusions and you were right . . . it was just a place two lovers had met for the first time."

But he wasn't convinced.

# CHAPTER THIRTEEN

In September Silas got his first taste of rural schooling. He thought he'd pretty much lord it over all those farmers' boys until a couple of older fellows took him out behind the privy and had a word or two with young Si. A single black eye and a bump on the jaw dented his spirit a little, but eventually he was accepted by the other children. Much of that was due to Courtney Downing's friendship with the newcomer. Even at such a tender age, Courtney enjoyed a great deal of respect from her peers.

September seventeenth, a fall-like Saturday evening, a grand party was held at Treemont. A party formally celebrating the engagement of Jennifer Downing and Chad Moran. It was no surprise for friends and neighbors, but the party was magnificent.

That night Maggie experienced her second nightmare in as many months. She envisioned a large bloodstone ring. The gold ring worn by Chad Moran only on special occasions.

Hunter got out of bed, covered his nakedness with a robe, and went downstairs to fetch a small portion of brandy. Returning to sit on Maggie's side of their large bed, he offered the glass.

Maggie took several small sips of the heady brew before setting the glass on the bed side table. "I'm worried for Jennifer," she said bluntly.

Hunter rocked back in surprise. "Jennifer? Because she's engaged to a man whose ring you dream about, little one? I'm sorry, Maggie, but that doesn't make much sense."

"It doesn't to me, either," she snapped and was instantly sorry. "Forgive me, darling," she whispered and stroked his arm beneath the bell sleeve of his robe. She shook her head, looking away, trying to gather her scattered thoughts.

And then she did something that aroused true concern in him; she reached up and fingered the faded scar that ran along her jawline. Hunter reached out and took that hand, pulling it gently away from her face.

"Is this what the ring has to do with, Maggie?" he questioned softly.

She frowned at him, clearly puzzled. "Pardon?"

"The ring—does the ring have to do with your scar?" And the rapist they never talked about anymore? he wondered.

Maggie stared at him as if he had just discovered the evolution of a species. "I don't know," she whispered as she thought back in time. "I said it was a ring that scarred me, but I don't know anymore if that's a fact, Hunter. I've had doubts for years. I don't remember the man or much about that day." And remembering suddenly seemed very important. Her hand pulled against the bedclothes in agitation. Ten years had passed. How would she remember now?

"Maggie . . ."

She stared at him, her lips forming into a sad, sad smile. "I'm half afraid I'll remember, darling," she whispered.

"You're thinking about Chad?" he asked perceptively.

Maggie nodded her head.

Hunter could not envision Moran concealing a violent nature, but one never knew what evil lurked in the hearts of men. "He was living in Richmond back then," he said gently.

"He returned frequently for visits," she explained.

Jennifer was awake with the dawn and soaking in a tub of hot, scented water while Hunter and her sister were trying to catch up on lost sleep.

She had a final fitting for her wedding gown at nine o'clock, and as the seamstress lived not far from Stonehall, she had decided she would stop in and pester Chad for a time.

She found him in his study, laboring over the farm accounts.

He looked up and smiled, offering his customary greeting. "Thank the Lord you've arrived," he teased after a welcoming kiss. "I'm a man of the law, not of accounting. I hate these books."

Jennifer settled herself comfortably on his lap and looked at the large ledgers. "I don't mind," she said. "I'll take them over if you wish."

He *wished*. "You're a wonderful young woman."

"Loved only for my skills with arithmetic," she muttered.

Chad touched her temple and then her cheek, his eyes taking in the freshness of her complexion. "Oh, you possess a few other qualities," he said softly.

"You're stingy with your compliments," she said peevishly and turned her attention to the books on the desk. "Did Mr. Tandy keep these for you while you were in Richmond?"

"He did. He's decided they're my responsibility now that I've returned."

"Probably because he's watched you sitting on your rump, lazing the days away," she teased, returning her complete attention to him.

"You, my lass, are disrespectful," he returned harshly, but the sparkle in his eye gave away the fact that she could tease him about anything and get away with it.

"I respect you," she said. "I even love you."

*"Even?"*

She nodded. "And speaking of lazy . . . when are you planning to go back to work?"

The fun ceased with *that* question. "I work here," he said tightly.

Jennifer ignored the change in him. "I suppose Silas will miss Bramble, but we can bring her to the city once she's weaned."

"I *work* here now, Jen," he said quietly.

*That* tone was more difficult to ignore. "Don't you like being a lawyer?" she asked guilelessly.

That was hardly the point. One fact remained all too clear in his mind's eye; he just could not envision gaining control and enthralling a jury while rolling around the courtroom in his chair. Addressing a jury required a *stance* of authority, and he was a man who could not stand. The thought was painful enough to leave a bitter taste in his mouth.

"Chad?" she prompted.

"Let it go, Jen," he said harshly. And then, seeing the wounded look in her eyes, he softened. "I'm sorry, darling," he said, stroking the palm of her hand with his thumb. "I'm just not up for that one yet, love. All right?"

"I didn't mean to push," she said quietly. "I'm sorry, Chad."

Silently he wrapped his arms around her and pulled her against his chest. He loved her enough to die for her, and he was confident in her love for him. After all she had done, after all she continued to do for him, he could not believe what he had just done to her. "You're the last person I want to be angry with," he murmured.

"I know, Chad," she said softly, pressing her face against his neck. "I know you're not angry with *me*."

"My father used to say 'We always hurt those closest to us.' I don't want to do that. Not to you."

Jennifer pulled back until she could see his face. "If you do, my darling, I'll be forced to put you in your place."

He laughed, hugging her fiercely. "I do love you, Jen," he said.

The was a rapping of knuckles on the paneled door just then, and Jennifer jumped to her feet, darting behind Chad's chair.

He smiled, shook his head, and called out.

The door opened, and Gerome stepped just inside. "I'm going over to Culpeper to get some medicine for Cook," he said. "Need anything in town?"

Chad started to shake his head, but then a scathingly brilliant idea hit him quite soundly. "I've ordered a new leather bolster from the saddler for the tilbury that should be completed today," he said. "If it's not ready, would you mind waiting for it?"

Gerome did not mind at all. This gave him an opportunity to stop by the eatery for a good meal and another look at the pretty woman who owned the place. Whether the bolster was complete or not. "Good enough," he said and disappeared.

"He's such a nice man," Jennifer murmured as she wandered around to the front of the desk.

"The best," Chad agreed, grinning as if he had just out-philosophized Socrates.

Jennifer looked at his face and found herself smiling in return. "You're looking pleased with yourself."

"I am," he said and laughed. "That bolster was not to be completed until tomorrow. Gerome might have to wait for hours."

"Oh, Chad," she admonished.

"He won't mind, Jen," he explained. "Gerome has a new lady-love in Culpeper."

"Gerome?" she asked, obviously amazed.

"That shouldn't be surprising. The man is hardly ancient."

Jennifer shrugged reservedly. "I simply hadn't thought about him with a woman," she said.

"Well, think about this, my darling," he drawled, rounding the corner of his desk. "We are alone in this house."

She was clearly surprised to hear that. "Cook?"

"Sick with the sniffles," he said succinctly. "And tucked up nicely in her own little bed in her own little cabin."

"I've never heard such enthusiasm," she said laughingly. "Poor, sick woman."

But Chad had stopped laughing. In fact, he was staring at her quite seriously.

It took Jennifer a moment to descend from the natural buoyancy of frivolity, but inevitably her smile also disappeared. "What shall we do, Chad?" she asked quietly.

He shook his head, realizing she had become uncomfortable. He moved toward her and reached for her hand. "Nothing that you don't want to do, love," he said. "We can let it go."

She stared down at their joined hands and grinned lopsidedly. "Or we can be impulsive." But it wasn't impulsive. It wasn't even romantic. It was awkward and unnerving. "This is crazy," she said with self-annoyance.

"I've been waiting for this moment."

"Sit down, Jen," he said softly and moved close to the chair she chose, facing her.

"I feel like a child," she muttered.

"You're not a *child*," he told her. "That's the problem. We can wait a few more weeks, sweetheart. Until—"

"I don't want to wait," she said hurriedly. "I feel like I've wanted to be with you forever. I just hadn't prepared myself for today, and now I feel . . . I feel . . ."

"Feel what, darling?"

"Unprepared!" she blurted.

Chad smiled and shook his head, knowing she was nervous. As was he. Knowing she had a right to be. As did he. Knowing, too, that he would have to take control. Because he wanted her. He wanted her as he had never wanted any woman he had known in his lifetime. Knowing she *did* want to be with him. And knowing they would soon never be parted. Having come to a decision, he reached for her hand. "Let's go for a ride," he said and pulled her onto his lap.

Jennifer hooked one arm loosely around his neck, and he pushed his chair toward a corner of the room. "Take the wine decanter and two glasses, would you, love?"

She looked at him askance, then did as he instructed. Holding the decanter between her knees, she reached out and took two long-stemmed glasses between the fingers of her right hand.

"On to the next," he said lightly and turned the chair toward the door.

"What does that mean?"

"You'll see."

Next, they entered the dining room, and Chad approached the table. "The candlesticks," he said with a nod of his proud head.

Jennifer smiled doubtfully but shrugged and reached out. "Here, hold the glasses for a moment," she said. When she had the candles in hand, she juggled things in her lap and took the glasses from him. "This is insane!" she said.

"This is fun," he returned.

She smiled at him. "Yes, it is."

He moved out to the hall and stopped before the newly installed lift. "Now we'll take a ride with Otis," he said dryly.

But once he maneuvered them into position inside the small compartment, Jennifer's feet would not allow him to close the gate. "Move them or lose them," he teased.

She laughed and drew her knees up almost to her chest.

"I suppose we're about to redecorate your room?" she asked tentatively when he raised his eyes to hers.

"It's needed something in the way of decoration for a long time now," he said.

"Perhaps we'll scatter a few garments about?"

"If that's what we feel like doing, Jen, then, yes."

Before another full moment had passed, they were sitting in the middle of the master bedroom, staring at each other in wonder.

"I can't believe we're alone," she said softly.

"You don't have to whisper." When she didn't answer, he took her hand firmly in his. "I want to make love to you, Jen," he said. "But I also want some quiet time with you. Sometimes it's nice just to hold each other." After they'd been married for fifty years and the passion had cooled, perhaps. He mentally shook himself, knowing he was half attempting to back away from doing this. He had rehearsed making love to her a hundred times in his mind; that did not seem to be helping him now. He was just plain scared he wouldn't be man enough for her.

"Will we make love to each other?" she asked softly, drawing his attention.

"If we feel it's right. If it's what we both want. There are no obligations."

"Are you nervous?" she asked with a small frown.

He nodded his head, admitting the truth. "In a way. Are you?"

Jennifer responded in kind.

"It's almost like the first time for both of us," he said ruefully.

"You find that funny?" she queried.

"In a warped sort of way," he said. "Yes. I do."

She thought about that for a moment and realized this would be a very different experience from any other he had known. "I don't want us to be nervous," she said tenderly. "I simply want us to be together, and I don't think there's anything to fear."

"There really isn't anything to fear," he murmured in an attempt to convince himself all would be well. "We'll take our time," he added, moving toward the bed. "We'll get to know each other a little more intimately than we have in the past."

Jennifer grinned crookedly and blushed. "It seems to me you know me intimately enough."

He smiled softly and began to relieve her of her burdens. "I don't know you nearly as well as I will. Will you pull the drapes?" he asked.

While Jennifer moved across the room and enclosed them in near darkness, Chad lit the candles and poured the wine. He held out his hand in invitation when she hesitated to return.

Once she was sitting on the side of the bed, he gave her a glass and raised his own in a toast. "To us, love," he said in a strong voice. "To our long life together. To our happiness together. And if we stumble, may we never fall."

Jennifer looked at him with equal determination and touched her glass to his. "We won't, Chad," she said. And suddenly, before she had even sipped her wine, Jennifer lost all sense of the anxiousness she had been feeling. She drank, set her glass aside, and proceeded to turn the quilt and cotton sheets back on the bed as if she had performed the chore a hundred times before. "Do you need me to help with anything?" she asked.

He caught her arm before she could move around to the other side of the bed. "I've just needed you here," he said quietly.

She smiled and lightly kissed his forehead. But before she moved away, she dropped to her knees and removed his boots. "There!" she said triumphantly, standing the high boots side-by-side near the door. "You're on your own."

He watched her from across the bed, smiled when she smiled, and wondered if he should ask her to leave him for a short time. But they would soon be sharing this room and she would learn a great deal about him and about his . . . condition. There was little use in trying to hide anything from her now. Except, of course, the wedding was still five weeks away. She could cry off, if she chose. But he didn't think that would happen. Jennifer was neither weak-kneed or spineless, and he was convinced that a little awkwardness on his part would not frighten her away. So he wasn't about to run across fields of clover to snatch her up in strong arms and whirl her in circles on strong legs. That did not diminish his love for her.

She returned to his side of the bed and smiled uncertainly as he removed his shirt. "I'm yours to command," she said lightly as she held his chair steadily in place.

Chad pushed off from his chair and pulled himself into a sitting position on the bed. "And if you think I believe *that* . . ." he teased.

Jennifer stepped out of her own boots and moved forward quickly to help him prop the pillows behind his back.

He smiled at her then, loving her, holding out a hand and helping her up beside him. "Kneel over me and be comfortable," he said softly.

She placed her knees on either side of his thighs and rested back. "Lord," she breathed, "I could be breaking your knees and we wouldn't even know it."

He laughed. "As light as you are, Jen? I don't think so." He stared into her eyes, smiling slightly as he reached out and brushed at the wispy hair near her temple. "Am I still easy to be with?" he asked.

"Yes," she said.

"Liar," he whispered tenderly and pulled her forward into his arms. "It will get easier, love. I promise."

He kissed her then, savoring the softness and the warmth of her. Feeling her press her firm young breasts eagerly against his chest. Feeling the intensity with which she returned his adoration.

But it was moving too quickly. Their breathing became short and labored, and the powers of passion threatened to cheat them of prolonging this, their first true moments of intimacy.

Chad pressed against her shoulders and moved her back, smiling as he reached for the buttons of her shirt. "Be easy, Jen," he whispered. "We have time."

Jennifer swallowed painfully and nodded. And then she reached out and eased her fingers through the dark hair on his chest, feeling the powerful toned muscles beneath his shoulders and biceps.

He pushed the boy's shirt over her shoulders and forced her hands away from him while he pulled the sleeves over her hands. She wore only a thin chemise, and the nipples of her breasts were already budded and begging for attention. "Will you be naked for me?" he whispered.

A mere breath and she had moved away from him, standing at the side of the bed as she unfastened the buttons of her breeches. She never removed her gaze from his as she slowly removed the remainder of her clothing.

Chad moved down on the bed, unfastening his own trousers, pushing them from beneath his buttocks. He sat up then and pushed the garment along the length of his legs, eventually tossing it away.

Jennifer removed her drawers, her final piece of clothing, and moved over him, turning to lie by his side. She had not taken the time to inspect him; indeed, she had barely looked. But now that she was lying beside him, she devoted her entire attention to his body. "I would never have believed a man could be so beautiful," she murmured.

He laughed and grasped her hand, resting it on his belly as he caught his breath. She was here, beside him, and she was his. That was all he could think about for several moments. Suddenly he propped himself on an elbow and turned toward her. "Lie back," he ordered softly.

She did.

There commenced a lengthy visual inspection on his part before he reached out and touched. "You are so amazingly beautiful," he breathed as he watched his fingertips circle a proud nipple. He petted and caressed her. "I've wanted you so much," he said, smiling and staring into blue eyes that appeared drugged with passion. He kissed her tenderly and with passion, and when Jennifer groaned in the throes of sweet distress, his lips moved down the length of her body, taking his time to savor the smooth texture of her skin. To enjoy the sweet essence of woman. Then he positioned himself between her thighs.

When he started to lower his head, Jennifer started and would have protested.

"It's all right," he murmured. "Just let me love you," he breathed before he began a thorough caressing of her secret place.

Jennifer was more surprised than frightened, but soon all thoughts left her mind and she concentrated only on what he was doing, only on that which she felt. Her body flushed with heat and coiled within itself, and she closed her eyes and moaned, pressing her head back into the pillows. And, quickly, all too soon, she exploded into glorious, quivering misery.

Her cry was more than the startled sob of climax, and Chad instantly identified her reaction. He pulled himself up along her side and wrapped her into a warm, firm embrace. "Sssh, love," he whispered.

Jennifer curled against him and buried her face in the hollow between his neck and his shoulder. "Chad."

"I'm here," he said simply, his voice harshly broken with his own need. She was still shocked and glowing from the aftermath of climax when he raised her head until their lips could meet. "I need you," he breathed.

He placed his hands beneath her arms and guided her, silently positioning her over him as his hands and mouth continued to caress her feverishly. "Oh, God, Jen," he breathed.

She was quick to understand what was needed and took command, caressing him as he had caressed her in many ways. She admired him without shyness as her long, slim fingers explored his muscled chest and ribs. She kissed him, too, as her hands moved downward and tentatively, experimentally, touched his erection.

Chad bent at the waist at the same time he pulled her hips forward. He assisted her with softly spoken instructions. "Go easy, darling." He had a fleeting moment of fear, of hurting her, as his hands guided her hips.

Jennifer barely hesitated. Her eyes raised to his when she felt some resistance within her own body. But then she leaned forward, wrapping her arms around his neck as she pressed downward, and it was done. She rested briefly against him, until the aching diminished and she sensed being filled with him. He whispered something to her and she nodded. "I'm all right," she whispered and turned her head to slant her lips across his. She felt his hands caress her back, her ribs, and eventually he captured her breasts as she began to move on him. Tentatively and then with more assurance, she loved him well and ardently, feeling her own passion soar as their hands mutually stroked each other.

And then Chad's body seemed to buck beneath hers, and he was pulling her fiercely against his chest as he shuddered violently.

Jennifer held him, acutely aware of every movement, every nuance of this thing that was happening to him.

And then he sighed, tightening his arms around her as he curved back into the pillows. "Oh, my love," he breathed.

Jennifer was so emotionally moved by what had taken place that she could not trust her voice to speak. She just continued to hang on to him.

Eventually their breathing slowed and their heated, sated bodies began to cool. Chad turned her head and kissed her tenderly as his hand stroked her back. All hint of doubt that he had harbored was now banished. His love was now free to occupy the entire universe of his heart and mind and soul.

Jennifer raised her head, suspicious of the small catch she detected in his breathing, and when she looked into his eyes, she glimpsed a small bead of moisture resting on his lash. She smiled lovingly. "Oh, Chad," she whispered as she reached up and removed the single tear with the tip of her finger.

His steady, loving gaze locked with hers, and he was unashamed. What he had privately seen as a barrier between them had now been breached, and he sensed the ease and freedom, the comfort, between them. Never again would he doubt his ability to satisfy her in this way. Never again would he doubt his maleness. Never again would he feel as if he were a sexless member of humanity as he had once felt. He was a *man* and never again would he doubt the fact.

Jennifer's forearms rested on his shoulders, and her fingers stroked the soft hair over his neck as she smiled sleepily at him. And then that enchanting look turned to dismay as she felt him slip from within her. "No," she breathed unhappily.

Chad smiled his understanding and pulled her against his chest. "I know," he whispered. "I feel the same." He turned his head and whispered against her ear. "I like being inside you."

Jennifer smiled and whispered in like fashion. "I like having you there," she returned with no hint of shyness.

Eventually other needs drove them momentarily apart as Jennifer supplied Chad with water and towels before entering the bathing room, off the master bedroom, to see to herself.

But soon she was back beside him, settling back as he pulled a light quilt up over her breasts. He lay on his back, resting one hand on his flat belly as he pulled her firmly against his side. "You're all right, darling, are you?" he asked softly. "I mean, you don't hurt?"

Jennifer shook her head against his shoulder. "This is positively the best day of my life," she murmured. "This and the day I knew I'd fallen in love with you." She tipped her head back and smiled up at him. "I've had a lot of glorious days because of you," she said sincerely.

Chad smiled in return and lightly stroked her cheek. "Me, too, love. Because of you."

She moved her head back onto his shoulder and watched her fingers toy with the hair on his chest. "You didn't want to fall in love with me, did you, Chad?"

He was silent for a moment, thoughtful. "No," he said quietly.

"Why?"

"Because I thought it would be too complicated. I thought my *life* was already too complicated."

Jennifer understood; life continued to be complicated in unfair ways at times for him.

"I didn't think I could give you much of a life," he continued. "I was challenged personally by so much, and I didn't think I was fit to start a relationship."

"You know better now, don't you?" she asked, raising up to rest on his chest.

He looked at her, touched her hair, and smiled. "I know better now, Jen," he said softly.

"I know that things may not always be easy," she said.

"They won't. Not always."

"But we'll share the good and the bad."

He raked his fingers through her hair and held on. "I believe you're strong enough to be with me, Jen . . . with a man like me. Otherwise we wouldn't be here like this, and we wouldn't be counting the days to our wedding. I love you too much to lead you into an unhappy life."

Warmed by his words and the loving look in his eyes, Jennifer pitched upward and kissed him. "An 'unhappy life' would be one without you in it," she whispered. "Do you know what I want to do?" she asked softly.

"What do you want to do, sweetheart?"

"I want to sleep beside you forever."

# CHAPTER
## FOURTEEN

Silas stabled his horse and entered the house through the back way. He was surprised that no supper was being prepared. Surprised even more to find the cooking stove cold.

He wandered through the lower rooms of the strangely silent house, puzzled that there seemed to be no one about.

But when he stepped up to the open door of the master bedroom, he saw them. A golden couple lying within the shelter of each other's arms, soundly sleeping.

He stared at them a moment before silently backing away and returning to the kitchen. He entered the pantry and fetched himself a glass of milk and a handful of cookies before settling himself on a high stool in front of the island work counter.

He wasn't shocked that Chad and Jennifer had been together. "Even animals do it," he muttered before drinking deeply. What bothered him was the *way* they were together. He'd never thought about men and women wanting to actually sleep together; to lie there like that as if they never wanted to let go. His experience had been that a man and woman disappeared into a back room or an alley, and a few moments later they emerged and went their separate ways. It was far different, this thing between Chad and Jennifer. He'd been puzzled by them for a long while.

He was also confused by a worrisome feeling he'd had of late.

Chad was the first to awaken, reluctantly drawn from comfort and warmth and contentment to the harsh reality that they had slept the afternoon away. "Jen," he whispered as he gazed in disbelief at the small clock beside his bed. "Jen."

"Mmm?"

"We'd best get up and get dressed."

Jennifer turned her nose against his shoulder and shook her head.

"Si will be home."

She was completely unresponsive for a dozen ticks of the clock, and then she raised her head in alarm. "Oh, my God," she breathed.

He laughed as she jumped up and scrambled over him.

"There's no fire, love," he teased.

Jennifer snatched up her clothing and stared at the open bedroom door before racing across the room to close the thing. Dropping all but her drawers back onto the floor, she danced on one foot and then another before she pulled the garment over her hips. "Do you think he saw us?" she asked frantically.

"I don't even know if he's in the house yet, Jen," he said ruefully. "Relax."

"He'll know," she said worriedly as she donned her shirt.

Chad held out his hand. "Come here," he said. "You haven't thought about this, obviously." When she was sitting on the bed, next to his hip, he took her hands in his. "He's going to know, love. If not today, then in the near future. We're going to be living together in this house and you are going to be sharing this room with me. Si may be lacking in a number of ways, but he is not a stupid boy. Nor is he too young to know about this sort of thing."

She stared at him as he spoke. "You're right," she said. "I simply hadn't thought about it." She leaned toward him and kissed him affectionately before pulling on her breeches. "I'll start some supper while you're getting dressed," she said. She moved his chair parallel against the side of the bed and retrieved his clothing from the floor. Smiling down at him, she asked, "Do you need me?"

He grinned and responded succinctly. "Yes."

She laughed. "I don't mean *that!*"

He nodded. "You go along."

She could not keep herself from kissing him one more time before she left. "I love you," she whispered, and then she was gone.

Silas was dwelling over his second glass of milk, his original thirst satisfied, when Jennifer danced into the kitchen and stopped in her tracks.

"Oh, you're home," she said stupidly.

Silas turned his head in her direction, smiling mysteriously. "Been sitting here for a while," he said.

Jennifer blushed lightly and turned away, walking into the pantry. She needed to collect her thoughts. He knew! She just knew he had seen them. "What would you like for supper?" she called over her shoulder. "We're cooking for ourselves tonight."

"If you're askin' *me* to cook," he called, "you better not be hungry!"

It was enough to ease the tension.

Jennifer returned bearing a platter of cooked ham. "What do you think?"

"I like it," he said. He watched her digging through bins, sorting potatoes and onions, wondering how a woman like her could sleep with a cripple. And then he corrected the thought; Jennifer did not like him referring to Chad as a *cripple*. She'd told him often enough. Chad was *disabled*. The fact that Silas was willing to use the term told him that his ways were slowly changing.

Jennifer placed six potatoes and two knives on the counter between them. "This is a family effort," she said, nodding toward the knife.

"We ain't no family."

"Your language is atrocious, and we will be soon enough," she said as she pulled the remaining stool around and sat facing him. "Can you manage?"

"I can handle a knife," he said, reaching for a potato. Jennifer silently bet he could. Probably as skillfully as he could throw stones. But that was behind them. They worked in silence for a moment, each concentrating on peeling the skins from the potatoes. "Do you think you'll like being part of a family?" she asked.

Silas did not raise his head. "Won't know till I try."

"Will you mind having me living here?"

"Don't know that neither."

"You like me, don't you?" She sensed that he did, but this boy was not very giving.

"You're all right, for a woman." Fact was, he liked her a lot. He'd even given her a passing thought or two. She'd been kind and patient and had devoted much of her time to teaching him things. But he thought he was *soft*, thinking that way.

Jennifer smiled, content for the time being with what he had given. Giving cost Silas dearly and she had learned about that early in their relationship. She had learned to identify small tokens from him and accept them as all he could share at the moment.

Chad joined them then, and Jennifer raised her head and smiled.

He looked from boy to woman and decided they were relaxed enough; Silas must have just arrived home. "How was school?" he asked as he approached the island work station.

"It was all right," he muttered and reached for another potato. "Courtney brought me some cake with lemon stuff in the middle."

Jennifer grinned at Chad before turning her attention on Si. "You like Courtney, don't you?"

Si raised his head and frowned. "I do not!"

Jennifer was visibly shaken by the heat of his denial.

"Don't speak to Jennifer in that tone," Chad warned.

Si turned his anger on his guardian. "Girls are for fuckin' and nothin' else!"

Chad's arm shot out, and he easily pulled the boy off the high stool. "Get into my study!" he roared.

"Chad..." Jennifer could see his ready anger and feared what he would do.

He looked over his shoulder as he followed the boy toward the door. "We're going to have a word, he and I."

She slipped from the stool and walked toward him. "Wait here," he said softly.

"You won't—"

"I won't hurt him," he muttered. He might tan the boy's hide, but he wouldn't do any permanent damage.

Si stood defiantly in the center of the room.

Chad closed the door behind them and turned to face the recalcitrant youth. He was amazed that Silas had not tried to bolt. "There are a few rules you will abide by in this house, Silas," he said evenly. "First, you will never use offensive language nor will you shout at Jennifer again."

Si shifted his weight and stared in confusion. "I don't see what's so—"

"You will treat her with respect," Chad insisted angrily.

"She's just like any other girl," he said simply.

That stopped Chad cold. "What do you mean by that?"

"I already said what girls is for," he explained. "You don't want me sayin' it again, you said."

Chad could not believe what he was hearing, and he felt his anger beginning to drain away. It took him a moment to latch on to his next thought, but once he formed the pattern in his mind, he nodded his head toward the nearest chair. "Sit down, Si," he said and moved his chair forward. It occurred to him that Silas had reverted to being a boy from the streets a few moments ago; he had reacted the way he had seen other men react.

Once they were sitting, face to face, Chad leaned forward and propped his elbows on his knees.

Si looked down at those strong hands, the fingers knitted together, and wondered if he were about to discover this man's true might.

"What made you flare up like that?" Chad asked.

"Jennifer was simply taking an interest in you."

"Likin' girls is sissy," he said petulantly.

"And you're anything but a sissy," Chad murmured.

"I know what girls is for."

"So you keep telling me," Chad said wryly. He was beginning to regret his explosion of anger, but he had been so incensed by Si's rudeness to Jen that he had reacted without thinking.

"You know, too," Si said. "You weren't just sleepin' all afternoon in that big bed o' yours," he accused quietly.

Chad remained calm and showed no surprise that he and Jen had been found out. "You know, Si, Jen and I are about to be married. We love each other very deeply."

Si raised his head and shot Chad a crooked smile. "I mostly hear it called something else," he said.

Chad nodded his head. "Yes, I understand that. Does it bother you that you found Jen and me together like that?"

"Nah. I don't care about that. I already told you I've seen more than that. Done it, too."

Chad very much doubted that; Silas could be full of sheer bravado at times.

A moment later the boy's eyes narrowed in curiosity.

"You treat her funny, though, sometimes."

Chad's brows arched upward in surprise. "Funny? In what way?"

He hesitated to use the word, but Chad had asked. "You treat her sort of soft."

A slow smile of understanding tilted the corners of Chad's mouth. "Like a *sissy*?"

"Well," he drawled, "now that ya mention it."

"How is a man supposed to treat a woman?"

"Well, I seen plenty o' girls get knocked around. And *up*!" he blurted, laughing at his own joke.

Chad frowned and Si's smile slowly disintegrated.

"I guess that's not fittin' talk, huh?" Si asked.

He did not bother to respond to that; the boy knew. "I know you've seen a different side of life from what you see here at Stonehall, Si," he said. "But there are several things I would like you to remember." He paused, ensuring that he had the boy's undivided attention. "First, it doesn't take much of a man to hit a woman. You will never see me treat Jennifer in that way. I don't think women enjoy roughness or harshness even though some women eventually have to accept that in their lives. Jennifer is not one of those women. We will not be rough or harsh or use offensive language in front of her. And you've been here long enough to know the difference."

Silas looked as if he would have to chew on that one for a time.

"A *real* man has enough confidence to admit that he not only *likes* but loves his woman. A *real* man respects his woman for a lot of reasons. And he just naturally wants to treat her well and gently."

"That sounds like a lot o' work to me," Si returned.

Chad laughed and straightened in his chair, resting back. "It isn't when you're in love, son," he said. "When you're in love, being 'soft' with her just comes naturally."

"But Jennifer's not like some little prissy thing," he pointed out. "Jennifer's smart."

"Yes, she is. Jennifer is a lot of things that I respect. Her intelligence is only one of them."

Silas thought about that for a moment. "You think she likes all that *lookin'* and soft-like *touchin'*?"

Chad had truly come to enjoy the way Silas could turn a phrase. "I think she does," he said. "And remember that we're talking about two different things here; my love for Jennifer and your relationship with her as well. I think you would like Jennifer to be your friend, and there is nothing 'sissy' about that. I suspect she would even be willing to talk to you about how you're going to get on together when she lives here with us."

"Oh, no," Si said, shaking his head. "I ain't havin' no sissy talk with no girl."

Chad crossed his arms over his chest and sighed dramatically. "It's too bad you feel that way, son," he said. "Jennifer thinks very highly of you. Having a confidential talk with her might just reap you a few rewards. Like maybe being on the receiving end of one of her special hugs."

Si's nose wrinkled with distaste, and he scoffed. "Like I was her son or somethin'?"

"Just exactly like that," he said quietly.

"Nah. I think I can live without it."

*You little fraud.* Chad thought affectionately. "Well, think about it," he said. "You might want to take advantage of some of the special things that come with having a friend like her."

"I can't think of nothing 'special' offhand that I'd be wantin'."

"It might come to you in time," Chad said wryly. "In the meantime, I would like you to go out there and apologize to her."

Si's eyes grew large and round. "What'd I do?"

"I think you know."

"Well, it's about time she got used to the way a *man* talks," he said firmly.

"Jennifer is accustomed to the way a *gentleman* talks," Chad returned. "I think she would appreciate a little more refinement than you demonstrated a while ago."

Silas slumped in his chair, knowing he would be forced, eventually, to make amends. "Well, she won't find 'refinement' everywhere she goes," he said. "You best warn her about that. I don't think Jennifer's too smart about people sometimes."

"What are you talking about?" Chad asked seriously.

"There's a non-gent around here, and he's watchin' her."

The tone of their conversation had taken a dramatic turn, and Chad leaned forward, intent upon discovering what this was all about. "Who's watching her?"

"Somebody who don't treat women soft-like."

"Who?" he asked with growing alarm.

"I see him lookin' at her all the time."

"Silas . . ."

"Tandy," Silas said. "I think he's got the—"

"Charles?" Chad returned with disbelief.

"He's not soft-like with women," Silas added.

"How do you know this?"

"I saw him smackin' a girl while he was—"

"Where? Where did you see this?"

"There's an old wreck of a place back by—"

"A church? Do you mean the old church ruins, Si?"

Silas nodded.

"He was hurting a woman?"

"I didn't say that. She seemed to be likin' it well enough."

Had she "liked it"? Chad wondered. Or was that Si's interpretation of what he had seen? "You say Charles watches Jennifer?" he asked, half fearing the answer.

Silas nodded his head. "I think he'd like to get at her, you know? And seein' as she's yours and so soft and all, I don't think neither one o' you'd be happy if he took after her."

The boy had a gift for understatement.

"Will you go out and apologize to Jennifer?" Chad asked distractedly.

He was not even aware of Silas leaving the room.

Later that night Gerome White entered his employer's library and found Chad drawing thoughtfully on the stem of his pipe.

Chad looked up when the man approached. "You saw her home?"

Gerome nodded.

"You waited until she was inside the house?"

"Just as you asked," the man said.

"I need to ask something of you," he said. "Something beyond our agreement of your duties."

Gerome shrugged casually. "Ask. I can only refuse."

"I need you to watch my future wife."

# CHAPTER FIFTEEN

Diana Chester walked slowly around the dress form openly admiring the blue silk wedding gown. "Jen, you are going to look exquisite." Gingerly she touched the large puff of a leg-o'-mutton sleeve as she inspected the ribbed lace inset of the square neckline. The fitted waist tapered down to a vee in front, and the bell skirt boasted a long, dramatic train. The gown would set off Jennifer's small waist and generous proportions quite stunningly.

Jennifer was sitting in front of the dressing table in her bedroom, brushing her long, dark-blond hair. "Courtney's gown is of a paler blue, and Everett will be in a black velvet page suit. They'll both look adorable."

Diana placed a small boudoir chair where she could face her friend. "And Chad has that little ruffian standing for him?" she said in wonder.

Jennifer smiled at her friend and lowered her brush. "Silas is not really a bad child, Diana. He's rough, but he's had to be, and we're working on his refinement."

Diana's personal opinion was that "refinement" was a long way away. "You really care for him?"

"Silas? Of course. He's learning to bend, and once he learns that it's all right to give and accept a little honest affection, I think we'll get on very nicely as a family."

Diana shook her head in disbelief and stood, moving behind her friend. "You want your hair up?"

Jennifer nodded and passed the brush over her shoulder.

193

"You know I want the best for you, Jen," she said quietly as she set to work. "You're my dearest friend. But it worries me that you're taking on so much."

Jennifer frowned as she raised her eyes to stare at her friend in the mirror.

"It seems to me that being someone's wife is adjustment enough. I mean, moving away from family into a new home, getting used to a man's ways, and I'm certain there are a thousand other adjustments. But you've got young Silas to contend with and . . ."

Jennifer waited, but her friend failed to continue the thought. "And Chad's disability? Is that what you're try-ing to say?"

Diana nodded slowly and met her friend's reflected gaze.

Jennifer sighed. "No one seems to understand. I could wish him out of that chair, for his own sake, but that is not going to happen, so there is little use in wasting energy on the thought. I think he has adjusted well to the . . . challenges he's been faced with," she said. Except she had not been effective in having him think about returning to law. Not yet. "I've learned a great deal as well, and we manage the inconveniences. He's a wonderful person and a good man and he loves me. And I love him just the way he is."

"What about children?"

"We plan to have several."

"I guess that answers *that*," Diana said wryly.

A sparkle danced in Jennifer's eyes as she laughed.

"You're as bad as Maggie," she said lightly. "My dear sister has been worried about the same thing but could not work up the courage to speak to me about it until last evening."

"A heart-to-heart," Diana murmured. She stopped fuss-ing with Jennifer's hair then and rested her hands on her friend's shoulders. "I've always regretted telling you about my first . . . encounter, Jen. I hope it hasn't put you off or made you afraid," she added worriedly.

Jennifer's expression softened. "Sit, Diana," she said. "I'm going to share a thing or two with you."

"The way Florence and Maggie are fussing around upstairs, I think we should have set this ceremony for later in the day," Hunter said lightly. He poured two glasses of wine and turned toward his future brother-in-law.

Chad reached out and accepted the drink. "I'm looking forward to seeing Florence after all these years."

Hunter sat in a chair where he could face the younger man, crossing his legs at the knee. "You won't know her, I'd wager. Our shy little Florence is more beautiful than ever and is quite the confident, accomplished young woman. She's enjoying a modicum of success with her writing, and she tells us she has an admirer. I suspect we'll be holding another of these affairs at Treemont in the near future."

"That's wonderful," Chad murmured into his wine-glass.

Hunter laughed. "Man, you are the picture of the ner-vous bridegroom."

Chad lowered his glass, grinned, and nodded. "Just like any man, I should imagine."

Hunter sobered somewhat but continued to smile as he caught Moran's meaning. "Just like any man."

The two men had become quite good friends over the course of the past months. On occasion they had resorted to playing the odd game of cribbage during an evening while Jennifer and her sister talked and planned for this day's occasion. They had given up trying to teach Jennifer to play bridge. Unlike her sister, Jen simply possessed not one wit of card sense.

The men also shared a secret. Rather, they shared a *suspicion.*

Chad had approached Hunter to discuss his concerns shortly after Silas had revealed his observations about Charles Tandy. Chad had been careful to make no reference to the fact that he and Jennifer had any firsthand knowledge of what had been going on at the old church ruins. He had no evidence, after all, that the stained drawers they had found had any connection to Tandy having been at the church on occasion. But he did make it plain that Silas had observed Tandy's latest interest. He had also revealed his decision to have Jen watched closely. Chad had begged Hunter to aid in that cause. While he felt reasonably confident that Tandy would not dare to approach Jennifer, once she was under his protection, Chad continued to worry.

It did not take an investigative genius to raise still another suspicion. Hunter told Chad of Maggie's dreams and of the possible connection to Moran's ring. Before the younger man could become defensive, Hunter had asked one simple question: "Is it at all possible that another man could have had access to your father's ring?"

Chad had agreed it was entirely possible. He had lost track of the thing for years.

So the men had one more suspicion and still no substantive evidence.

Chad added more fuel to the slowly building fire by telling Hunter about Jennifer's friend who had been "set upon."

It puzzled both men that Charles Tandy, or any man, could have possibly been molesting young women for years, and there had been no outcry in the area. It made them doubt their own notions. But it also made them angry that there was a possibility that such occurrences had continued. It also made them determined to either prove or disprove Tandy's connection to any wrongdoings.

It was agreed that they would keep all these bits of information to themselves for the time being. And after the wedding Chad would attempt to discover the identity of Jennifer's friend and arrange to speak with the young woman.

Maggie remained ignorant of these speculations.

And Jennifer continued to be blissfully happy.

"Could I do that?"

Jennifer turned from the feminine dressing table that had been recently moved into Stonehall's master bedroom and smiled. She stood and walked slowly toward the large bed which was currently inhabited by her naked husband. "Promise me you won't ever wear a nightshirt," she said softly.

Chad laughed as she stood looking down at him. "I don't believe I own one, love," he said.

"That's good," she said succinctly, giving over her hairbrush. "I like looking at you." She sat on the side of the bed and presented her back.

The room was cozy-warm from the fire that burned in the grate, and slim candles cast soft yellow light that played at the edges of the shadows. It was a large room that felt instantly familiar and comforting although she had only been there once before.

Jennifer's head tipped back and her eyes closed in weary ecstasy as Chad ran the brush from her temple down the full length of her hair.

"Your hair is so beautiful," he murmured. He loved the healthy glow of it, and there was something exceptionally sensuous about the texture when he touched it.

"Thank you," she said softly.

"You're tired," he said, knowing he was suffering the same.

"It was a lovely day, though, wasn't it, Chad?"

"It was, sweetheart," he said warmly. "It was just too full of people and things to do."

"Damon was a bore," she said flatly. The young man had taken advantage of his host's hospitality and sampled far too many libations.

"You should have told me he was so in love with you, Jen," Chad admonished.

"It simply hadn't occurred to me," she said quietly. "We've been friends since we were children and I have never felt romantically involved. I knew Damon had other thoughts, but I thought we had reasoned it out."

"Love isn't always reasonable."

"Lord, that's true." She was thinking of her love for her husband; she would have died had she not been successful in winning his love. Jennifer opened her eyes narrowly and stared at the fire across the room becoming half-mesmerized by the dancing light. "I'm glad we were together before tonight," she said quietly.

"Are you, darling?" he asked as his gaze followed the movement of the brush.

"Mmm-hmm. Now I can enjoy you and not be nervous."

He smiled, set the brush aside on the nearby table, and eased her back against his arm. "It hasn't taken away from our wedding night? It hasn't destroyed the anticipation?"

She smiled softly. "I'm full of anticipation," she said. "I remember how you made me feel. I think about that night."

"Do you?" he questioned softly as he looked into her eyes. He remembered how frequently he thought about her and *how* he had thought about her. "Do you have tender reflections of that night?"

"I remember how you made me feel," she said. "I remember how gentle and sweet and considerate you were with me even though you were anxious, too."

He stroked her cheek with the backs of his fingers as he continued to smile at her. "You are far too perceptive," he said.

"I seem to be when it comes to you."

"That's just another reason why I love you," he said.

Jennifer sighed as she stared up at him. "There is no rush, is there, Chad?"

"None, darling."

"We can make love all night long."

"We can."

"I'm enjoying lying here admiring you," she said. "It's making me wild."

He laughed. "Wild?"

"I don't know how else to say it," she muttered and took his hand, placing it over her breast. "Feel?"

Her heart was racing at an alarming pace.

She turned her head, pressing her lips just below his right breast. "I can feel your heart, too," she said softly. And when she looked up at him again, she was grinning. "There is also something else I feel," she said brightly.

He laughed again and pulled her up against his chest, whispering against her ear. "I think I've been in this state for hours."

"Only hours?" she teased.

"At a time, on and off, for weeks," he added.

Jennifer giggled. "Me, too."

"Women have an advantage in that their need is not obviously apparent," he returned as he moved his head back to look at her.

"Not so," she said, shaking her head. "You have no idea how many times lately someone has tried to carry on a conversation with me and my mind has been miles away."

"Really?" he queried.

Her head bobbed a time or two. "Thinking naughty thoughts," she added blatantly. "I kept thinking, frequently, about sneaking out at night and coming to you," she admitted.

Chad set aside his teasing attitude. "I wish you had," he whispered. "I've needed you."

"Me, too," she murmured.

The glow in his eyes took on a deeper tone as he eased her upward. "Come up here," he said huskily.

Jennifer stood, long enough to shed the peach-colored wrapper that matched her lace and silk night dress. And then she was joining him on the large bed, easily pulling her skirt out of the way as she straddled his thighs.

He stared at her, placing his hands on her bent knees as he examined the look of her in the garment. "It's beautiful," he said. "You're beautiful. Enticing."

Jennifer stared lovingly at his face as he lifted his hand and traced the ridge of lace along the square-cut bodice of the gown.

Eventually Chad raised his eyes to hers. "I love you in it," he said. "But I would love you without it even more."

Jennifer smiled and nodded.

He reached for the hem and skimmed the flowing material up over her thighs, her waist, her breasts, and eventually pulled it over her head.

She sat there proudly, unashamedly as naked now as he. "I don't know where to start with you," he muttered as he openly admired her. "I want to touch all of you at once."

Jennifer solved the problem for him by easing slowly upward on his legs until his engorged manhood was safely nestled in the junction of her thighs. She tipped forward then, pressing her breasts against his chest as he wrapped his arms around her.

They worshipped every inch of their upper torsos with fingers, palms, and lips until the heat of their bodies became unbearable and their harsh, uneven breathing became quite discernible, intermingled with their soft whimpers of mutual need.

Chad pulled her forward until she was kneeling tall so that he could fondle and caress her breasts. He pulled one taut nipple into his mouth and teased her until she cried for equal attention to the other breast.

When the passion of their play threatened to overwhelm them, he breathed in deeply, staring into her desire-filled eyes as he gently pressed her downward. He guided her and eased her way, and then pulled gently on her hips until she fit tightly against him.

"Oh," she sighed, wrapping her arms around him as she savored the fullness, the depth of him.

Chad shuddered as he fought to maintain control. He did not want either of them to move; not yet. He reached between their bodies and touched her, and when she started, he soothed her with rasping, yet softly spoken words. "Just let me touch you, darling," he breathed. He sensed the tension building in her, and the anticipation heightened his own exhilaration. He felt a drawing, deep within himself, and knew they were matched in this most exquisite torture. He could wait no longer, his senses were too overwhelmed by her. "Come with me," he breathed. He felt her explode and knew she was moving, tightening around him. He cried out as he burst into a rapid succession of quivering spasms and he poured his very life into her. Frantically he pulled her against him, pressing their joined bodies tightly together before wrapping her solidly in strong arms as if, in this way, they would never have to be separated.

Jennifer lay limply against his chest, her fingers digging into his shoulders as she strived to remain at the height he had taken her.

Slowly, warmly, they drifted reluctantly downward.

Chad pressed a tender kiss on her shoulder. "Roll onto your back," he whispered at last.

She shook her head, bumping his upper arm with her chin.

He took a great gulp of air and pushed gently on her shoulders. "Remember what we talked about?" he asked in a low-pitched, broken whisper.

Jennifer's eyes opened wide, knowing exactly to what he was referring. She eased upward and then rolled away to lie beside him.

Chad rolled to his side and moved into the extended invitation of the arms she held up to him. He rested his chest on hers, pressed his cheek against hers, and flattened the palm of his hand against her belly. "You need to keep me inside you," he said softly.

They had talked about making the babies they both so desperately wanted and had concluded that this was necessary to achieve their goal.

"We could be starting a little Chad," she said with a smile.

He raised his head and smiled down at her. "Or a little Jennifer."

She lay there looking exceptionally beautiful, flushed from passion, and extraordinarily pleased with herself.

"Perhaps one of each."

Chad shook his head. "I don't wish that upon you," he said. "Birthing one child must be difficult enough."

"I'm already a mother," she said pompously.

Chad's brows shot upward as he propped his head on his hand. "What? To Silas? Some affectionate son he is proving to be."

"He'll come around," she said as she smiled up at the ceiling and enjoyed the feel of his hand drawing small, gentle circles on her abdomen. "I'm going to bombard him with affection and shower him with love."

"Just brace yourself for his reaction," he said ruefully.

"I think it's important that Silas feel loved before *our* baby comes along," she said thoughtfully. "And I think we should include him in everything *family*. Talk to him about the baby as if it will be an addition to his life as well. That sort of thing."

Chad had a sudden concern about the way she was talking. "Jen, don't get your hopes up just yet, darling. It could be months before we actually manage to do this. It's easy for some couples and not so easy for others. I don't want you to be disappointed."

She stared up at him then, loving him, and said quietly, "We'll know soon enough."

Chad was surprised by the comment and looked it. "What?"

"I'm approaching my monthly," she said. "If it doesn't come in a week or two, we'll know, won't we?"

Affectionately he smoothed fine wisps of hair back from her forehead. "We'll see, darling. We'll see."

Jennifer drifted slowly out of the haze of deep sleep, aware of the warm, firm flesh beneath her cheek. She breathed in the scent of him and smiled against his skin as the mellow fragrance of male stirred her. She felt drawn to move closer against his side as a barrage of feelings and sensations threatened to overwhelm her. She opened her eyes and found herself staring at the fine matt of hair on his chest, and she moved her hand to touch the springy mass.

Suddenly a large, strong hand covered hers and she tipped her head back, raising her eyes to find him smiling lazily at her. "Good morning," she whispered. Her blue eyes positively glowed with the overwhelming love she felt for him. He made her feel cherished and *special*. He was strong and tender and he was hers.

"Good morning, yourself," he said affectionately.

"It's wonderful waking up beside you," she breathed and raised herself upward on his chest until she could reach his lips.

Chad tipped his head forward, meeting her halfway and savored the warmth of her, fresh from sleep. The flesh of her back was warm and silky smooth beneath his hand, and her full breasts were flattened temptingly against his chest. He had awakened pleasantly aroused, and his need had grown stronger as he had watched her sleep. They had loved and dozed and had awakened to love again throughout the night. It was as if they couldn't get enough of each other, as if they had to be continuously touching to reinforce the reality that they were finally together; that they needn't ever be separated. The months of emotional and physical need they had both endured should have been fulfilled, but he knew they had only begun. They had a great deal more to learn about each other, and for the most part, it was going to be a glorious discovery. The reality was that there would be moments of disappointment and frustration because of his disability, and Chad had never fooled himself about that. He could not, however, entirely set aside the apprehensions as the reality of Jen discovering his limitations nagged at him.

At this moment he would dearly love to pick her up in his arms and dash into the bathing room to share a warm scented bath with her. But that was not possible, and the surge of resentment that washed over him occasionally as he moved through his days struck him anew. He tightened his arms around her and pulled her firmly against his chest, successfully quashing the bitter thought in favor of lying there, enjoying the feel of her. She had become a safe haven for him almost from the first day she had teased him about sitting around on his rump. He felt he could be himself with her, could talk to her about his innermost feelings, his joys and disappointments. But more important, at least to Chad, was his overwhelming need to cherish and protect her. He had no intention of sheltering her or impairing her strength of will and individuality in any way. She was a woman of substance and backbone, and he admired that in her; he simply wanted her to have the very best that life could offer.

"It's curious that I feel right at home, waking up here," she said softly.

Chad's gaze dropped to the top of her head. "You're surprised by that?" he returned.

Jennifer's head nodded, her cheek moving against his chest. "I thought it would be strange not waking up in my own room." She raised her head and grinned at him. "It must be the company I keep," she teased.

His own eyes sparkled with joy as he beheld her obvious happiness. "You're a bit of a Saucy Sue in the morning, aren't you?"

Jennifer giggled, but her smile wavered in the next instant as the door leading to the bathing room closed. Her startled gaze darted in that direction, beyond the foot of the bed.

"It's all right, Jen," Chad said quietly. "It will be Gerome preparing the bath."

She turned her head and grinned at him again, her entire countenance positively glowing with pleasure. "*Our* bath?"

He laughed shortly. "You are a bold one," he said, but it was obvious he did not mind her boldness one bit.

"It was just a thought," she returned hopefully.

Chad shook his head, his smile altering to one of regret. "I'll bath after you're done, sweetheart," he said.

Jennifer realized that the teasing and fun had suddenly gone out of the morning. And all because of something that most people took for granted as a simple, daily task. Here was something with which she could not help; he would need Gerome's greater strength. She also knew that there must be a better way. A way that her husband could bath with little or no assistance. She knew Chad was often too close to his own difficulties to see ways around them, and if she could resolve this dilemma, she could restore another small portion of his independence. She would give the matter some careful thought.

They lay there, wrapped in silence and each other's arms until the door leading from the next room to the hall closed with a reverberating statement.

Jennifer smiled as she stared in the direction of the bathing room. "I suppose that's the signal?" she asked, striving for a lighthearted tone. She turned back to him then, moving her lips very close to his. "I don't want to leave you," she whispered.

"I know," he said, lightly touching her cheek. "I feel the same." He kissed her then, pressing his lips firmly against hers, breathing in deeply as if he could take her inside himself and hold her there. After a moment he pulled away from her, pressing his head back into the pillows as he smiled his understanding into sorrowful blue eyes.

"Off you go, sweetheart," he said reluctantly.

"I know we have to move and start our day," she said as she pushed away from him. "But I don't have to like it," she added as she darted across the room.

Chad raised his arms and cradled the back of his head with his hands, grinning with delight as he eagerly viewed her softly rounded buttocks before she disappeared beyond the doorway. The clock on the table beside the bed had ticked but once or twice before he heard the soft splashing of water, and he envisioned her lowering herself into the large copper tub. He closed his eyes and imagined the sheen of water cascading over her skin and beading on the ample swell of her breasts.

He waited.

He listened.

He heard soft, mellow tones of humming, and he was soothed.

*Lord, it's good to have her here.*

# CHAPTER SIXTEEN

Jennifer returned to the dining room to join her husband over coffee while he sorted through the mail. Passing behind his chair, she dropped a quick kiss on top of his head before returning to her seat at his right.

"He's off, then?" Chad asked.

She nodded her head and grinned devilishly. "He's a funny boy, you know? He insists on groaning every time I send him off to school with a hug and a kiss, but I think he actually likes it."

He reached across the table and briefly squeezed her hand as he teased. "I groan, too, when you give me hugs and kisses."

Jen laughed. "That's a different sort of *groan*, darling," she said.

"Whether he groans or not, I've seen a change in Si the past few weeks. I think you've made a difference."

She couldn't deny she felt the same and nodded as she reached for the silver coffeepot. "I think so, too," she said.

While she refilled their cups, Chad returned his attention to the letter he had been reading.

"Anything interesting?" she asked hopefully; he was normally very good at sharing interesting bits of news with her.

He was, however, reluctant to share this particular letter with her. "Just a letter from someone I've never heard of," he said as he folded the square of paper and set it aside.

Jennifer's brows arched. "Why would someone you don't know write to you?"

He should have known he wouldn't get away without appeasing her curiosity. He also suspected what would happen once she learned the contents of the letter. Still, the topic would arise time and time again until she gave it up. And until Jennifer reached the point of knowing her arguments were fruitless, he knew he could not run from the issue, or her. Displaying a smile of resignation, he passed the letter to her.

Jennifer scanned the letter thoroughly, raising her eyes briefly to his when she came to the reason behind this man's, this James Hope's, reason for writing to her husband. She read carefully, taking a moment to digest the contents before setting the letter aside. "Are you familiar with this Homestead Strike?"

He nodded and reached for his pipe and pouch. "It was written up in *Harper's Weekly* this past summer," he said as he concentrated on pressing tobacco into the bowl of his pipe.

Jennifer quickly got up and fetched a dish and matches from the sideboard. "I've never heard of a place called Homestead," she said as she returned to her chair.

"Thank you," he said, taking up the box of matches. "It's an industrial town built by Andrew Carnegie in the early eighties, I believe." He looked at her askance as he touched flame to tobacco. "You've heard of Carnegie?"

Jennifer set her cup on the saucer and nodded. "Steel," she said succinctly.

He smiled and nodded as he watched a puff of smoke drift above his head. "Carnegie built his steel plant and a small town for the workers upriver from Pittsburgh. I recall reading about it at the time. Innovative idea, actually. The theory was that the relocation of industrial factories and towns would get the workers and their families out of the overcrowded cities and into a better life. It was hoped that workers would be more content if they had small houses of their own, yards for their children, and a small parcel of land to garden. Carnegie went so far as to have parks, a library, and even bowling alleys built in Homestead. But the town is a *company town* and there have been problems inherent in all such places that have been built. The companies have too much of a hold on the workers and their families, even going so far as to dictate where food will be purchased and at what price. As I understand it, there had been problems at Carnegie Steel over employment and dismissals, and then, in July, the company cut wages. The steel workers went on strike."

"How did this man come to be charged with murder?" She was growing more and more intrigued as he talked. His days had once been filled with situations like this, and Jennifer did not understand how he could bear to give it up.

"I only know what he wrote in his letter. James Hope was obviously one of the picketers during the strike. Carnegie had hired something like three hundred Pinkerton guards to protect his plant from the strikers. When the guards arrived, all hell broke loose. The picketers fired on the Pinkerton men, and there was a day-long battle. Seven guards and two strikers died that day. James Hope is one of several men charged with murder."

Jennifer's gaze dropped thoughtfully to the letter for a moment. When she looked at him again, she studied the strong, relaxed fingers that held the bowl of his pipe; she loved the rich, fragrant odor of his tobacco. "How did Mr. Hope come to write to you?"

"I don't know, Jen."

"I think you must have quite a reputation as a defense attorney," she said bluntly.

Chad merely shrugged his shoulders casually.

"Yes, I think you must," she murmured. "And this man needs you."

"There are plenty of lawyers——"

"Not like you," she interrupted. "I just know it."

"You're biased, darling," he said fondly.

She reached for the letter and scanned the middle paragraph. "It says here there are several men who need your help."

"Jen . . ."

She put the letter aside again and sat back in her chair, staring at him with determination. "I don't think you'll be able to sleep at night if you don't go."

"Trust me," he said, leaving his pipe in the small dish before pushing back from the table. "I'll sleep."

Jennifer jumped to her feet and followed. "Well, I would like to watch this trial," she said.

Chad laughed shortly and shook his head, pushing mightily on the wheels of his chair. "Then, my darling," he drawled, "you must go."

Jennifer stopped in the open doorway of his study. "My interest is piqued," she said doggedly.

Chad positioned himself behind his desk and looked at her from across the room. "Don't play those little games with me, Jen," he said shortly. "They won't work."

She gave up her imploring approach and abruptly altered her tactics. Slowly walking toward the desk, she asked, "Do you honestly have the heart to write to Mr. Hope and turn down his request? Obviously someone went to a great deal of trouble to provide him with your name and address. You must come highly recommended, Chad. These men are probably filled with hope that you will represent them. Aren't you just a little curious about this case? Doesn't the thought of returning to your career hold any attraction for you?"

"Frankly, no," he said as he began sorting through a small stack of bills.

Jennifer reached across the desk and stayed his hand. "I believe your reputation must be known far and wide. I believe you must be brilliant as a defense lawyer."

"I don't think quite that highly of myself," he said, refusing to raise his eyes to hers.

"What bothers you about going back, Chad?" she asked softly. "How can I help?"

He did look up then. "I don't need help," he said tersely. "If I return to my practice, it will mean moving from Stonehall again. Can't you be content living here with me?"

"I can," she said softly. "The question is, darling, can you?"

With that she turned and left the room.

She was there at the back door, just as she had been every day when he returned from school.

"Hello," she said gaily, holding the door for him. "How was school?"

Silas turned sideways and slipped past her into the kitchen. "School is school," he said. He looked at the island work station with eager anticipation; every day she had a snack prepared for him. Every day she sat opposite him on the high stools and indulged in a glass of milk while he ate. Today there was milk, cinnamon rolls, and fresh butter. He set his canvas school sack aside and climbed up to his usual perch. "They're goin' to do a dumb Christmas play," he grumbled as he reached for a roll.

Jennifer hid her smile and sat across from him. "Which 'dumb' play would that be?" she asked.

Silas shrugged, his mouth full. Once he had swallowed, he reached for the glass of cool milk. "Somethin' outta the Bible."

She nodded.

"Courtney's goin' to be Mary," he went on.

Jennifer's attention perked up. "Is she? Courtney will be a terrific Mary. Who will be Joseph?"

"They asked me," he grumbled, wiping away a milk mustache with the back of his hand. "I told them to stuff it."

Jennifer groaned silently over this typical response from him.

"I'm not actin' like some stupid husband and starin' at some stupid baby."

Everything was stupid. "*Stupid*," she said. "I agree."

He looked at her suspiciously.

"They can find someone else," she continued. "And I'll explain how you feel to Chad, if you like. I'm certain he won't be too disappointed."

There was a long moment of silence as Silas tried to reason out her scheme. "Why would he be disappointed?" he asked at last.

"Chad is proud of you, Si. You must understand that. I think he would be very pleased to watch a play in which you are participating."

Silas narrowed his eyes and dropped both hands to his lap. "Lady," he drawled. "I think you play dirty."

Jennifer grinned and nodded. "Yep. But I'm proud of you, too."

That night Jennifer sat on the side of the bed while Chad painstakingly brushed her hair. It had become a nightly ritual between them, and it never failed to make her tingle with anticipation of what would follow.

"Did you write to Mr. Hope?" she asked, breaking a long silence between them.

"No," he said quietly.

"Do you feel that I'm nagging, Chad?" she ventured.

"Yes," he said succinctly. "But I know why you're doing it," he added.

"I'm doing it because I love you."

Chad placed his hands on her shoulders and turned her to face him. "I know that, sweetheart. But, Jen, you've got to leave this one to me. Please. You're hurting me by pressing."

This was not the first time she had wanted to cry and wail against what had happened to him. But this time the pain was more intense. This time she actually felt she was *feeling* his pain. But she would not cry. Not in front of Chad. "I'm sorry," she said softly. She put her arms around him then and rested against his chest. "I've been thinking of a way to resolve the bathing problem."

Chad closed his eyes, wearily resigned to the fact that she would not let it go; any of it. He also knew his life was better because she wouldn't. "How?"

"I haven't worked out all the details yet," she said.

Lord, she was incredible. "Well, tell me what you've got so far."

"Promise you won't be angry?"

He laughed skeptically, wondering if he was going to be humiliated as he had so often in the past. And yet, it was Jennifer who took so much of the sting out of mortifying situations. "I'm not promising anything."

She hesitated a moment before dropping the proposal blatantly between them. "A sling and a pulley," she said.

"What?!"

She raised her head to look at him. "You said you wouldn't be angry."

"I said no such thing," he returned, but he was laughing. "You're not putting me in any damned sling!"

Jennifer sat up then, drawing up one knee and pressing it against his hip as she faced him. "This is how I envision it working——," she started.

"No," he broke in, crossing his arms over his naked chest.

She ignored him. "The sling will be like a pendulum that we can push over the tub and——"

"No," he said again.

Jennifer's eyes developed a decidedly mischievous glitter. "We can have much more privacy if we don't need Gerome's help in the morning," she said easily.

Chad simply stared at her, hiding his amusement.

"I can't seem to help thinking about sharing a bath with you," she said brazenly.

He laughed openly then. "You're an audacious little thing," he said indulgently.

"I'm a woman driven by need," she said resolutely, making him laugh all the more.

"You are indeed a *woman*," he said when he could speak. "A very clever woman and you make me very happy."

Jennifer stared closely into his eyes, studying his expression. "Do I, Chad?"

"You do."

"I hope I always will, you know?"

"I know, darling," he said softly. "And I want the same for you." Her eyes were shining with desire as he stared back at her. She was wearing a fine cotton nightdress, and even though her breasts were not quite touching his chest, the heat of her radiated through the cloth and over his body. His semi-erection grew instantly more demanding. Her next words, however, forced him to quell his ardor.

Jennifer was not certain how best to approach the subject, this being the first time she had been forced into thwarting their love play. "I hate it that we can't make love tonight," she whispered with obvious disappointment.

Chad understood, of course. "For a few nights, Jen?" She nodded and then laughed at herself when she felt a heated blush. "I don't believe it!"

"Struck by the intimacy of it?" he teased, capturing both of her hands in his. "There won't be much we won't know about each other in time, darling."

"I know," she said, growing at ease with him once more. "And I'm glad for that."

"Come lie beside me," he said softly. "Let me hold you."

Jennifer needed no coaxing, but first she dashed across the room and fed another log onto the fire before returning to him.

Gerome purposely stacked smaller logs there, knowing Jennifer would be the one to get up in the night if they should need heat. He had supplied the lighter logs at Chad's request, but the older man doubted that the young couple would have much need of heat, other than what they would, undoubtedly, create on their own.

Jennifer snuggled next to Chad, purposely keeping her lower body a small distance from his hip; she had suffered a fleeting concern earlier in the day that Chad might be offended by her state.

He was instantly aware of what she was about and pressed a firm hand on her buttock, fingers splayed. "Get over here," he ordered lightly.

Jennifer breathed a relieved sigh and moved closer, resting her head comfortably on his shoulder.

"Don't ever be embarrassed," he said softly. "Not with me."

"I won't. It was foolishness," she said quietly.

"Are you disappointed there's no baby?"

She thought about how to respond; she had no concerns about babies happening, and she didn't want him to worry, either. He had enough on his plate. "I felt a pang of disappointment this morning when it started, but I'm not worried."

"That's good," he said concisely. After a moment he said, "I have something to ask of you."

Jennifer was warm and tranquil and growing sleepy already. "Mmm?"

"You once told me about a friend who had been . . . as you so delicately phrased it . . . 'put upon.' "

Jennifer's eyes popped open. "I remember."

Jennifer raised her head, frowning in earnest. "I don't think it would be right of me to tell."

"Why?"

He shrugged, bumping her shoulder. "Call it curiosity."

She shook her head. "Not good enough, Mr. Moran."

He sighed heavily. "All right. Call it a lawyer's need to uncover the facts."

"You didn't feel the need to 'uncover the facts' about Homestead," she pointed out.

Now Chad was frowning. "These are two entirely different issues."

"Are they?"

"Yes," he said firmly. "Suffice it to say that I don't like the thought of this man roaming the area. There are other women, besides your friend, who could be in jeopardy."

Jennifer gave his explanation a moment's thought.

"Why is this striking you now?"

Chad's dark brown eyes burned into hers. "Because now I have something very dear to protect."

"Me?" she questioned with disbelief.

"You."

The thought was ridiculous. "But, Chad, I would never be in the same situation as . . ."

"Yes?"

"My friend," she finished. "I would never flirt with another man."

"Perhaps no teasing or flirting would be required to set this fellow off," he suggested. "Had you thought of that?"

"I just don't understand why you're asking about this now," she said quietly.

"It hasn't ever left my mind, sweetheart. I've asked myself if I shouldn't be doing something to protect the women who live hereabouts. Indulge me."

Jennifer shook her head, loyal to the end. "I'll have to speak with her," she said. "I'll have to ask her to come to you.

"No!" Diana Chester said emphatically. "I'll not tell anyone else about what happened to me. Absolutely not!"

"But Chad is a lawyer, Diana," Jennifer reasoned. "He knows what is legally right and what's not. He only wants to prevent some other poor woman from——"

"No!" she said again, whirling her horse away from her friend's. "No one will believe me over the man," she said heatedly. "If I confess, I'll only ruin my own reputation. Nothing can be done about *him*."

"Diana, Chad wouldn't ask you to come forward if he didn't think something could be done."

"Don't give me away, Jen," her friend returned heatedly. "You promised."

Jennifer shook her head. "I won't. I swear."

# CHAPTER SEVENTEEN

Chad had been agonizing over the plight of the men of Homestead who had been accused of murder. He was half annoyed that Jennifer could plant a seed in his thoughts that would give him no rest. He was also a whole lot in love with her for doing so.

It was true, he missed the challenges of his profession: the need to know; the digging for clues and evidence; the craft of defending those who were innocent; and the desire to see justice fairly done. The Homestead case would be one of great challenge, for, surely, there was guilt on both sides: the *company* with little apparent care for the respect men thrived upon, and the workers who rebelled with violence. Such positions would only bring more deaths unless precedents could be set and awareness brought to the attention of the nation. There was the possibility of avoiding further violence if powers of negotiation were granted both parties in such situations. There were several other industrial towns like Homestead, and it was to be hoped that the example set that July day near Pittsburgh would not be repeated.

The challenge of the case nagged at Chad, and he knew he had to make a decision and provide James Hope with a response to his letter.

But the challenge and the intrigue did not negate the fact that Chad was facing a personal struggle. To say *no* to James Hope and the other men would be easy. To say *yes* would mean personal anguish and a struggle Chad was not certain he was prepared to face just yet. He was not a cowardly man, and he knew that. But should he return to the courtroom and not succeed in demanding, and receiving, a position of respect in the eyes of the court, he would be forever crushed by the experience.

"What is it, Chad?" Jennifer asked quietly. "What has you puzzling so?"

Chad raised startled eyes; he'd been so deep in thought he had failed to hear her enter the room. "I thought you were helping Silas with his reading."

She smiled as she sat in a chair very close to him. "I gave him some time off for good behavior," she said lightly. "He's improved a great deal. He's gone to his room, and I'll bet he's going through that new picture book you gave him, for the hundredth time."

It was a book about horses, and it hadn't come cheap, but Chad had hoped to fuel the boy's growing interest in the animals. "Hunter has agreed to take Si under his wing and teach the boy all he knows about horses," he told her.

Jennifer had heard that just this very day, from Maggie. "He couldn't have a better teacher. Hunter saved Treemont from financial ruin with his knowledge of horses and his understanding of the needs of breeders."

"Yes, I know."

Jennifer had been watching him closely from the moment she had entered the room. Something was troubling her husband deeply and had been for several days. "Could we converse?" she asked seriously.

Chad smiled crookedly in confusion. "I thought we had been," he said. "We were talking about Silas."

Jennifer shook her head and drew one leg up under her, leaning on the arm of her chair as she clasped her hands together. "We were *talking*, but I think we've been talking around an issue for several days, Chad. What's wrong? How can I help?"

He looked away from her, frowning as he stared out the double glass doors of the study, feeling as bleak as the late fall day had been. "There's nothing," he said.

He was shutting her out and that hurt. Jennifer's eyes roamed over the profile of his face, a face she loved, the face belonging to the man she loved without question. It saddened her that he was suffering an inner struggle that he could not seem to share with her. She would fight all the armies of the world for him; surely he knew that. "Whatever battles you wage, I wage as well," she said softly. "Whatever pain you suffer, I suffer, also."

Jennifer was too damned perceptive where he was concerned; he could seldom hide much from her. And normally she was so easy to talk with. But he had never shared his innermost feelings about the one thing she could not understand; his fear of returning to work.

Chad also knew he was at the point of needing to talk with someone. Of needing to speak the words and thereby, hopefully, regain his perspective on the matter. Who else should he talk with except the woman who loved him, regardless of his faults and shortcomings?

He turned his head and Jennifer was shocked by the anguish that she read in his face. "Oh, Chad," she whispered as she stared into the dark brown of his eyes.

He grinned in self-ridicule. "You've married a coward, my love," he said.

"I have not!" she returned heatedly.

Chad's head nodded, once. "Is it better to try and fail or not to try at all, Jen?" he asked.

Jennifer was becoming increasingly concerned for him.

"I think you know the answer to that," she said softly.

Chad laughed shortly. "Oh, yes. I do. But to try and fail will mean shutting something out of my life forever. Something I once cared about very much. Whereas, if I don't try, I can always assume that, one day, I'll go back. I won't be locking it entirely out of my life or out of the realm of possibility."

Now Jennifer understood. "Your work," she said without question. Leaning forward, her expression intense, she asked, "Explain this to me. Help me to understand why this is so difficult for you, darling. You haven't lost your skills as a fine lawyer."

"I've lost the use of my legs," he said flatly.

Her frown of confusion deepened. "But you don't need the use of your legs," she pointed out bluntly. "You need your mind, and there's nothing wrong with that."

Striving for patience through this most painful of confessions, he said, "You've seen how people react to me. They see a man in a chair. Often they talk to me as if I'm also deaf or dim-witted. As if they assume I've lost more than one faculty because of one disability. I need to stand tall in a courtroom, Jen," he said intensely. "I need to command attention, not to my physical situation, but to the questions I'm asking and the evidence I'm disclosing. I have to command respect for my craft and convince a judge and jury to listen to me as an authority. They aren't going to see that first. They're going to see this chair first."

"So, let them have a good look and get that out of the way," she said forcefully.

He looked at her with disbelief and then laughed shortly, shaking his head.

"What you fail to understand, Mr. Moran," she said forcefully, "is that you are a commanding figure whether you are sitting or not. Your very presence in a room demands attention, and your voice lures people to listen." Her eyes sparked with mischief suddenly and she grinned. "You certainly gain all of my attention when you speak."

He did laugh at that; they both knew damned well that she might listen, but then she did exactly as she chose.

"You are possibly the most intelligent human being I have ever met," she added. "You'll bowl them over the moment you arrive in the room." She spoke with confidence because she was now convinced that he would be returning to the law in the near future.

He stared at her for a long moment as he wondered, not for the first time, how he had been fortunate enough to have her fall in love with him. "If I were the devil's own son, you'd back me up."

She smiled. "Possibly."

"You would," he said with certainty.

"I'm going with you," she said quietly.

Chad's brows arched in question and surprise. "Going where?"

"Pittsburgh or wherever we have to go to help James Hope and those other men."

"I haven't said I'm prepared to defend James Hope or anyone," he said firmly.

"You will."

He laughed shortly as they continued to look at each other. There was no contest, he decided. "You're a cheeky little wench," he teased as he held out his hand to her.

Jennifer moved from her chair to his lap with practiced ease. Her arms went around his neck as she smiled her understanding of his doubts. It would be difficult for him, she knew. She had only to place herself in his position to imagine what it would feel like to wheel that chair into the center of a room full of people. To say that one would feel self-conscious in Chad's situation would be an understatement. But she also knew that he would take command of the situation, and once he set this first encounter behind him, he would be free of any doubts or concerns. He had overcome so much in a very short time, and he was not a man to hide safely behind the walls of Stonehall and allow life to pass him by. He would live and work and enjoy life to the fullest and to hell with what others thought. "It's a big first step," she said.

He understood her meaning exactly, and he knew he would not fail. He also knew he would have eventually returned to his practice in any event, but having her there beside him, loving him and believing in him, would do much to ease his way. "And then it will be behind us," he said softly.

She smiled, loving the fact that he had used the word '*us*.' She hugged him, pressing her cheek against his as tears welled up in her eyes. She appreciated his understanding of the pain she suffered on his account, even though she was careful never to let him see how she agonized at times. She hated most of all that he had to endure so much. Losing the use of his legs was only one trauma he'd had to undergo. Putting one's life back together and tolerating the many changes was another thing entirely. But she would be there beside him no matter what life threw in their direction. She had made that decision quite consciously the very day she realized she was falling in love with him.

Chad closed his eyes and pulled her tightly against his chest, pressing his cheek more firmly against hers. It was continually amazing how she could soothe his torment and rebuild his inner strength with only a few words, a soft smile, and an embrace. She made his life whole, and that would have been the case whether he had *walked* into her life or *wheeled* his way in. "You don't see the chair, do you, Jen?" he asked softly.

She shook her head slightly against his and pressed a lingering kiss on his neck. "I haven't from the first," she said. "I only saw a very terrific man."

"I've been short-tempered and testy at times."

She moved her head back and grinned at him. "That's true."

"But it didn't drive you away."

"I didn't take your anger personally, darling," she said. "And I felt you were entitled to those moments."

"You're a very *mature* woman," he said, smiling.

"Watch how you say that," she returned with feigned ire.

He laughed. "What?"

"Are you implying that I'm *old?*"

"No!" he said, laughing again. "I'm 'implying' that I think you're wonderful."

Jennifer's arms were draped over his shoulders, and her fingers gripped his hair. "I believe I can accept that," she said cheekily.

He looked at her face, examining the clarity, the softness of her complexion, the pale blueness of her eyes. Eyes that stared back at him with such unadultered love it made his heart twist. He reached up and caressed her cheek with his fingertips, his eyes following the path of his hand. "I love you so much sometimes it hurts," he confessed.

"Me, too," she whispered.

"I just want to keep you all to myself and protect you against everything bad."

"You can't do that, darling," she said. "But I thank you for the thought."

His hand moved downward, gently smoothing the long column of her neck, and his gaze followed. He boldly traced the outline of her breast, and he heard her breath catch. "Every time I look at you or touch you, it's as if I'm discovering a whole new wonderful world," he murmured.

"You make my world spin crazily, my friend," she gasped as he pressed his thumb against her rigid nipple.

Chad raised devilish, sparkling eyes to hers. "*Friend?*"

"You know what I mean," she said huskily as she pressed toward his hand.

"Do I?" he asked as he continued to tease her. He raised his other hand and gave her other breast like treatment. "Am I your *friend*, Jen?" he coaxed.

"My lover," she whispered.

"And what do you say to your lover?"

Jennifer's head dropped toward his shoulder. "You make me ache," she whispered.

Hearing those words, the way she said them, caused Chad's own breath to quicken. She could arouse him with just a look, just a whisper, and he never seemed to get enough of her. He pressed her back against his arm, holding her firmly while he stared down at her. "How can this be?" he questioned softly. "How can I love you so much? How is it I always need you more?"

Jennifer smiled her understanding. "How can this be?" she returned. "How can I love you so much? How is it I always need you more? And more?"

He grinned then, even as his lips moved closer to her. "I think we're oversexed," he said.

"Lord, I hope so," she breathed as his lips touched hers.

He broke the kiss off immediately as he laughed and hugged her fiercely. "Close the draperies while I lock the door," he said softly.

Jennifer frowned up at him as he loosened his hold.

"Pardon?"

"You heard me."

"But why?"

"Because I'm going to make love to you," he said frankly.

Jennifer's eyes became large and round. "Here?"

He simply continued to stare, giving her time to decide if she wanted him badly enough to risk discovery from others in the house. The hour was not late, and Silas or Gerome might seek them out for any number of reasons.

Suddenly she giggled and jumped up from his lap, racing toward the glass doors.

Chad moved quickly across the room and turned the large key in the lock.

They met beside a straight-backed, armless chair in front of his desk. "Let's move this near the fire," he said and they did.

At his request Jennifer moved across the room and poured a single glass of brandy as Chad transferred to the chair. When she returned to him, she placed the glass on a small table nearby and stood smiling down at him. "I feel positively wicked," she said.

He grinned knowingly. "Stimulating, isn't it?"

Jennifer nodded and took a step closer. "What should I do?"

He continued to look up at her as he reached for her skirts. "Just stand there a moment," he said. His hands moved unerringly up her naked thighs until he found the drawstring of her drawers.

Jennifer looked down at him, placing her hands on his shoulders as he worked his magic under her skirts. The teasing glint in their eyes changed to dusky, sensuous heat as Chad made a protracted ritual out of this process of ridding her of one simple garment.

His hands cupped her naked buttocks before he skimmed the fine cotton down the length of her legs until the drawers dropped to her ankles. He took his time then, his eyes never leaving hers as he studied her reaction to the movement of his hands. The texture of her skin was like nothing else he had ever touched as his fingers traced a pattern up her thighs and around her hips. He teased her with the tantalizing threat of touching her womanhood before sliding his hands away. He retraced the pattern and moved toward her secret place again. "Do you want me to touch you?" he asked huskily. She nodded her head.

Jennifer could not trust her voice. She nodded her head.

When his fingers met her warm, moistened flesh, she jumped as if she'd been struck by a lightning bolt.

Chad smiled passionately in the face of her condition.

"You'll never be able to hide your need from me," he said. "You're too fiery a woman."

"Is that bad?" she moaned softly as her eyes closed and she concentrated on the sensations that were growing more demanding.

"That's very, very good," he whispered as he moved his hands slowly down her thighs again.

Jennifer opened her eyes and frowned her disappointment.

"Soon," he said as he reached for the top button of his trousers. But he did not want this to move quickly, in spite of his painful need of her. He wanted to prolong the moment, building on the tension that went along with the perceived risk they were taking. They had never made love outside of the master bedroom, and he knew the risk of discovery, however slight, would increase their anticipation and, ultimately, their gratification.

His eyes smoldered as Jennifer dropped to her knees in front of him and her hands replaced his in the management of the small trouser buttons. There was no shyness between them, none at all, as she boldly exposed his engorged manhood. Chad caught his breath and held it as she touched him, gently guiding him from within the sheltered confines of his clothing. "Oh, Jen," he breathed, lightly stroking her cheek. His hand turned and cupped her chin as he leaned forward and pressed his lips lightly against hers. "Go slowly, love," he encouraged. "I want you slowly," he murmured before pulling her upward and across his lap.

Jennifer had thought to take him as she settled herself against him, but Chad had other thoughts and positioned her so that he was snuggled warmly against her moisture.

He raised his head and pulled her down toward his lips, kissing her tenderly before allowing his arm to drop and his hand to caress her breast. "Let me see," he said.

Somehow he managed not to touch her as Jennifer unfastened one button after another down the length of her blouse. She had little need of the long, whale-boned corsets worn by most women and, indeed, Chad discouraged her use of such garments, proclaiming them unnatural and unhealthy. Jennifer opted instead for a much lighter, cotton bust bodice that was boned at the sides, providing more comfort and yet support for her ample breasts. This garment, too, she unbuttoned.

Chad reached for the brandy she had left on the small table, never taking his eyes from the progress she was making. She had caught his game now, he suspected, and was revealing herself to him slowly, with deliberate movements. He raised the glass and sipped and their gazes met briefly, heatedly, before he looked again at her hands and the pale, full globes that were being revealed to him.

Jennifer would never have believed such actions could be so stimulating. Just having him look at her with such intensity was akin to having him touch her everywhere. "I'm feeling very bold," she whispered, even though she hesitated in pulling the sides of the bodice away.

Chad raised his eyes and reached up to touch the side of her neck. "You must do anything you wish to do, darling," he said in a voice gone deep with passion.

Jennifer felt her complexion warming and dipped her head, lightly brushing her lips across his. "I might do something you don't like," she murmured.

Chad smiled, very much doubting that. "I would tell you," he said simply.

Jennifer stared into his eyes before placing a forefinger beneath the glass he held and slowly guiding the drink upward toward her mouth.

He allowed her to sip the fiery brew once, twice, before she felt she had had enough.

Brazenly she stared at him, watching his gaze drop to her breasts as she revealed them fully to him. More brazenly still, she brought his free hand up to touch her. She closed her eyes as the palm of his hand warmed her, and then she jolted forward as he lightly pinched her rigid nipple and sent a shock of sensation through her. "Oh," she groaned and braced her hands on his shoulders.

Chad continued to play with her, eventually setting the brandy aside and concentrating on pleasuring her with both hands.

Jennifer's passion grew to such a monumental pitch that she began to shift on his lap, pressing her lower body against his and moving upward along his length. A tiny spark startled her when the vital bud of her center came in contact with him.

Chad understood her gasp of surprise and reached under her skirts, placing one hand on her hip as he reached between them. "Lift up a bit," he murmured hastily. And when she did as instructed, he guided himself inside her. "Easy," he said throatily. "Take your time."

Jennifer's forehead pressed against his, her breathing short, quick, and painful as she lowered herself upon him, taking all of him. "Oh, God," she breathed as she dipped her head and pressed her lips against his neck. She was aware only briefly of his fingers touching her intimately before she was racked by explosive spasms that rocked her body against his.

Chad pulled her body tight against him, knowing the movements of her body were taking him close to his own climax. He reached for that same gratification now, even as she settled upon him.

Jennifer felt her body tighten around him and heard his surprised intake of breath. She felt drained of all ability to move, but she was also very aware of her desire to fulfill his need. She moved upward and lowered herself, feeling her body tighten around him reflexively once again.

Chad was totally consumed by her, drawn demandingly inside her. He sensed the explosion coming and frantically wrapped his arms around her waist and hips, pulling her down on him as his upper body jerked in spasm and he poured himself into her.

They rested weakly within the shelter of each other's arms, gasping for air as the warm flow of afterglow washed through their bodies. Every nerve ending seemed to react independently as slowly they drifted back to the real world, to the room that sheltered them and the nearby fire that warmed them.

Wearily Jennifer murmured, "I pity Diana." She instantly regretted the words, of course, but neither could she take them back. Startled by her own stupidity, Jennifer's head came up and she looked into his eyes.

Frowning his confusion, Chad asked, "What about Diana?"

She had been thinking only that her friend deserved to know the kind of loving she had just experienced, rather than that first and only painful episode of passion Diana had explained.

"Diana Chester, Jen?" he probed. "What about her?"

"Nothing. It was just a stupid thought."

"You were thinking about a woman?" he queried.

"That's not very flattering, darling."

Jennifer dropped her head to his shoulder and tightened her arms around his neck. "It was just a brief thought," she whispered close to his ear, "that Diana could know love as I do."

Chad ignored her comment, not wanting to emerge from the heat of passion with thoughts of others intruding between them. He pampered her with softly spoken words of love and touched her, caressed her with languorous strokes of his fingers. When reality encroached, he silently helped her make herself presentable, kissing her tenderly between the careful fastening of each button.

His inquiring legal mind was a little fogged by residual passion, but it took only moments for his thoughts to shift into some semblance of order. Once he, too, was fully clothed, Chad pulled her onto his lap and reached for the remainder of their brandy. "Why pity?" he asked, before raising the glass to his lips.

Jennifer made a great show of straightening her skirts.

"Let it go, Chad. Please."

She refused to look at him and that made Chad more curious than ever. "What kind of loving did you mean, Jen? Surely not physical loving? Diana isn't wed. Nor has she been, as far as I'm aware."

"I think we should speak to Silas about adoption before we leave for Pittsburgh," she said firmly. But before she could distance herself from him, Chad had a firm, but painless, hold on her arm.

"You like making love with me," he said.

Jennifer did look at him then. For a moment, "I like everything about you," she said with soft-spoken sincerity.

"You liked what we just shared," he added pointedly.

Jennifer turned her head toward him and smiled. "And we didn't get caught," she chirped.

"Jennifer . . ."

"I spoke out of turn," she said firmly. "Please don't question me."

"Diana is the one, isn't she?" he asked gently. "Diana is the friend who was put upon."

Jennifer raised a hand and wearily stroked her brow. "I swore I wouldn't speak of it," she said.

Chad set the now empty brandy snifter aside and cupped the side of her face with his hand. "Jennifer," he said softly, turning her head toward him. "I'm not about to cause

Diana any harm. She's your friend and you obviously care deeply about her."

Her frown deepened with worry. "I've just broken a confidence," she said miserably.

Chad smiled his understanding. "In the heat of passion, darling." Trying to lighten her mood, he added, "I think it quite a compliment, actually, that you think so highly of our lovemaking you would wish the same for a cherished friend."

She smiled pitifully.

"I won't reveal Diana's secret," he said seriously. "If there is any *revealing* to be done in future, it will have to be by Diana herself.

She nodded her head in agreement. "I trust you."

"I should hope so," he returned ruefully.

"She's so worried about how she will explain her lack of . . ."

"Virginity?" he supplied.

Jennifer nodded her head. "To a future husband," she said, completing the thought.

"I suggest she tell the man outright, before it gets to the point of discovery on their wedding night."

"What if he doesn't want her if she's not a virgin?" she asked with hasty concern.

Chad shrugged. "Then perhaps he's not the right man. If he loves her, the question of virginity will not make a difference."

Jennifer frowned as she thought about that. "Would you have married me if I'd been in Diana's situation?"

"Without question," he said easily. "I would have wanted to shoot the man who hurt you, however."

Jennifer settled back comfortably against his chest and stared into the dancing flames of the fire. "I truly think he did hurt her," she said quietly. "I don't know what the experience is going to do to her future associations with men."

Chad wrapped his arms around her and took her hands in his, resting them against her belly. "Perhaps if you tell her of your own experience, she won't fear," he said softly.

"I've done that," she said, rotating her head against his shoulder. "But I don't think that mere words can blot out a bad experience. I don't know that she believed me when I told her how wonderful it is when one's in love and has a considerate lover."

Chad weighed the information he possessed over his need to discover the identity of the man who had forced himself upon Diana Chester. It was entirely possible, if he spoke now, that Hunter and Maggie Maguire might never speak to him again. Not only would he have earned their wrath, he would hurt his beloved Jennifer in the process. Still, he felt it imperative that the true nature of Charles Tandy be brought into the daylight and closely examined. If the man was, indeed, a rapist . . . if the man continued to take advantage of unsuspecting young women . . . if he were permitted to continue to hurt naive women, both physically and emotionally, Chad knew he would not be able to live with himself.

Taking a deep, cleansing breath, he prayed he would not do more damage to innocent souls. "Darling, you must tell me who the man is who hurt your friend."

Jennifer tipped her head back until she could see his face. "But I don't know who he is," she said guilelessly. "Diana would not tell me."

"Then we must convince her to tell us, before more women are hurt."

Jennifer sat up and turned to face him. "Why are you so intent upon this?"

Chad took her hand and slowly, methodically stroked her knuckles with the pad of his thumb. "Because I love you," he said, looking directly into her eyes. "Because I want to protect you. Because I'm beginning to believe this man has done more than force himself upon a naive young woman who is now blaming herself for the incident."

Jennifer's heart twisted painfully as she sensed his feelings of genuine concern. "Chad . . . ?"

He shook his head and continued. "Because I think this man remains close by," he added. "Because I think this man is capable of rape." He felt her fingers tighten around his and knew his words had greatly impacted upon her.

"What's made you think this way?" she demanded quietly. "Why are you so insistent?"

He hesitated only briefly, knowing he would hurt her but feeling he had little choice. He told her all he knew; about the mysterious disappearance of his father's ring years ago, about Maggie's dreams and the rape of ten years before.

She cried then, shocked and grievously sorrowed over her sister's pain. "That explains the 'accident,'" she said, weeping against his chest.

"Maggie never wanted any of you to know."

"I remember she didn't want to marry Hunter," she said brokenly. "Now I understand why."

"But he's been good to her," he said.

Jennifer's head moved. "Oh, yes. He's been wonderful, and I know how much she loves him."

"There is more, my love," he said quietly. He told her about Silas's wise observations of Charles Tandy and the boy's well-hidden concern. "He's a smart little monkey," Chad said. "He knows enough to understand that Tandy's interest in you is not good or natural."

"But Charles has never approached me," she said logically. "I've never *felt* that he's had an interest in me."

"He wouldn't dare approach you. And I've had you watched closely," Chad explained.

"We have no proof against him, do we?" she asked at last. "The law is on the side of men, isn't it?"

He couldn't deny that. The evidence against Tandy would be circumstantial at best, and Maggie could not remember the identity of her attacker, if she ever knew the man. Diana would be discredited in a moment in a court of law; she was a woman who played a dangerous game and lost. She would be looked upon as having teasingly drawn the man into an affair. "If Charles Tandy is the man who forced your friend, then perhaps we can find a way to discover more about him. I can't promise that we'll manage to convict him of raping Maggie, but the very least we can do is have him openly accused and see that his reputation precedes him wherever he goes. We'll do our best to see that no other woman suffers at his hands."

Jennifer curled up against him. "I'll invite Diana for lunch tomorrow," she said wearily.

A totally unsuspecting Diana Chester joined Jennifer and Chad Moran for luncheon two days later at Stonehall.

They feasted on small sandwiches and a hearty vegetable soup.

When they adjourned to the study for coffee, Jennifer sat on the settee beside her friend and braced herself for her husband's gentle assault.

Chad had positioned his chair in front of the two young women and smiled encouragingly at his bride before turning his attention upon Diana. "We've asked you here because Jennifer cherishes your friendship, Diana," he said thoughtfully. "And we hope—we *both* hope—you will return to visit us often. But there is also something that needs to be discussed."

Diana stared curiously at her friend's husband before her attention was drawn to the woman at her side. "What's this about, Jen?"

"Diana," Jennifer said quietly as she reached for her friend's hand. "Please tell him."

Now Diana was truly confused. "Tell him what?"

Chad gently demanded her attention. "Jennifer cares very much about you, Diana, and I want to say at the outset that she has not purposely betrayed your confidence."

The young woman continued to look confused.

"I did not mean to give away your secret," Jennifer whispered.

Diana's head swiveled toward her friend. "You told him?" she whispered in disbelief as a heated blush stole upward from her neck to her forehead. There was little doubt of the subject under discussion; Diana had only one true secret. "How could you?" she breathed brokenly.

Jennifer's hands tightened around Diana's. "I—".

Diana attempted to break free of Jennifer's hold, to move from the place where she was seated and bolt from the room, from the very house.

"I forced Jen to reveal your identity and with very good reason," Chad said quickly. "There may well be an issue of greater magnitude than you believe, Diana. Please stay and allow me to explain."

He was wonderfully compelling when he spoke, and Jennifer's eyes began to glow with pride as she felt her friend relax as Chad spoke to her.

He explained it all in a gentle yet professional tone that relieved Diana of much of the embarrassment she was feeling. There was an issue to discuss and information to be gathered, and he made that very plain. There was no conspiracy to disgrace or humiliate her and the confidence she had placed with Jennifer would now bind Chad as well. Her name would not be revealed beyond the four walls that provided them with privacy this day.

It was stressed to Diana that there was a suspicion that the man who had taken advantage of her was possibly

capable of an even harsher crime. Chad protected Maggie's identity but easily made his point with the young
woman. Eventually he asked for the man's name, and she
gave it.

Diana turned to her friend after she had spoken and
cried on Jennifer's shoulder.

Chad's head was bowed as he listened to her pained
sobs. The evidence he possessed was flimsy at best, but
it was enough, as far as he was concerned, to fire Charles
Tandy and see the man away from Stonehall. Still, that
would be tantamount to turning a demon loose, and
Chad's conscience simply would not permit him to drop
the matter. If he could not obtain enough evidence for
a conviction, he would, at the very least, leave Tandy
fearing for his freedom.

At the very least, Chad knew the concept of Natural
Law must be applied: principles used to determine what
is right and what is wrong as written by the definitive
Author of nature. God.

After consulting with Hunter and the local constable,
Chad set several wheels in motion.

He had a frank discussion with Silas.

And he hired a Pinkerton man.

# CHAPTER EIGHTEEN

"We'll talk to him in the morning, before we leave?" Jennifer asked as she lay curled up in bed beside her husband.

Chad was well sated and drowsy after their lovemaking, but he managed to nod his head.

The trials of the steelworkers had been postponed until the New Year, and finally they were packed and prepared to travel to Pittsburgh. Chad had engaged a junior lawyer in that city to gather critical evidence prior to his arrival. Once there, he would closet himself in the young man's office and prepare his theories and trial notes.

They had been married for less than three months and Jennifer's pride and love of her husband had grown even stronger, if that were possible. They had conquered many tribulations in the short time since Chad's return to Stonehall, and when her heart hurt over his struggles and humiliations, she drew her strength from him. Likewise, Jennifer knew she was a source of strength for her husband. And she knew because he told her so often.

They had argued heatedly over only one issue to date, and that was the question of whether or not Jennifer would accompany Chad to Pittsburgh. There was no question, as far as Jennifer was concerned; she was going.

She pointed out that she would be there to share his triumph.

He pointed out that he could fail. And, secretly, he was determined not to have her witness such an event.

She turned his own words of months ago around and retorted, "We might stumble, but *together* we will never fall."

She would be by his side.

They were mutually supportive and respectful of each other's needs, and they conferred regularly in their roles as acting parents to Silas. And as she lay contentedly within the protective embrace of her husband and lover and friend, Jennifer realized she had never expected life to grant her such excessive happiness. Life was not perfect—*perfect* would get Chad out of his chair—but it was grand.

"Are you asleep?" she whispered.

There was a momentary silence before he answered, "Yes."

She giggled and propped herself on his chest. "I've missed my monthly," she informed him.

Chad's eyes opened and he stared at her in silence for a moment while he considered the passage of time. "Just barely, Jen," he said softly.

"Yes, but it's a good sign," she said, refusing to be daunted.

He smiled, touching her cheek tenderly, knowing how much she had come to love Silas and knowing, too, how much she wanted a child of her own. *Their* child. "I don't want you to be disappointed, darling," he said. "You could be late for any number of reasons."

She shook her head. "I'm never late."

He stared at her frankly, lovingly, having the idea of a child settle delightfully in his mind.

"Would you be happy, Chad?"

"Yes, love."

She laid her head down, just beneath his chin, and wrapped her arms around him. "I'm going to pray it's true," she whispered.

Chad's hand moved in small, caressing circles on her back. "Me, too, Jen," he said.

"You'll have to watch me grow fat," she warned lightly.

He grinned. "I think I could tolerate that."

She immediately lifted her head and frowned. "Having a baby growing inside me won't stop us from . . . ?"

"From what?" he urged when she faltered.

"Will we continue to make love?" she questioned with obvious concern over that matter.

Chad took a chance at second-guessing her meaning. "Are you asking whether or not it will be safe to continue?"

"Yes," she breathed.

He laughed lightly at her. She was acting as if this were a matter of dire need. "My understanding is that it is safe to continue for quite some time, darling," he said fondly.

Jennifer released a *whoosh* of pent-up air. "Good."

Chad laughed again but completely understood her concern; it would be difficult to abstain from their play even for the short time he knew it would be necessary. He was like a man addicted to drugs, where she was concerned; the more he had, the more he wanted. Still, there was little use anticipating something that may not happen for months.

Jennifer had returned her head to his chest, and they lay together in a thoughtful, comfortable silence. They frequently savored moments like these, after the headiness of loving had drained their bodies and before sleep could overtake their tender thoughts. They simply enjoyed the feel, the sight, the smell, and the warmth of each other.

"What will Silas think of a baby?" Jennifer questioned softly.

Chad grunted softly. "We're not even certain, as yet, what Silas thinks of *us*."

"Are you certain I should be with you when you talk to Silas, Chad?"

"There's a possibility of you becoming his mother, Jen. I think you should be there. Just brace yourself in the event he wants nothing to do with adoption." Chad feared that, actually. He knew just how very hurt she would be if Silas decided against their offer. He also knew that the boy had become fond of Jennifer, whether Silas could bring himself to acknowledge a bond between them or not. It was now a matter of just how much of a bond existed.

The following morning Chad asked Silas to join them in the library.

At first the boy looked wary, as if he might expect bad or unpleasant news. But as Chad explained the reason for their *chat*, Silas seemed quite overwhelmed and remained silent for a good, long time.

Jennifer had pulled a chair close to Chad, needing to be near her husband as she watched Silas mentally struggle with what was being said. She found herself drawing in a deep breath and holding it when no sign of warmth or happiness or assent was forthcoming from the boy.

Eventually Silas had to ask the question and hear Chad's response before he would actually believe. "You want to adopt me?"

Chad's head nodded firmly, once. "We do, if you're of a mind to agree. You wouldn't have to take my name if you decided otherwise. But you would legally be our son and would live with us until such time as you're ready to be on your own."

The boy's eyes narrowed. "Who decides *that?*"

Chad smiled, understanding the concern behind the question. "You do," he said. "With our guidance, of course."

"Maybe I don't want no 'of course' about it," he said.

Chad knew there was a tough spot that would never be knocked out of this boy. He had known that before he had even anticipated having this conversation. "Make no mistake, Silas. We care for you or we wouldn't be suggesting such a step. But we expect respect, at the very least, in return. While you are in this house and under our care, you will behave according to the guidelines we set out. There may be rules you do not like, but you must understand that Jennifer and I will do as we feel best for you. You may never come to love us, but I'm asking that you have some regard for our feelings toward you. If you feel you cannot do that, then you must return to Richmond and your fate will be in the hands of the courts once again."

Jennifer's heart twisted at the very thought, and unconsciously she reached for Chad's hand, holding on tightly. She knew those words had been as difficult for him to say as they had been for her to hear. What she did not know, and what she feared, was Silas's reaction to them.

Silas looked at Jennifer and found her staring intently in his direction. It was true she had done more for him than anyone else in his young life. She had tutored him and seen him properly dressed, even if it had been with Chad's money. In the beginning she had done much to smooth his way at Stonehall and had often intervened on his behalf when Moran would have taken a firm hand with him. She had been as tender as he would allow her to be, and yet he suspected she could offer much more in the way of motherly love. He simply wasn't certain he wanted all the sissy stuff. Her hugs were warm and she smelled real good, but he would die before he would let anyone know that he liked that sort of thing. It had been particularly hard over Christmastime to remain aloof and detached, he recalled now. Jennifer had made a big thing about *family* over the season and an even bigger thing about the thrill of selecting gifts for those she loved. She included him in all her Christmas secrets and made it difficult for him not to show his growing excitement. Silas had thought it strange when Jen had first asked him to help her haul pine boughs and holly, but Chad had not seemed to mind that his house was being filled with half of the nearby forest. Jen went wild with the stuff; everywhere Silas looked there was another display of vibrant color—green plants and huge red bows and miles of ribbons. Eventually he did admit that the decorations made the house smell nice, but that is all that he would admit.

And then Christmas morning, Jennifer had come creeping into his room just as the sun was rising.

"It's Christmas," she had said in a hushed tone. "Hurry!"

Silas opened one eye and frowned before burrowing deeper beneath the quilts. "I don't have to go to school," he muttered.

Jennifer giggled and pulled on one of his wrists. "Of course you don't, slugabed. Get up! Chad is waiting for us downstairs."

"Jen . . ." Silas groaned.

"Come on," she coaxed. "There just might be some surprises down there for us."

It took a moment, but eventually Silas rolled onto his back and stared up at her, apparently now quite coherent. He had seen everything she had purchased for Chad and Maggie and all the rest. What could be such a surprise? But he could not help but question. "Surprises?"

"Of course," she said lightly. "From Santa Claus."

"Jen," he drawled, attempting to roll away, "I think you need some sleep or somethin'."

Jennifer held fast to his wrist and dropped down onto the side of his bed. "You're certain you're not interested?"

Silas snorted derisively. "Santa Claus? Jen, that's dumb."

She appeared quite serious all of a sudden. "Is it?" she asked. "You're quite certain?"

Silas decided to end this nonsense so he could get back to sleep. "Well, he never left me no surprises before," he pointed out brusquely.

"*Any* surprises, Si," Jennifer said, again showing the soft smile that somehow seemed secret. "He didn't leave you any surprises because you moved around too much. He didn't know your address."

Silas could not suppress the chuckles that came out as two abrupt barks. "And he does now?"

"Obviously!" she chirped as she whisked the quilts to the foot of the bed. "Come on now, dear boy," she teased, pulling him to his feet.

Silas scrambled, dancing in place to allow his nightshirt to straighten and drop below his knees.

"The sweet rolls are growing cold," Jennifer added.

Silas put on the robe she had retrieved from the foot of the bed. "Sweet rolls?"

With a knowing grin, Jen dropped to her knees in search of his slippers. Silas might not believe in Santa or gifts or surprises, but he sure believed in sweet rolls, and he liked them hot.

Triumphant, she pulled the slippers out from beneath the bed. "Here. Hurry."

"Hurry, hurry," he muttered as he balanced on first one foot and then the other.

Jennifer put one hand on his shoulder and waited until Silas looked up at her. "Aren't you just a little bit excited that today is Christmas?"

Suddenly even the air around them seemed sober.

Silas shook his head.

But Jennifer knew in her heart that it was a doubtful reaction. "You are just not a believer, I suppose," she said softly. With a sudden, brilliant smile she reached for his hand. "I'll just have to show you!" she added, laughing as she pulled him toward the door.

Silas had found himself running in her wake, flying down the stairs and skidding to a halt just inside the door of Chad's study.

Jennifer released him then, plopping down on the settee beside her husband. "I had to bribe him with sweet rolls," she said with well-feigned seriousness. "Silas would rather sleep than celebrate."

Chad grinned at her and winked before turning a serious eye in the boy's direction. Both he and Jen had slept little—it was her fault—in anticipation of morning. They suspected Silas had never received a surprise gift before coming to them, and now he was about to receive several—and that was Chad's fault. Their anticipation of the youth's reaction was great.

But Chad's words died in the back of his throat as he stared at the boy he now thought of as his son. Silas was staring openly at the tree Jennifer had taken such pains to decorate. Fifty tiny candles glowed on the tips of the wide branches, and strings of glass beads reflected the light. The boy's eyes roamed slowly, carefully examining everything in the room that had not been there the night before. "Looks pretty good," Chad observed.

Silas could feel the warmth in that room like nothing else he had ever experienced in his lifetime. A chill of wonder made his shoulders shiver once, but then he stiffened his spine, unwilling to allow any softer emotions to be detected. "Somebody did a lotta work," he said. His steely coolness was demolished, however, when his voice cracked.

Chad understood the boy's stiff stand, or thought he did. "Well!" he said, clapping his hands and then rubbing his palms together. "Let's get down to some serious fun."

Silas turned his head and frowned, one brow arched skeptically. "Serious fun?"

"Certainly," Chad returned as he tucked Jen under his arm and squeezed her shoulder in expectation. "What do you think of that saddle over there?"

Silas's gaze followed the direction of the man's pointing finger, and he stared a moment before walking a few steps closer to the tree. "Wow, Jen. That's a beauty," he breathed as he took another step.

Jennifer's eyes clouded as she briefly took in the sight of his thin legs peaking out from beneath the hem of his robe and nightshirt. "Jen?" she asked. "What has that saddle got to do with me?"

Silas turned his head in her direction, his long lashes shadowing his confusion. "It's not yours?" he questioned.

She smiled. "It's not a gift for me, Silas."

The boy seemed to back away then, as if doubting some wild thought that had just invaded his mind.

"It's for you, Si," Chad told him at last. "You've shown admirable responsibility in caring for your little mare. You've earned that saddle."

His brooding eyes drifted slowly from Jennifer to Chad and settled there.

"Go ahead, son," Chad said softly. "You can take a closer look."

Silas stared in disbelief for so long that Jennifer felt tears well up in her eyes.

"I didn't do nothin' to earn it," he said. "I just liked her."

Chad nodded, understanding. "You just have to be yourself to 'earn' a gift from us, Silas. We're giving it because we love you."

Silas wasn't ready for that. Abruptly he turned away, his attention landing on the tray of sweet rolls. He snatched one up and stuffed it in his mouth, a distraction that did not work. His eyes continually drifted back to the fine, coffee-colored saddle.

They watched, silent and warm, wondering what was going through the boy's mind. Finally, Jennifer ducked her head briefly to dry the moisture on her cheek against Chad's shoulder.

He grinned as he felt the dampness of his shirt. "Thanks," he said sardonically, but he pulled her tight against his side.

Silas had forgotten their presence by now and had stepped closer to the saddle which rode upon a waist-high sawhorse. He reached out gingerly and touched it with the tip of his forefinger; it was cool and smooth. And then he bent over it and breathed in deeply—a rich smell of leather. His head turned after another moment and his gaze settled on the couple on the settee behind him. "Is it really mine?" he asked softly.

Chad and Jennifer both nodded their heads.

Slowly, cautiously, Silas allowed a small grin to wreathe his mouth. But the telling moment of acceptance came when he rested the palm of his hand on the saddle seat.

Jennifer laughed, breaking the tension, before jumping to her feet. "I saw something else here," she said gaily as she began to search beneath the tree.

Silas continued to hold onto his saddle as Jennifer turned toward him with a cloth-wrapped package.

He took her offering in his free hand and stared up at her. "This is for me?" he asked in wonder. "People get all these presents? I mean . . . this many seems . . ."

"Oh, there are more," she blurred. "Courtney made you something very special and . . ." Jennifer stopped, seeing that this was a good deal more than Silas could comprehend. "This one is something we knew you really wanted," she said kindly before turning practical to ease the situation. "Open this one and then drink your milk."

Silas could not seem to remove his hand from the saddle, so he leaned against the leather as he untied the red ribbon. Now this gift had him totally baffled. He thought it must have taken guts to give him such a gift. Either that or she was dumb enough to trust a kid like him.

Jennifer had given him a hunting knife he had admired in the store.

And Silas had decided weeks ago that Jennifer wasn't *dumb*. Therefore, she must trust. It had been the most amazing day Silas could remember. Somehow Chad and Jennifer had managed to almost pull him completely into their world. Not with the gifts; those were special even though he had difficulty admitting to that openly. It was the warmth, the joy, and the sharing that had caught his attention. It had been there all along, of course. Well, almost all along. But he had watched them tease and laugh and ogle each other this Christmas Day and, for the first time, he had allowed himself to join in. He had allowed himself to trust, and he accepted their trust in him. That was another *first* for Silas: having someone trust him. It made him think he might just want to hang around and see what else could come out of this relationship.

But the concept that these two people sitting in front of him now actually cared enough to want him to stay was just hard to figure. "I put you in that chair," he said, hoping his defiance would somehow save him some hurt if this all turned against him.

Jennifer squeezed Chad's hand, but her husband easily retained control. "You didn't purposely choose to hurt me or anyone, Silas," he said quietly but firmly. "I understand that. I suppose we could say that Fate chose me."

"I'm a criminal," the boy added flatly, as if he were trying to dissuade them from this foolishness.

Jennifer blinked in surprise.

"Perhaps in the past but not in this case. There was obviously no evidence of *mens rea*," Chad told him, and then realized he had spoken from years of habit. "That means there was no criminal intent," he explained.

Silas refused to look at Jennifer, and she understood he was afraid of making himself more vulnerable than he was already.

After another long, painful silence Silas asked Chad, "What do we have to do?"

With obvious relief both Chad and Jennifer relaxed back in their chairs.

"I will write to Judge Lang and explain our intent," Chad said. "However, we may have to travel to Richmond to appear before him."

Clearly, Silas did not think much of that idea. "Why?"

"We have to have his permission to proceed with the adoption," Chad explained.

"I don't see it's none o' his business," Silas said baldly.

Chad didn't particularly care for the boy's tone, but he remained patient. He leaned forward, resting his elbows on his knees as he loosely knit his fingers together. "I don't think you understand your relationship with the judge, Silas. Judge Lang was acting on behalf of the state when he sent you here. He was applying a philosophy known as *parens patriae*, which means the state becomes a parent. When a child goes astray and it is clear that there is lack of parental guidance, the courts take over the parental role for the good of the child. In a manner of speaking, Judge Lang has been your parent since you first appeared before him. Now we must obtain his permission to alter your status."

"I don't think I like that," Silas grumbled.

"That's the way it is, boy," Chad said not unkindly. "Not everything in life is to our liking."

Silas looked from Chad's legs to the wheels of the man's chair and understood.

"Shall I write to the judge?" Chad asked.

Silas looked at Jennifer then, silently begging her not to go all mushy on him, as she was sometimes tempted to. "Sure. Why not?" he said casually. But with those words his heart thumped firmly in his chest as he experienced another *first. Joy.*

Silas was to remain at Treemont while Jennifer and Chad were away, and to that end, Jennifer had helped him pack his clothes, and his meager treasures, the previous evening.

Now she entered the room that had once been hers and would be his for the next few weeks. "Maggie has done a good job of redecorating," she murmured as she looked around. "It looks more like a boy's room now than a girl's."

Silas nodded silently as he opened his suitcase on the bed.

"Shall I help you?" Jen asked, stepping up beside the boy.

"Naw," he said. "I can do it."

"You won't mind staying here for a bit, will you, Si?"

Again, he shook his head. "I can learn lots from Hunter while I'm here."

"I'm sure you will," Jennifer said, feeling awkward. She reached out and ran her finger along the open edge of the case as Silas turned toward the chest of drawers with a load of underwear. "I'm very happy that you decided to go ahead with the adoption," she said quietly.

"Yep, well, it seemed like the only thing to do," he said casually before returning to the bed and reaching for his neatly folded shirts; Jennifer was always so neat, he thought.

"I want you to know that Chad and I love you, Silas," she said softly. "I want you to know that we'll miss you."

Silas stared at her askance, unable to fathom so much in just one morning. Eventually he admitted, "I don't want to hurt you, Jen, but I can't say what you're askin' me to say."

Jennifer looked wounded and tried to save them both.

"I'm not asking—"

"Yep, you are," he said with conviction and wisdom that went beyond his years. "But I don't know how."

She smiled then, feeling her hurt assuaged. "I understand. Maybe, until you learn that it's okay to tell people you love them, you could just give us a hug once in a while?"

He flushed with the thought of how weak his old friends would think him if they ever discovered he would even think about such a sissy thing. But then, his old friends had never truly been friends except when they were up to some scheme that inevitably landed them in trouble. Chad and Jennifer were his friends now, and Silas had witnessed, on many occasions, that there was no shame between the two adults when they were showing affection to anyone who touched their lives. He thought a hug might make Jennifer feel better, after his failure to return her love. They were alone, after all. Maybe it would be all right.

He turned to her, refusing to raise his head to look at her before his arms went around her waist.

Jennifer's arms went around his shoulders, and she smiled as she hugged him close. "We love you, Silas," she whispered. "I hope you'll be happy with us."

There was only so much he could take of this first excursion into the world of open affection, and after a brief moment he broke away. "I'll go downstairs and say goodbye to Chad," he muttered.

Jennifer encountered Maggie at the bottom of the stairs a moment later and promptly plucked Jason from his mother's arms. "You've just fed him?" she asked.

Maggie nodded and placed an arm around her sister's waist, steering the younger woman toward the front door. "Everyone is outside," she said.

Jennifer stopped just short of stepping out onto the front porch. "Maggie, what's it like to nurse your babies? Is it as wonderful as I think?"

Maggie was taken aback by the questions and laughed briefly. "Well, Jen, I don't know what you *think*, but, yes, it's wonderful. I don't know that I can explain it, but—"

"You don't have to explain," Jennifer said hurriedly. "I think I might be finding out for myself in a few months."

Maggie's eyes locked with those that mirrored her own in color. "You're pregnant? So soon?"

Jennifer laughed and bounced Jason a time or two as he rode her hip. "Well, we're not certain yet. But my husband is pretty terrific in a lot of ways," she said.

"Obviously," Maggie returned dryly.

"We're happy to have Silas, but we want children of our own, Mag," Jennifer explained.

"Of course you do," her sister said with a smile. "I hope it's true, Jen. I really do."

"You were surprised," Jennifer accused.

Maggie could not lie about that; her amazement had been obvious. In the dead of night, in the privacy of their master bedroom, Maggie had expressed her concerns about the quality of Chad and Jennifer's love life to Hunter. Now it appeared that her worry had been for naught.

Jennifer laughed at her sister's frown of confusion and realized Maggie did not know what to say. She returned Jason to the arms of his mother and lightly kissed Maggie's cheek. "It's okay," she whispered. "I know you must have worried about it."

"Worried about what?" Maggie asked indignantly.

"About Chad's ability to father children," Jennifer said blatantly. "I had some concerns of my own, once upon a time."

"Jen, that is entirely between you and Ch—"

"And I will tell you something else," she said with a girlish giggle. "He's a wonderful lover."

Before Maggie could voice her disapproval, Jennifer pecked her quickly on the cheek once more. "Take care. I love you!" she whispered before she danced down the steps of Treemont's front porch.

Silas was seated inside the closed carriage on the seat opposite Chad, talking quietly. He felt the sway of the vehicle as Gerome took his place up front beside the driver and, turning his head, noticed Jennifer moving away from her sister. Time was marching on, and still his decision was not made.

"If you need anything," Chad was saying, "you have only to ask Hunter."

Silas nodded his head.

"And you've got the name of our hotel," he added. "It would make Jennifer very happy if you would write to her occasionally."

Silas raised his head then and stared at the man who might possibly become his father in the very near future.

"Would it make *you* happy, too?" he asked doubtfully.

Chad was genuinely surprised. "Of course it would, son." he said.

"You don't blame me for what happened to you, do you?"

"No, I don't," he said honestly.

Silas shifted his eyes away, and when he looked at Chad again, he had decided to take an emotional risk for once in his life. "When the judge does that adoption thing, would it be all right for us to ask him to make my name the same as yours?"

Chad's complexion instantly flushed with pleasure. "It would be *very* all right, Si," he said quietly. "And it would please me more than I can say."

The boy's head began to bob in awkward acknowledgment.

And then, instinctively, Silas knew their time was up; that they would not see each other for possibly weeks or months. His mind made up, he moved across the small distance between them to Chad's side before throwing his arms around the man's neck.

Chad was momentarily stunned but quickly engulfed the boy in his arms and returned the hug.

"Jennifer said this was okay," Silas muttered.

Chad smiled, closing his eyes. "I think it's more than *okay,* son," he said, and then he opened his eyes and stared directly into the shining, smiling face of his beloved wife as she watched them from the open carriage door.

Silas moved away then, refusing to look anyone in the eye as he dived out of the carriage. "Give 'em hell!" he bellowed as he charged toward the house.

Hunter and Maggie and their children moved close to the side of the carriage, and Jennifer sat beside Chad and straightened her skirt.

"Don't worry about anything back here," Hunter told Chad pointedly.

Chad nodded. "There will be a report coming to you before the end of the month," he said, referring to the investigation by the Pinkerton man he had hired. "Share it with me if there is anything of interest," he said.

Jennifer knew of the situation, but Maggie seemed to frown in confusion. It was only in that moment that Jennifer realized her sister was not aware of the subject under discussion between the two men. Silently she decided that Hunter's protective instincts were to be honored. She grinned broadly and said to Maggie, "I'll write to you and report anything of interest."

Maggie laughed and stepped back, pulling her children back away from the wheels of the carriage. "Take care!"

Jennifer twisted at the waist and waved just before Hunter closed the door, encasing her and Chad in a dark, warm cocoon.

As the vehicle moved forward, Chad shook out a lap robe and shared it with Jennifer as her feet found the warming pan beneath her skirts.

"I suppose it will be much colder in Pittsburgh," she muttered as she squirmed against his side and settled under his arm.

Chad smiled down at her. "Considerably, I should think."

Jennifer tipped her head back and grinned up at him.

"I didn't think he would do it!"

Chad's browns arched in question. "Who? Do what?"

"Silas," she said with exasperation. "I really didn't think he would ever hug you."

He smiled at that. "Neither did I. It was quite a surprise."

"You're happy that he's coming around, though," she said knowingly.

He was. And he told her so. "He wants his name to be Moran. The same as ours."

Jennifer's eyes shone with love and admiration. "No. I think Silas wants the same as I wanted, but for different reasons. I think he wants his name to be the same as *yours*."

# CHAPTER NINETEEN

Jennifer was going to become a crusader. Chad had seen that coming within hours of commencing their trip. Every time he encountered a barrier that prevented him from going where he wanted to go, Jennifer would grow red-faced with anger. She knew some of what he was feeling in these situations. He understood that. It was something akin to being in a room from which one desperately wanted to escape and being able only to stare at the back side of a door that could not be opened. But Chad was too busy trying to calm his dear wife to give much thought to his own feelings.

Chad knew that most disabled persons were confined to family homes or institutions and that fact seemed criminal considering the day and age. But they both came to understand why institutions were full to bursting as trains and buildings and streets failed to accommodate his needs. And he frequently thought the general population who came in near contact stared askance, as if Chad had a lot of nerve merely entering *their* world. Jennifer said very little, but he knew what she was thinking.

The trip was grueling and exhausting, and their tempers were sorely tested by the time Gerome saw them safely ensconced in their hotel room.

Jennifer stored the last of their cases beside a chest of drawers as Chad examined the notes he had placed on the table near the single window.

"Would you like a bath?" Jennifer asked as she approached from behind. "I could give you a nice sponge bath, if you like," she added, placing her hands on his shoulders.

"I'm quite capable of bathing myself," he said harshly.

Stung, Jennifer pulled her hands away, as if some wicked witch had twitched her nose and turned his body into a red-hot stove. "I know exactly how capable you are," she snapped tiredly.

Chad turned his head, frowning at her over his shoulder.

"What does *that* mean?" he questioned accusingly.

"Chad, for heaven's sake . . ."

Now he turned his chair and glared at her. "Just what is it you think I'm not capable of, Jen?" he asked tightly.

"Nothing," she said forcefully. "I wasn't insinuating anything. Chad, you're exhausted—"

"And you're not?"

"Would you tell me why we're fighting?" she asked more reasonably. "I'm on your side, remember?"

"Are you?"

Jennifer's hands fisted at her sides, and her complexion darkened. "Perhaps you *should* bathe yourself," she said angrily. "And I hope you damned well fall face first into the basin! Maybe that will bring you back to your senses." She turned on a heel and marched toward the closed door leading to the hall.

"Wait!" he called before she could leave. "Jen, wait! I'm sorry."

She stood there, staring at the closed portal.

"We've stumbled, Jen," he said with soft spoken conviction. "And it's my fault. I'm sorry."

She turned toward him, and he saw clearly how very much he had hurt her. "Aw, Jen," he groaned, holding out a beseeching hand. "I'm a fool. Please, forgive me."

"You've never spoken to me like that before," she said unhappily.

"I know," he said, shaking his head as if even *he* was amazed by what he had done. He felt exhausted and beaten before he had even started the case that would demand much of his time and strength. He could barely admit to himself that one simple trip had taken such a toll on his energy reserves. How could he admit as much to her? And yet, Jennifer was the one person with whom he could admit his weaknesses. "There is no excuse for the things I just said," he admitted.

Jennifer began walking slowly toward him. "No, there isn't," she said softly. "But I think I understand. And I forgive you."

When she stood in front of him, Chad grasped her hand as he looked up at her. "I love you, Jen."

"I know, darling," she said softly.

"Perhaps we could spend a quiet evening here together? If you can find the wherewithal to remain in my company, that is."

"I think I can manage," she returned as she fought the urge to smile over his attempt at being humble.

"Perhaps I'll find a way to apologize for being an absolute . . ."

"Stinker?" she supplied.

He blinked in surprise. "What?"

"That's a *Silas* word," she said cheekily. "It means—"

Chad held up an arresting hand. "I believe I know what it means."

"Are we even?" she teased.

He laughed.

Jennifer bent at the waist, locking her elbows as she planted the palms of her hands on his knees. "I'm going to ask Gerome if he would mind very much eating alone tonight," she whispered, her lips very close to his. "And then I'm going to arrange for our supper to be brought here to our room. Along with a very nice bottle of wine. When I return, you'd best be finished in that bathing room," she warned, her head tipping briefly toward the ensuite room. "Because once I invade it, it's completely, solely, wholly mine."

His eyes took on the sparkle of anticipation. "Really?" he drawled. "For what purpose."

"My darling," she murmured, "you are far too exhausted to care."

He could have disputed her words, knowing he would never be too exhausted to *care*. But for the first time since she had become his wife, Chad Moran thought he just might be too tired to *do* anything about it.

That night, when he pulled her against his side as they settled in the large, foreign-feeling bed, Chad could feel her entire body shivering as if she had caught a chill.

"You're shaking," he stated with concern as he pulled the quilts securely around her shoulder.

Jennifer nodded. "This happens sometimes when I'm extremely tired," she explained.

"You're too busy taking care of me," he said flatly.

"You're not taking care of yourself."

"That's not true, Chad."

He felt her trembling down his entire length and in the mattress beneath them, and he tightened his arms around her. "What can I do, Jen?"

Jennifer turned her lips against his neck. "You're doing it," she whispered.

But the statement her body was making caused him concern. It brought home the fact that, while she appeared strong and healthy, she, too, had her limitations. "Promise me you'll take care, love," he whispered, holding her close. "Promise me."

The following days were hectic and filled with people coming and going from their room as Chad interviewed one strike witness after another. Additionally, Chad was almost constantly accompanied by Joe Devine, the young lawyer he had hired to assist him.

Jennifer simply tried to stay out of the way.

Her usual spot was across the room from where the men sat at the table covered by papers and very legal-looking documents. She would pretend to be reading, but not a page in her book would turn hour after hour as her attention became caught up in the conversations that were taking place.

Chad was brilliant, as far as she was concerned, and the workings of his mind left her in awe.

Joe appeared almost as overwhelmed by Chad's exceptional bend of mind. Jennifer realized that from the first day the two men sat down together to work. Well, young Mr. Devine would benefit greatly from her husband's experience, and his association with Chad on this case would not do his reputation any harm, either.

There was a tangible tension in the room the evening before the trial was to begin. Jennifer could feel it, and subsequently, once they were alone, she respected Chad's need for silence.

She wanted to do more for him; she wanted to ease his way and share his burdens. But she could not.

The devils that tormented him would be met face to face on the morrow. In a courtroom. He would overcome them, she knew. She also knew Chad was not feeling that way, however.

When it came time for bed, Jennifer simply curled up beside her husband, and they held each other through a long, sleepless night.

They went early to the courthouse the following morning. Chad wanted to be settled and reviewing his notes before the throngs of curious overtook the place.

Jennifer found a place behind him, behind the wooden barrier that would keep her separated from him. The wooden barrier that separated the onlookers from the participants in this trial.

The jury selection took two days.

And the tension in Chad grew.

On the day of his opening statement, however, he shone with a confidence bordering on arrogance. This was where he belonged. This was his niche and he was *good*. And Jennifer's pride in him welled up inside her like lava building inside a volcano that was about to erupt.

He approached the male jury and stared at each man in turn before he even said a word.

He boldly moved his chair back and forth in front of the jury box, staring them down, and Jennifer looked around, finding every pair of eyes in the room following her husband. She could barely tear her attention away from Chad even to satisfy her curiosity.

And then Chad was moving back, positioning himself where all could see and, when he spoke, he spoke with an authority that demanded attention.

"Gentlemen of the jury!" he said in a strong, deep voice. "Before this trial is over you will have walked in the shoes of the accused. You will have relived the passions of these men," he added, pointing to those men he represented. "You will understand their need for self-defense. You will *know* the heights these men strived for in defending not only their very lives, but their need to protect their livelihood and, more so, provide for the protection of their families!"

Jennifer's skin popped gooseflesh, almost in defiance of the warm woollen dress she wore. He was masterful with this jury. He was emotionally moving every soul that had crowded into the room that day. She found a restriction in her throat that prevented her from swallowing as she watched. And, upon hearing his final statement, she was forced to look down so that no one could see her face. She studied the dark gloves on her hands before removing the left glove. The glove that covered the ring that Chad had placed on her finger. Suddenly the gold became misty as tears of pride filled her eyes.

"Gentlemen!" Chad demanded. "At the conclusion of this trial you will *not* find these accused guilty!"

And they did not.

All those accused of murder during the Homestead strike were acquitted.

Chad could have celebrated anywhere in the city that night, based on the raucous and numerous invitations he received.

But there was only one place he wanted to be.

Jennifer followed him into their hotel room and stood silently near the door, watching as Chad made his way across the room. He just stayed there for a moment, also silent, as he stared out the window. She doubted he was seeing much of anything out there; he'd been quiet and pensive since they had left the partylike atmosphere of the courthouse. Once the verdict had been read, the place had exploded with happy shouts and cries. And the tears of the women whose men had been on trial flowed freely. Jennifer had watch her husband receive his just dues, his moments of tribute. The men and their families had paid homage to Chad, and she had stood by, smiling and radiant in her pride.

Only she had had an inkling of what it had taken for Chad to participate in the trials, and only she had an inkling of what this verdict meant to him. He had seen justice done, but he had won so very much more for himself.

Chad pushed back on one wheel of his chair and turned to face his wife. She was standing across the room, smiling softly and awaiting some word from him. She hadn't even removed her heavy coat.

He loved her so damned much.

Chad held out a hand, beckoning her, and she came.

He lightly squeezed the hand she gave to him before he began to unfasten the buttons of her coat; one at a time, and slowly, as he stared up at her. Once she had shrugged out of the thing, he pulled her down onto his lap and wrapped his arms around her, burying his face against her breasts. Chad proceeded to do what he needed most in that moment.

He just held on.

Jennifer wrapped her arms around his neck and pressed her cheek against his, unwilling to break this silent communication that told more about how he was feeling than any words ever could.

"I love you," he whispered.

"I know, darling," she said softly. "I love you, too."

"Going into this trial was the most difficult thing I've ever done in my entire life," he confessed.

"I know."

"I've been a bear to live with," he stated flatly.

"No," she whispered emphatically.

"Thank you for being there."

Jennifer straightened, pulling away from him until she could see his face. She smiled as silent tears rolled slowly down her cheeks. "Where else would I be?" she whispered. "I'm so proud of you, Chad, I don't know where to put myself."

He framed her beautiful face with his hands and smoothed away her tears with the pads of this thumbs before locking one hand at the back of her neck and pulling her slowly down to meet his lips.

The kiss they shared was sweet and lacking in urgency. He slanted his lips across hers and honored her as the woman he loved. It was a tender kiss that reflected the depth of his feelings for her; that told her they would go on forever.

A light tap on the door interrupted the moment, and Jennifer smiled regretfully before removing herself from him and crossing the room.

Gerome. Dear, thoughtful Gerome. He had arranged a private dinner for them, complete with champagne and candlelight. Jennifer stood back from the door as the feast was wheeled into the room on a two-tiered trolley that was covered by a crisp linen cloth. She grinned at Chad as he impatiently watched the waiter set the table near the window. Once the man had received a tip and the door was closed and locked, Jennifer returned to his side. She allowed her hand to rest on her husband's shoulder as she surveyed the meal.

"Gerome has outdone himself," she said softly.

"Mmm."

She laughed softly, looking down at him. "Which feast shall we partake of first?" she asked lightly. "The food or each other?" Chad had been exhausted, and they hadn't made love for two nights; they were both in dire need of each other.

Chad smoothed her hip with the palm of his hand. "You're in need of food, I think."

"I'm in need of you, too," she admitted.

He grinned and nodded his head, feeling the same. But he also knew she needed nourishment. He had been mentally caught up in the trial, but now, as he watched her pull a chair close to his, it dawned on him that they had been away from home for *weeks*. "I've been sadly lacking as a husband," he said quietly.

Jennifer, in the act of spreading a napkin across her lap, looked at him askance. "You?" she asked with disbelief. "Hardly, darling."

His brown-eyed gaze collided with hers. "You *are* pregnant, aren't you, Jen?"

Jennifer had kept confirmation of her condition close to her heart, until the time that he could be free enough to think about it, to talk about it. He had known all along, of course. They were far too intimate a couple for Chad to have missed it. But, of necessity, his mind had been devoted to other things, and she had waited patiently.

She grinned foolishly.

"Aw, Jen," he breathed, leaning toward her and kissing her lightly. "I must have known, but—"

Jennifer pressed her fingertips against his lips, silencing him. "Of course you knew. You've simply had a thing or two on your mind," she said easily. "All I want to know is, are you as delighted as I?"

He took her hand and raised it to his lips, his eyes shining with euphoric brilliance. "I'm more than delighted," he murmured. This, too, had been something he had doubted he would ever achieve. "Less than a year ago a door closed on my life," he said quietly. "Now there are windows opening all over the place. I have you and now a child on the way."

"And you've proved to yourself that you're still a brilliant lawyer," she said happily.

"I'm a very fortunate man."

"You made it all happen, Chad," she said with serious intensity.

He thought about that and grinned mischievously. "I did, didn't I?"

Jennifer laughed as she watched him reach for the bottle of champagne. "Now he's going to crow!"

"Damned right!" he returned, sending the cork bouncing off the far wall.

It was a night of celebration, of champagne and love-making. In the small hours of the morning, when she was glowing warm and sated, Jennifer turned in her husband's arms. "When will we move to Richmond, Chad?" she whispered.

It was spring and she wanted to be home, but *home* would be where he could carry out his life's work.

# CHAPTER TWENTY

Before starting for home, Chad suggested they detour and visit with Florence, a suggestion eagerly accepted by Jennifer.

They found her sister caught up in her work but also radiantly in love. Gone was the shy, retiring girl Jennifer had grown up with. Florence had become a beautiful, confident woman.

"We want to come home to Treemont for our wedding," Florence told her sister.

"You'd better," Jennifer said succinctly.

Chad and Jennifer had instantly taken to Mark, the love of Florence's life. He, too, was a writer. A reporter with the *Herald*. And he very obviously, without doubt, worshipped Florence. Jennifer was content in knowing that her sister was loved and would be happy.

Their homecoming was filled with noise and laughter. Jennifer did not know who to hug first, but she quickly made her choice and made a beeline for Silas.

"We missed you," she said, having given him a forceful greeting.

Silas had missed them, too, but he *wasn't* about to make a fool of himself by admitting as much. "I've been keeping kinda busy," he said.

Jennifer smiled down at him, understanding. "Have you learned a lot about the horses?"

Here was something he could not hide: his new love. "I've followed Hunter almost every minute," he said, displaying the first signs of excitement Jennifer had ever seen in him. "And Bramble is all broke in."

She smiled, her hand squeezing his shoulder. "Are you pleased with her, Si?"

The boy nodded his head, his hand squeezing his shoulder. "She's a good one. Hunter said so."

"Then it must be so," she said softly before bending and whispering close to his ear. "I have gifts for you when we get home."

Silas watched in stunned silence as she turned away to greet all those milling about on Treemont's front lawn. Chad and Jennifer had been generous in the past, providing all that he needed. But he hadn't expected *gifts* brought from some faraway city. These two, these guardians of his, were frequently a source of surprise. They treated him as if he belonged, as if he were actually a member of the family. As if they were proud of him and cared about him, and having them return after months of absence forced his thoughts and emotions back into a pell-mell confusion. He didn't know how to react or what to say, and sometimes, when he wanted to return Jennifer's signs of affection, he felt unhappy because he could not.

Chad watched as Silas remained off to the side of the commotion. He studied the boy's look of concentration and wondered what Si must be thinking as Jennifer made the rounds of her family to give and receive greetings and signs of affection. He understood that this open display of love might be just a bit overwhelming to a street urchin; a child who lived by his wits and had learned to suppress life's softer emotions. And then he saw signs of distress steal across the boy's face as Maggie pointedly asked Jennifer if she was with child. Silas's troubled stare only darkened when Jennifer confirmed her sister's suspicion.

Chad knew instantly that he and Jennifer had some work ahead of them, and it must be done quickly. Silas must be reassured that the baby would make no difference to his status in their lives.

Jennifer dug through their cases, snatching up the things she had purchased for Silas before running back downstairs to Chad's study. When she entered the room, she immediately saw that her husband and the boy were deep in conversation, and she stopped in her tracks near the open door.

Chad raised his head and motioned for her to join them. "Come in, Jen," he said. "This concerns you, too."

Silas was sitting, head bowed, on the settee, and Chad had moved his chair close in front of the boy.

The contents of her hands forgotten, Jennifer walked slowly, and with curious concern, toward them. "What's wrong?" she asked, staring at Chad and then Silas as she sat beside him.

Chad leaned forward, propping his elbows on his knees. "We were just about to come to that part," he said as he stared at the frowning boy who refused to raise his head. "Weren't we, Si?"

Silas did raise his head then, and the depth of his anger was unleashed upon Chad. "I think it's disgustin' that you knocked her up!" he spat.

Jennifer's complexion deepened heatedly as she rocked backward on the settee. She was shocked, not so much by Si's chosen language, but by the ferocious verbal attack on her husband.

Chad, however, seemed undaunted, as if he had been expecting this. "Why do you think it's disgusting?" he asked quietly.

"Just like animals," Silas railed insolently.

"Si," Jennifer breathed, but Chad was shaking his head, asking her to wait and listen and be silent for just a moment.

"Like people in love, Si," Chad said patiently. "People in love want children."

"You got me!" he hollered.

There it was. It was out.

Now Jennifer understood. She reached for his hand and gripped it hard against her knee. "Yes, we do," she said softly. "And we still want you."

Silas cast her a quick, doubtful look.

"Silas," Chad said, gaining the boy's attention. "When you first came here, you and I had our problems. Do you remember that?"

His head turning to stare out the window, Silas managed a brief nod of acknowledgment.

"Judge Lang is a very wise man," Chad continued conversationally. "He knew we would have to face each other and sort out our own personal demons. I suspect he hoped we would go beyond our dislike and distrust and come to terms with what you meant to me and what I meant to you back then." Chad smiled ruefully then, winking at Jennifer before returning his attention to the stone-faced boy. "I doubt, however, that he ever thought that we would come to love each other."

Si's head snapped around. "I never said I love you!" he said defensively.

"You've never said you love Jennifer, either, but I know you do," Chad returned. "It's all right to say the words, Si."

Jennifer could see the internal struggle that was plaguing Silas, and her heart twisted in her chest. "I love you, Silas," she said softly. "We both love you."

"Jen is right," Chad said. "We do love you."

Silas tore his hand away from Jennifer's and looked away again, frowning uncertainly.

With a weary sigh Chad tried again to reach the boy. "We don't want to hide our affection for you, Silas, but you make it difficult."

"Sissies hug and kiss," he mumbled.

"Do they?" Chad asked. "You've seen Jennifer and me together often enough to know that we're not afraid to show our love for each other. Do you think I'm a sissy?"

The man wasn't afraid to stick his neck out, Silas had to give him credit for that. "No."

"It takes an *animal* to *use* a woman, Silas," he said. "And I suspect that your experience has been in overhearing the braying of a good number of jackasses. But it takes a *man* to *love* a woman." Chad waited patiently, silently, for his words to be digested by the still-frowning boy. And when Silas finally turned his head, staring hesitantly in his direction, Chad smiled. "It isn't 'disgusting' that Jennifer is expecting a child, Si, is it? It's just a little frightening for you. But things won't change. I promise."

"But if you have your own kids—"

"We'll still want you, too," Jennifer said quietly.

"We asked you long ago how you felt about adoption," Chad said, "even though we hoped that we would one day have children of our own. Do you think we would have asked you that if we didn't want you to remain here with us? As part of our family?"

"I guess not," he said cautiously.

Jennifer smiled radiantly and leaned toward Si, daring to kiss his cheek. "How do you feel about having brothers and sisters?" she said teasingly.

Silas wrinkled his nose, feigning revolt. "I'll have to get used to the idea," he said.

She laughed and reached for the gifts she had set beside her. "Do you want to see what we brought you?"

He did and he was overwhelmed. Jennifer had shopped during many of the days Chad was working. There were shirts and pants and books. But the thing Si loved most was an ebony carving.

Chad sat back, smiling contentedly as a ring of smoke from his pipe rose above their heads. Jennifer was as excited as the boy as they dug into the box that contained the carefully wrapped carving.

"Do you like it?" Jennifer asked excitedly as Silas turned the small horse over and over in his hands.

All the boy could do was nod his head and admire the piece.

"Chad picked this one," she said.

Silas raised his head and stared at the man who sat a few feet away. "Thank you," he said politely.

Chad laughed, delighted by what he was sharing with these two people he loved. "You're very welcome."

That evening Chad and Jennifer saw a change in Silas. They both understood it wasn't the fact that they had lavished material gifts upon him; Silas had received another gift today, and he was adjusting to the fact that he was wanted and loved.

At dinner he chattered incessantly, bringing them up to date on all the happenings in the area and at school during their absence.

But there had been one event he had not talked about and would not discuss in front of Jennifer. He rose from the table, said a polite good night, and hesitantly hugged Jennifer before going to his room.

He would talk with Chad, alone, when the time was right.

Chad smiled, reaching for his pipe as he watched his young wife follow Silas from the room with her eyes. When she turned to face him, Chad saw exactly what he had expected to see. "You're looking all misty, darling," he teased softly.

"I think he's actually becoming our son," she said.

"He'll make it, Jen. He might need a bit more time, but Silas will be fine with us."

Jennifer placed her elbow on the table and propped her chin on the back of her hand. "I think you're wonderfully perceptive, Mr. Moran," she said. "How did you know Si was upset about the baby?"

"I saw his chin fall to his knees when Maggie guessed at your condition," he said, reaching for her free hand. "Perhaps I had been anticipating his reaction. I don't know."

"Well, I think he's feeling better," she said softly. "Do you think you could do the same for me?"

He laughed at her suggestive tone and the wanton look in her eye. "What is it I could do for you, my love?"

"We haven't made love in our own bed for ever so long," she said sweetly. "I just know you could make me feel so much better."

"Really?" he asked, laughing again.

"Mmm-hmm."

"Do you choose to walk or ride, madam?" he questioned as he set his pipe aside and rolled back from the table.

"I'll ride, please," she said, rising from her chair and walking the two steps that would take her into his arms. "It keeps me that much closer to you," she whispered as her arms went around his neck.

# CHAPTER
## TWENTY-ONE

Stonehall had easily become home to Jennifer, although she was trying desperately not to become any more attached to the place than she was already. Even though Stonehall piqued her homing instincts, Jennifer knew that Chad and Silas and the baby were her home, and she would be content anywhere as long as she was with them. She suspected it would not be long before they packed up their belongings and moved to Richmond, where Chad would once again build his legal practice. He had not discussed the matter with her as yet, but they had only been home for two days, and she suspected he was mulling his plans over in his mind. Jennifer thought she would remain silent on the subject of Richmond until Chad was ready to talk. She did suspect, however, that they would not be moving before the birthing of their baby.

It was Sunday and exceptionally warm for springtime as Jennifer took a basket and walked away from the house toward the chicken coop. Life could not be more wonderful, and her thoughts were pleasant, her expectations high.

Silas had already run off to be with his beloved Bramble. It was somehow ironic that a boy who had once seen horses only as a target for stones had turned about so completely and could now barely talk of anything else. Chad had been more than a little wise in giving the filly to the boy.

Jennifer approached the fork in the dirt trail that would lead her either to the barn or the smaller outbuildings and stopped as her child gave a mighty kick or two. She smiled, caressing her belly. "We'll see that you get a filly of your own, too," she said softly.

Silas emerged from the barn, saw her standing there wearing a funny grin, and raced to her side. "Are you okay, Jen?" he asked with obvious concern.

Jennifer nodded, continuing to smile. "He's kicking me," she said.

Si's eyes lowered, and he gazed in wonder at her barely swollen middle for a brief moment. "Really? Does it hurt?"

"No. Not at all."

"You want me to get Chad?" he asked hurriedly.

Jennifer laughed lightly. "No. Chad has felt this before, Si. There's nothing wrong, I promise," she added reassuringly. She reached for his small hand then and placed it on the side of her abdomen. "Feel?" she asked.

He remained silent and still, staring at their hands until he felt a distinct movement beneath his palm. "Wow," he breathed in wonder. "Wow, Jen."

Jennifer felt closer to Silas in that moment than she ever had and took a chance by casually draping her arm across his shoulders. "I remember when Maggie was expecting Courtney. I think I drove her crazy always asking to feel the baby move."

Silas nodded his head. He could understand that; this was special.

"So, what do you think?" she asked. "This is your brother or sister here."

He turned with her, automatically walking on as he became aware of the warmth of her arm on his shoulder. "It's not like I'll really have a brother or sister," he said. "Just as good as, Si. I might need your help with the little ones now and then. That's what big brothers do."

He stopped and stared up at her. "Little *ones*? You mean more than one? You mean you're planning to do this again?"

Jennifer laughed at his hurried speech. "Of course! We want lots of babies."

Silas thought they would get them, too. They were always touching and kissing! "Well, Jen," he drawled benevolently, "I guess if you're willin' to do the hard part, the least I can do is help."

"Thank you," she said wryly.

They approached the chicken coop, and Silas unhitched the wire door. "Are you afraid?" he asked quietly.

Jennifer stepped beyond the door and turned to face him. "Of what?"

"Having the baby?"

Jennifer noted the slight pinkish tinge to his complexion then. He also refused to look at her, and that made her realize he was uncomfortable with his own curiosity. "I'm not afraid, Si. I might be anxious when the time comes, but only because I want a perfect, healthy child. Maggie had three babies with little trouble," she said, smiling as she added lightly, "and whatever Maggie can do I can do better!"

He smiled but continued to look doubtful, and Jennifer felt her heart expand. Bending, she kissed his cheek and whispered, "I love you for worrying, but don't *worry*, dear."

Silas blushed heatedly over the endearment. "Aw!" He turned toward the first row of laying hens, presenting his back to her.

Jennifer stood back, grinning happily, and allowed him to gather what eggs there were.

A few moments later Silas looked askance as Charles Tandy took his time passing the chicken coop, staring at Jennifer all the while.

Silas hid his frown from her as he remembered that he really must talk with Chad.

Chad was at his desk reviewing long-ignored accounts when Silas stepped into the open doorway.

"I need to talk to you," Silas said.

Chad raised his head, frowning in curiosity over the boy's serious tone. "Of course, son," he said, closing a large, leather-bound tome. "Come in."

Silas closed the door behind himself, ensuring their privacy. He walked slowly across the room and settled his forearms on the large mahogany desk before saying another word. "I guess with Jennifer expectin' and all, she's kind of airy."

"Airy?" Chad asked, bewildered for the moment. "Do you mean delicate, Si?"

"Yep. Like that."

Chad smiled crookedly. "Well, we don't want her working too hard, and we'll have to watch and see that she takes care of herself. But Jennifer is strong and healthy. Is that what you wanted to discuss? Are you worried about her, son?"

There was that word again: *son*. Silas was beginning to like having Chad call him that, but it still continued to throw him off balance. In time, however, he thought he might become accustomed to being this man's *son*.

"Well, that," he admitted, "and I had something to tell you I didn't think maybe Jennifer should hear 'cause it might get her all nervous or somethin'."

Chad sensed the seriousness of the discussion that was coming and moved from behind his desk. "Sit down, Si," he said quietly as he positioned his own chair so that he could face the boy. "What's troubling you?"

"Courtney and me went fishin' out at your pond here the first hot day, and while we were sittin' there old Tandy came along."

Chad felt an instant tighting in his chest. "When was this?"

"A few days ago. The old bugger was lookin' funny at Courtney just like he does at Jennifer sometimes."

"What did you do?" he asked with obvious concern.

"I stared him down," Silas said. "I just kept lookin' until he stopped starin' at her and looked at me. He looked real mad before he left."

"You've stayed away from him, I hope?"

Silas suddenly looked very uncomfortable. In the old days he would have lied without so much as a twitch. But Chad had confided in him, had trusted him, and had said he loved him. How could he lie to this man now? Besides, he had admitted to himself while alone in his bed that he did love Chad and Jennifer. "Well, I figure when Tandy gets to lookin', it means he's *needin'* a girl, you know? I took Courtney home and then I came back here."

Chad was angered that the boy had possibly placed himself in danger. "Silas, I told you—"

"I didn't go near him," he hurried to explain. "He didn't see me, and he didn't do nothin' that day anyway, so I went back to Treemont. I warned Courtney, too. Well, sort of," he added. He tipped his head when he raised his eyes to look at Chad. "She's kind of young, you know, Chad?"

Chad smiled his agreement, although he thought Si's comment incongruous to say the least; there was something about a child referring to another child as *young* that struck his sense of the absurd. But the matter under discussion was raising Chad's anger and his fear, and these emotions took precedence over all else.

"I don't know whether she really understood, but I told her that men can be bad sometimes, and I made her promise to stay away from Tandy," Silas added.

Chad took a moment to think about this conversation and this boy who was soon to become legally his son.

"Are you sure you're only twelve years old?" he asked.

Silas thought that was a stupid question, so he ignored it. "The day before you came home I saw Tandy ridin' across the fields with a girl. She was all flirty and smiling like he was something special, and I just knew where they were goin'. He likes to take them to that old church back of here, so I ran along the edge of the trees so he wouldn't see me," Silas studied Chad's expression to see if he was digging himself into trouble, decided he was not, and continued. "By the time I got there, he was on her, you know? And she wasn't smilin' anymore. He was hurtin' her and she was cryin'."

Chad closed his eyes and bowed his head as bile rose high in his throat. Another young woman foolishly trapped in her own game. And soiled because Charles Tandy obviously had no sense of honor, no conscience. The bitter truth was, however, that the girl would be seen as cooperative and willing by most who heard the tale.

It also angered Chad that a twelve-year-old boy should be witness to such a thing. It was safe to say that Silas had witnessed and experienced much more in his young life than other boys his age, but that did not negate the fact that he should not be witness to violent behavior against women. Chad could no longer tolerate these goings on at Stonehall. His voice was deep and deliberate when he asked, "Do you know the young woman?"

Si shook his head. "But I'd know her if I saw her again."

"I won't have this going on," Chad said. And he would no longer wait for the Pinkerton man to build a case. "Something has to be done about Tandy and quickly."

"I'll say," Silas agreed angrily. "He's still gawkin' at Jennifer."

Jennifer knew that something was being kept from her. There was a tension in the air around Stonehall that she could almost feel. Chad and Silas had driven off the previous day without a word of what they were about, and her curiosity had instantly piqued.

Chad, however, was remaining frustratingly close-mouthed, and even young Silas had obviously been coached to silence.

She had tried cajoling her husband into revealing the secret, waiting until he was at his most vulnerable: while he was making love to her.

"I think I'm more sensitive than ever," she breathed as Chad's tongue circled her rigid nipple.

He cupped her breast in the palm of his hand then and placed his lips close to her ear. "They're bigger," he whispered.

Jennifer grinned as he raised his head and look down at her. "Does that make them better?" she asked boldly.

Chad laughed lightly, looking down at the pale, heavy globes. "Anything more than a handful is a waste," he teased.

Jennifer cuffed his naked shoulder.

He laughed again, pulling her against his chest and rolling onto his back. "God, I love you, woman," he whispered.

Jennifer settled comfortably on his chest and smiled at him. "Chad, what's going on?"

Every grain of merriment and passion disintegrated in an instant. "Nothing," he said.

"Darling—"

"Let it be, Jen," he said quietly but firmly.

"I think it's Charles Tandy again," she speculated.

Chad's eyes narrowed and he frowned. He supposed he'd been foolish to think he could keep anything from her; they were too close and she read him too well. "Yes," he said softly. "It's Tandy."

"Why did you take Silas with you yesterday, Chad? What does he have to do with Charles?"

He sighed wearily, raising his arms and cupping the back of his head with both hands. "Si witnessed another of Tandy's seductions," he said bluntly.

"Oh, Chad, that boy . . ."

He understood her concern bordered on alarm and brought one hand forward to gently stroke her hair. "I know, darling. I've talked with him. You know, we can only speculate on all that Silas witnessed before coming here," he said thoughtfully. "He learned about life on the seamy side, for certain. A year ago Silas would have accepted Tandy's behavior as normal and acceptable. Now he knows it's not acceptable for a man to force a woman or to hurt her. I think he's learned that there's a difference between being physical and being loving."

"He's learned that from you," she whispered before gently kissing his chin.

Chad's fingers lightly combed through her hair. "I've just cause to fire Charles as far as I'm concerned, but Hunter and Peter Williams, the sheriff, have convinced me to hold off for a day or two. They're looking for this last poor girl to see if she'll tell them her story."

"Like Diana," Jennifer said unhappily.

"Like Diana. If these women won't talk, Jen . . ."

"And you still won't prove that it was Charles who . . . I mean, Maggie still . . ."

He shook his head. "She can't remember, sweetheart," he said gently. "I don't believe she ever will."

Jennifer flattened her hands on his chest and lowered her chin, resting there, silent and thoughtful. "The only way is to force him to confess."

Chad grunted angrily. "That would never happen, Jen. We have no evidence, and Tandy's smart enough to know that. And with the other women, it's their word against his. Who would be believed?"

"Not the women," she returned with disgust. After several moments of silence, Jennifer raised her head to look at him. "Maggie deserves to see her attacker brought to justice," she said angrily.

"Certainly, love. No one is disputing that fact."

"Supposing I could trick Charles into confessing? If there was a witness, would his confession see him convicted?"

His smile was slightly patronizing even though he understood her motive. "How would you propose you might accomplish that?"

"By flirting with him."

Chad's eyes grew enormous, and deep wrinkles instantly lined his brow. "Absolutely not," he said rigidly.

"Why not?"

"You're pregnant."

"What does that have to do with this discussion?"

"And you're my wife," he said harshly.

"I'll keep that in mind," she teased.

"This is not a laughing matter, Jen," he said. "You just get this thought right out of your head."

"You're simply going to fire him and call that a just punishment?" she countered.

"You don't know the first thing about flirting with a man," he returned.

Jennifer grinned. "How do you think I got you?"

"Through persistence," he said in a lighter tone.

Jennifer was mightily offended over that comment. "Chadwick James Moran!"

He laughed. "Yes, dear?"

"How do you think I got our baby?" she said primly.

Chad lost his sense of humor. "That, Jennifer, is not a good argument in this case." Even teasing about such a thing caused fear in him. He had not forgotten that Silas had caught Tandy openly eyeing Jennifer, and if she could do to Charles what she did to *him* . . .

"Why isn't it a good argument?" she asked sweetly.

"Stop playing, Jen," he said severely. "You're not going anywhere near Charles Tandy. Do you understand?"

Jennifer sat up, staring at him angrily. "That's very high-handed of you," she said. "I don't take well to orders."

He knew he had gone too far and reached for her hand. "You don't realize how easily you can stir a man's passions, Jen. Think about what you do to me."

"That's different," she said shortly. "You love me."

Chad shook his head. "Yes, that is the difference. The *difference* is that I'm gentle with you because I love you. Tandy would not be gentle, sweetheart, if you tease him into satisfying his lust. You're my wife. I love you. You're carrying our child. Please forget this notion, Jennifer. I couldn't bear to have you hurt." And he couldn't watch her every single minute of every day. He could try, but he also knew the strength of her will. "Please."

"What about Maggie?" she asked petulantly. "You said she has the right to see justice done."

"Not this way, Jen. Not with the risk of placing yourself in jeopardy."

"I think he's the one," she said unhappily as Chad pulled her safely within his embrace. "It isn't right to let him go. It isn't fair."

He sighed. "No one ever said life was fair, sweetheart."

Jennifer tossed her idea around for the better part of that night and most of the following day. Obviously she could not discuss her plan further with Chad. Maggie hardly seemed the appropriate person in whom Jen could confide. Hunter would, no doubt, lock her up rather than give her an opportunity to attempt the scheme. And Gerome would run to tell all to Chad in a moment. That left only one person to act as witness.

Jennifer was standing out at the main road when Silas returned from school that afternoon.

"No!" Silas said firmly after hearing her out. "No, Jen. Lord love a duck. Chad would skin us both."

"Mind your language," she said absently; she had thought Silas, at least, would be willing, just for the adventure.

He stared at her in disbelief. "You're telling me to 'mind my language' and *you're* thinking about getting a man—a dangerous man—all hot and—"

"Never mind," she said quickly.

"Jennifer, I'm way younger than you—"

"Not so much younger," she interrupted as she flinched at the accusation.

"*But*," he added pointedly, "Chad says I've seen a lot. Way more than you, for a fact. You don't play with men like Tandy."

"No one else can come up with a better idea," she said shortly. "I certainly can't. And if he gets too . . . frisky, you'll just jump out of your hiding place. Charles will back off if there's a witness."

That seemed logical enough; perhaps it was the only logical thought in the entire crazy scheme. What worried Silas was, if he did not participate, Jennifer might try this on her own, without a witness, and get herself hurt. And Chad had already tried to talk her out of this, and she had not listened to *him*. She would never listen to a mere boy, even though, at this moment, Silas considered himself a good deal smarter than Jen.

"It won't take long," she added. "I'll know right away whether he's going to take the bait."

With a weary sigh Silas said, "Jen, you don't know nothin' about baitees and baitors."

She laughed. "Where did you learn that?"

"I don't know," he said, heart-sickened over this whole idea. This was a dilemma, to be sure. Even for a streetwise twelve-year-old.

Well, somebody had to watch out for her, and Chad could hardly hide in the barn loft.

"When do you want to try this crazy thing?" he asked miserably.

Jennifer smiled. "Tomorrow morning. You'll go off to school as usual and then sneak back."

He nodded. "And I'll be hiding in the loft with a mallet," he said.

And so would someone else, if Silas possessed any powers of persuasion at all. He knew he would need someone much larger than himself nearby if Charles Tandy really got his boiler stoked.

That night, after all in the house had gone to their beds, Silas tiptoed down the hall for a visit with Gerome.

Jennifer found Charles Tandy the following morning, leaning against the paddock fence, overseeing the breeding of a new mare.

*Perfect timing*, she thought ruefully.

She stopped several paces behind the man, halted by indecision. It was one thing to have knowledge of the event that was taking place before the eyes of several men, but she had never openly witnessed the breeding act. At Treemont, she had always kept herself from view of the horsemen during these times. Horses were powerful animals and watching them mate was not always a dispassionate phenomenon.

It took several moments for her to decide that she could carry on, regardless. In fact, as she walked closer to Tandy's back, she thought the scene he was witnessing just might turn the tide to her advantage if Charles was truly the lustful fellow everyone believed him to be.

It was a foolish thought, of course, because she could not hide the telltale blush that stained her cheeks when the man of her thoughts turned to face her.

But it was that blush of innocence that did more to aid her cause than any other single thing Jennifer could have done.

It was difficult for a man to think of a pregnant woman as innocent, but Charles felt that way as he carefully examined the pinkish tinge of Jennifer's complexion. Normally, he would have no interest in a female with a swollen belly. Truth be told, he didn't know how their husbands could have any interest, either. But Jennifer was different in his eyes this morning. And he not only liked what he saw, the horses had made him ready for any sweet thing in a skirt that crossed his path. "Mrs. Moran," he said in a strained tone.

Jennifer's heart pounded painfully in her chest as she attempted a seductive smile. "Mr. Tandy." She moved around him, taking the few steps that would bring her up against the paddock fence. "They're a fine breedin' pair," she drawled. She flinched when the mare squealed as the stallion bit into her neck.

Charles was now watching her and not the horses. "Don't fret," he said smoothly. "She likes it."

Jennifer looked at him askance for the space of a breath. "Does she?"

"Why, certainly."

"It seems to me he's hurting her," she returned softly.

"That only makes it better," he said, boldly testing her mettle.

"I find that difficult to believe, Mr. Tandy," she said.

Charles could hardly believe his luck. He was a little suspicious about her standing here talking with him like this after months of trying to capture her attention. But he was too intent upon getting what he wanted to allow the thought to burden him overmuch. "I think you must have a curiosity about it, Mrs. Moran," he said softly. "Otherwise, you wouldn't be standing here watchin'."

"We're watching *animals*, Mr. Tandy," she said pointedly.

"Yes, we are."

Jennifer's head moved fractionally, and she turned her eyes upon him. "I have the feeling we're not *talking* about animals, however."

"We're not, if that is your wish."

Jennifer almost choked over the comment; she doubted Charles Tandy cared about anyone's *wishes*. Turning, Jennifer braced her shoulder against the uppermost fence board and crossed her arms under her breasts in what she hoped was a seductive pose. "I'm a married woman, Mr. Tandy," she said. "I should not be discussing this with you at all."

"And I'm a married man. That doesn't mean I'm dead."

"Are you suggesting you cheat on your wife."

"My wife is fragile, Mrs. Moran. I'm a healthy man." Jennifer frowned appropriately. "I don't take your meaning."

Charles leaned toward her and questioned softly, "What about *your* man, Mrs. Moran?"

Jennifer could have happily shot him for the suggestion; instead she continued toward her goal. "As you see, sir," she said sweetly, caressing her slightly swollen belly.

Tandy wished she hadn't done that, drawing attention to her condition could be offputting. "A surprise, to be sure," he drawled.

Again, she felt anger welling up inside of her. "Chac is a very proper lover," she said shortly.

Tandy smiled. "Proper?" he laughed. "I think you deserve more than 'proper,' Jennifer." He watched as concentrated curiosity stole across her face, and then he dared to touch her wrist, just below her breast. "I think you *want* more than 'proper.'"

Jennifer allowed silence to work in her favor as she forced a slow smile. "He's very gentle," she whispered.

"I suspect a cripple could be little else," he said smugly.

For the first time in her life Jennifer knew the paralyzing affect of needing to do violence and being unable to respond to that need. But she would never have a second opportunity to discover the truth about this abominable man.

"I don't think you came down here to watch the horses or to entertain yourself with any of the boys in that paddock," Charles boasted arrogantly.

Jennifer could feel him moving in, in a manner of speaking. She raised her eyes toward the sky. "It's very warm under this morning sun. Would you agree, Mr. Tandy?"

He grinned lasciviously. "Oh, yes, ma'am."

"I think it might be cooler in the darkness of the barn," she murmured and turned, walking in that direction.

With a victorious smile Charles followed in her wake. Her slim-fitting, narrow skirt caused his imagination to run rampant. He liked his women to be facing him when he took them. Their expressions of pained ecstasy always heightened his own pleasure. But with Jennifer, it might be different. Hell, she was willing enough. He'd have her both ways.

Jennifer walked through the stable until she reached the spot near an empty stall where Silas told her to conduct her indiscretion. Indiscretion? *Folly* was a word that was now coming to mind as Charles moved very close in front of her.

He braced a forearm on the rough boards above Jennifer's head and smiled down at her as he boldly cupped her breast. "It took you long enough to seek out a real man," he murmured.

For *that*, Jennifer swore silently, he would pay. "I'm not certain I've chosen wisely," she said softly.

A flash of anger stole across his face, but Charles recovered quickly. "I've never had complaints," he said arrogantly. "Quite the contrary."

"Really?" she chirped, flinching as his hand tightened on her breast.

Again, he flashed that lecherous grin. "Let's just say I've practiced to become perfect."

He lowered his head then, and she knew she was going to be kissed. Steeling herself in order not to shudder with revulsion, Jennifer sought a means of diverting him. She reached up and caressed his chest with both hands. "I hope you'll have a care for my condition," she said.

He grunted. "Oh, I'll have a care," he said snidely before he attempted, ineffectually, to capture her lips once again.

His voice was becoming rasping, his breathing harsh, and Jennifer knew she was dangerously close to pushing him beyond any control she might have. Still, it would take a greater need before he would become foolish, and bracing herself in order to control the heaving of her stomach, she touched him through the material of his trousers.

Tandy's breath caught in his throat, and he pressed his lips against her neck, nipping her painfully as she caressed him. "God, woman," he breathed.

"Maggie said you were good," she whispered.

His head came up instantly, and he stared at her suspiciously.

"She remembers," Jennifer breathed. "She said you were g—"

"You're lyin'!" he rasped.

"No! Why do you think I came to you? She told me what you could do for me."

After a moment a lazy, impassioned smile turned his lips and his hand moved to her neck. "You're too prim to say the words, aren't you? Did *she?* Did Maggie? Did she tell you how I can make a woman scream when she comes?" In the next moment, however, his smile disappeared as he remembered back more than ten years and realized that this woman's sister had not screamed in climax. This woman's sister had been unconscious. "You bitch!" he hissed, realizing he had been stupid.

Silas chose that moment to drop from above. Unfortunately, he did little other than knock Tandy to the ground. When he gained his own footing, Si noticed fearfully that Jennifer had gone down along with the other man. "Get away from her!" he screamed as he raised his mallet to the ready position.

Violence from the boy was not necessary, however, as Gerome darted from within the blackness of the empty stall. It took only Gerome's superior weight, and a knee in Tandy's back, to have the man subdued, facedown on the stable floor. "Help Jennifer up," Gerome told Silas. "And get her to the house."

They stopped along the way while Jennifer was relieved of the contents of her stomach.

"I'll get Chad," Silas said worriedly.

"No! I'm all right. I don't want him upset."

Silas was stunned into a moment of silence. "You think he's not going to be *upset?*" he asked in wonder.

Jennifer's smile possessed a good measure of worry. "Perhaps a little."

"A little?" he returned. "Jen, you don't know much about that man."

"I don't know whether to shake you, spank you, or hug you," Chad said several hours later.

The excitement was over. Tandy had been taken away and would stand trial for, at minimum, the rape of young Maggie Downing. As soon as Gerome had explained what had taken place, Chad had sent word to the authorities and to Hunter Maguire. Hunter had walked into the barn where Tandy was being held and convinced Gerome to unlock the stall door that held the man prisoner. The moment the portal swung outward, Hunter stepped inside and felled Tandy with a mighty blow to the chin.

"You're fortunate I'm not going to kill you," Hunter said. "But I won't hang and leave my Maggie alone because of the likes of you," he added before he turned and walked away.

Now that they were finally alone, Jennifer's thoughts were taking over, and the impact of what she had done was causing her to shake. "I know you're angry, darling, but please—"

"Angry?" he said as he moved toward her; his throat was so dry with raw fear he could barely speak. "Every time I think about what could have happened to you I—"

"But nothing happened," she said quietly as he stopped in front of her.

"That's not the point."

"I know."

He stared at her for a moment, feeling his anger drain slowly away as she smiled miserably at him. "Aw, Jen."

"I'm shaking," she whispered. "I need you to hold me."

A worried frown creased his brow as Chad quickly positioned his chair so that he could transfer to the sofa. "Move down, love," he told her, and when she had shifted along, he swung his lower body onto the place that she had warmed. "Come here," he said wearily and pulled her into his arms.

Jennifer shifted until she could half lie against him, bending her knees and bringing her feet up to hide under her skirt. Her arms tightened around his back as she buried her face against his chest.

"Dammit, Jen," he said softly as a severe shudder rippled through her body.

"That sounds like a love word," she said, her words muffled against his shirt front.

"Dammit?" he asked in confusion.

"Mmm-hmm. It sounds like 'Dammit, I love you, Jen.'"

He laughed softly and pulled her trembling body closer. "That's what it means, all right," he muttered. And then he was calling, "Silas!"

A brief moment later the boy appeared in the open doorway, swallowing a mouthful of belated supper. "Here!" he crowed.

"Run and fetch a quilt, will you?" Chad asked quietly.

Silas frowned, seeing Jennifer curled up like a small, quaking animal. "Is Jen all right?" he asked.

Chad nodded and smiled, trying to relieve the boy's concern. "Just a little case of aftermath shakes," he said. He sincerely hoped that was all that was wrong.

Silas charged from the room.

"He's a good boy," Jennifer whispered wearily.

Chad's head lowered and tipped to the side in a vain attempt to see her face. "Are you falling asleep?"

"I think so," she muttered.

There was little use in his roaring in anger; she had done what she had to do. How could he fault her for that? And yet, when he had learned of the incident, Chad had almost been ill with fear. Only the fact that Jennifer had been standing in front of him, trying bravely to smile, had prevented him from losing his breakfast.

He tried now to turn his thoughts from what might have been. She was here and she was safe. *If* she was well. That thought had been plaguing him also.

When Silas returned with a down-filled quilt, Chad took the thing and whispered, "Ask Gerome to go for the doctor."

And when the boy blanched with concern, Chad took hold of his small hand and explained quietly, "Just to be certain, Si. Jen's all right, really."

"Then we don't need a doctor," Silas whispered in return.

"Just to be certain," he whispered again.

Silas was not gone long before Chad looked up to see him standing again in the doorway.

"Come sit with us," he told the boy.

Si moved quietly into the room and dropped to his knees near Chad's legs. He looked at the blanket-wrapped Jennifer, seeing only the back of her head. "Is she sleeping?" he whispered.

Chad nodded.

"Has she stopped shaking?"

"Yes. I think she's fine now. She's just very tired from her very *busy* day," he said pointedly.

Silas looked up guiltily. "Are you mad because I helped her?"

"I suppose, all in all, I'm grateful you were there," Chad admitted.

Silas felt a flash of pride, and his chest swelled out just a bit. "Really?"

"And if you ever let her talk you into another such harebrained scheme," he said fondly, "I'll paddle your backside."

The boy looked truly concerned for a moment, and then he caught a flash of understanding in Chad's eyes. Leaning forward, Si pressed his forearms into the padding of the settee at Jennifer's back. "I love her, you know?" he whispered as he tried to see her face.

Chad felt his heart go warm and moisture gather in his eyes. "I know that, son," he said softly.

It took a moment of concentrated thought and effort before Silas could raise his head and look Chad in the eye. "I love you, too," he said.

"I know."

He swallowed painfully and dug his fingers into a corner of the quilt that covered Jennifer. "I was wonderin' if you could ever forgive me for puttin' you in that chair?" he asked brokenly.

Chad reached out and gently gripped Si's chin, forcing him to look up. "Son, I forgave you a long, long time ago," he said. "You only had to ask."

# CHAPTER
## TWENTY-TWO

Jennifer was none the worse for her experience, although she paid the price of Chad's disapproval; he refused to make love to her for a week!

When he gathered her against his side and forced her hands away from him for the sixth night in a row, Jennifer rebelled.

"The doctor said I am fine," she said firmly.

"I'm beginning to believe you are."

"Are you going to punish me for the rest of my life?" she asked as she leaned over him in their bed.

"Probably not," he said wryly.

"Because if you are, I'll—" She stopped, blinking stupidly as she realized what he had said. "You're not?"

Chad shook his head. "Don't think I can stand another minute without you," he teased.

She cuffed his shoulder.

"Don't hit me. I'm in a delicate condition."

"*You* are?" She laughed, falling on his chest.

"I need you, Jen," he whispered.

Jennifer's eyes took on a mischievous glow as her hand slinked down the length of his torso. "So you do," she muttered.

"I didn't keep myself from you to be mean," he said hopefully.

"Really?"

Chad drew in a long breath and pressed his head back into the pillow as her delicate fingers wrapped around him. "Really," he breathed.

"You thought it was in my best interest?" she prodded.

"Yes."

"Cow-chips," she said bluntly.

"Jennifer!" He laughed.

"You wanted to be certain I was all right?" she asked.

"I did."

"And the baby?" she added.

"Correct."

"I don't think you're that damned noble, Mr. Moran," she whispered before pressing her lips against his.

"You have a very foul mouth, Mrs. Moran," he breathed lovingly as he pulled her on top of his body.

"What are you doing?" Chad asked as he returned to their bedroom.

"Pacing," Jennifer said succinctly as she turned and walked away from him. "It's so hot, Chad," she said miserably. "I was hoping the worst of the heat would be over by now."

"I've sent for the doctor," he told her, positioning his chair out of her way.

"And Maggie?"

"And Maggie. Jennifer, shouldn't you be lying down?"

She turned back, smiling at his concern as she crossed the room once more. "Maggie told me everyone wanted to put her to bed at the first sign of her labor. Hunter told them to let her walk around, if that's what she wanted to do. She did and it helped. So I'm walking."

Chad nodded but he was not at all certain about this. What was good for Maggie may not be good for Jen. And he was wishing the woman would get here. Hunter, too. He could use the moral support of a more experienced man.

Jennifer grinned as she stood beside him and bent to kiss his forehead. "Don't worry, darling," she said. But as she straightened, a band began to tighten around her back and her belly, and she steadied herself by gripping Chad's shoulder. "It's another . . ." She groaned through clenched teeth.

Chad's fear was instantly squelched as he strove to concentrate on Jennifer's needs. He gripped her free hand and held on as he took a quick look at the bedside clock to time her contractions. "Breathe," he reminded her. And when she let out a *whoosh* of pent-up breath, he added, "They're getting closer together. Seven minutes."

"Whew," she breathed. "That one hurt."

They all hurt, as far as he was concerned. Her belly got so tight it was like a huge rock. Placing his hands on her, Chad pressed his lips against the spot where their child labored. "Be easy, son," he whispered. "Go easy on your mother."

He *was* so loving and so worried. Jennifer smiled down at him, finger-combing his hair back from his forehead. "A little pain won't hurt me, darling," she said.

Chad's head snapped back, and he frowned up at her. "A *little?*" he asked incredulously.

"Certainly. And I'll forget it all after the baby is here. Maggie forgot between babies."

"But you're suffering *now*, Jen." And he didn't like it, not one bit. Her hard labor hadn't even started, and already Chad was swearing to himself that she would never go through this again.

Jennifer placed both hands on the small of her aching back and paced away from him.

Silas did not know what had awakened him, but the moment he stepped out of his room, he was drawn toward the light from the master bedroom. "What's going on?" he asked sleepily.

Jennifer turned toward the doorway and smiled. "We're having a baby," she said. "Come in."

The boy's eyes grew positively huge as he darted a startled glance toward Chad. "Wow," he breathed.

Things accelerated very quickly after that. Maggie and Hunter arrived, and Silas was turned out of the large bedroom.

Hunter took the boy down to Chad's study, away from the commotion.

"It's really hurting her," Silas muttered. "It's making Chad real upset."

Hunter's large hand squeezed Si's shoulder reassuringly. "They'll both get over it soon enough, son."

Maggie was preparing the bed while Jennifer watched, leaning on Chad's shoulder for support. "Mag, you're doing all right, aren't you?" she asked.

Maggie looked up from her chore and smiled softly. She understood the question and nodded her head. They had talked frequently about Charles Tandy and how Maggie was feeling about the "accident" of years ago coming to light. Now there was little that was not known by everyone close to her. And now there was little that was not known by Maggie herself. Tandy had admitted to "playing" with more than his share of the women in the area over the years. He relished in the details and also claimed that the women lauded his talents. He admitted to sporting the Moran ring whenever he had been out to impress a lady. It had made him feel good, he said. It had made him feel big and important. Like the Morans. And he had found it great sport when "old man Moran" would claim the thing missing, only to have it found again. On occasion Tandy had kept the expensive piece of jewelry for weeks or months. The *ring*. The ring worn on a hand that had savagely struck and scarred Maggie Downing Maguire for life. But Maggie's response to these discussions and the concern of her family was always the same: "I have Hunter beside me," she would say. Now they all knew that Charles was going to prison, but the sentence for his violence was not nearly satisfying enough.

Jennifer was rocked by a severe contraction just as the doctor arrived in the room.

"Time to take to your bed, Jennifer," he said. Dr. Hubert Cook was a man of sixty, a trusted friend, and the man who had delivered Maggie's children, along with countless others.

Chad backed off, remaining out of the way as they made his young wife as comfortable as possible. But Jennifer continued to stare at him, looking to him for moral support, and he gave it. His only desire, in that moment, was that he could do more. Maggie stepped between them, blocking their view of each other, and he said, "I'm here, Jen."

They had talked about this—whether Chad would remain with her. He wanted to be there, and to hell with convention. And Jennifer wanted him near her. Dr. Cook had already agreed.

Jennifer's hard labor extended into two hours before she screamed as her body gave up their son.

"A boy!" Dr. Cook crowed as he laid the child on Jennifer's belly.

Chad was laughing as tears of relief washed down his cheeks. He held Jennifer's hand and watched her hesitantly reach out and touch their son. "Oh, Jen," he breathed. He looked at her then. She was crying but smiling brightly, and Chad pressed his cheek next to hers. "It's difficult to believe," he whispered. "I love you," he said before kissing her damp cheek.

And then Maggie was taking the baby away to wash him, and Jennifer's body twisted painfully again. This time she gave up the afterbirth and then drifted back against the pillows in exhaustion. The last thing she remembered, before being pulled into much needed sleep, was Maggie gently placing her son in her husband's arms.

As soon as he knew all was well, when Jennifer and his son were comfortable and sleeping, Chad silently left the master bedroom and made his way downstairs.

Hunter took one look at him and turned to pour a healthy portion of brandy.

Si's eyes narrowed in disbelief. "You look awful," he said bluntly.

Chad smiled wryly. "Thanks," he said.

"Everyone is fine up there?" Hunter asked as he gave over the drink. They had already been told that Chad and Jennifer had a son.

"Fine," Chad said simply before tipping up the brandy snifter.

"Jen's really okay?" Silas asked.

And then Chad remembered how hard the waiting must have been for him. He reached for the boy's hand and looked at him. "Jen is all right, Si," he said earnestly. "She's sleeping now."

Silas seemed to wilt, quickly dropping wearily into a chair.

Maggie took over the running of the house that day, and her first orders were extended to Silas and Chad. "To bed and to sleep. Both of you," she said.

But Chad could not sleep. He took up residence in the guest bedroom that day, but the room and the bed were sadly lacking.

Jennifer wasn't there.

A few hours later he wheeled his chair into the master bedroom, determined not to wake her, but as he moved his chair next to the bed, Jennifer was smiling at him. "Hello, sweetheart," he said softly.

"Hello," she returned, and then her gaze dropped to the child in her arms; she was holding their son against her breast.

Chad was somewhat surprised by this, but it was a beautiful sight. "Do you have milk?"

She shook her head. "Not yet."

Chad's head bowed and he reached for her hand. "Jennifer," he choked. "You'll never know how happy I am."

She smiled softly. "I think I have a vague notion, darling."

"A short time ago . . ." He hadn't thought ever to see this day. Ever to have a loving wife and a son lying in her arms.

"I know, Chad," she whispered and squeezed his hand, hard.

And when he raised his head, he was crying without shame.

"Oh, Chad," she said, tugging on his hand until he bent to her, and she kissed him tenderly.

# ❧ EPILOGUE

"Lord, he's being greedy tonight," Chad complained.

Jennifer laughed and gave her son a delicate pat on his diapered bottom. "He's greedy every night," she said.

They were in the pretty blue nursery of their new home in Richmond, and the day had been long, for all the satisfaction they had derived.

Chad joined her here every evening while she nursed baby James and before they adjourned to their own room. It was a quiet time for them; time alone to talk quietly about the events of their days. He had reopened his law practice, and business was growing steadily and to his satisfaction. "Do you miss your family very much, Jen?" he asked as his fingers absently stroked her knee.

"My family is here," she said.

"But you miss Maggie and Hunter and the children," he said knowingly.

Jennifer shook her head. "Of course I miss them, but they aren't that far away, darling. We'll visit. And Florence and Mark will be coming to stay for a bit." Her sister had married shortly after James had been born. "And I won't be lonely with my *three* men around me," she said lightly.

Silas was now legally a member of the family. They had appeared that day in the chambers of Judge Herbert Lang.

"Come around here, son," Judge Lang had said to Silas.

The boy had walked hesitantly around the large desk until he was standing directly in front of the white-haired man. "Sir?"

The judge had blinked at that; he didn't recall Silas being nearly so polite just over a year ago. In fact, *that* boy had not possessed the social skills required even to imitate politeness. "I want you to tell me how things have gone for you," the judge had said.

"Well," Silas drawled, looking across the desk at Chad and Jennifer for support. "Chad and Jennifer got married," he said.

Patiently, Judge Lang nodded and continued to listen.

"So, now we have James," Si added.

The judge smiled. "And how do you feel about James?"

"He sleeps mostly, but he's interestin' to watch sometimes."

"Do you understand why we're here today?" the judge asked.

Silas nodded his head and smiled. "Sure. Chad and Jennifer are going to adopt me."

"And that's all right with you? Do you think you'll be happy living with this family?"

"Yep." He leaned forward conspiratorily. "Could you change my name to Moran, Judge?"

Herbert Lang picked up a very formal-looking document from atop his desk. "That's what this paper is, son," he said patiently. "When I sign this, you will become the son of these people. And this paper," he added, nodding to a second page, "will change your name to Moran."

Silas studied the two documents for a moment before looking at the older man. "Will you sign them, please?" he asked hopefully.

This time the judge smiled as he reached for a straight-nibbed pen.

Jennifer and Chad smiled at each other, and Chad welcomed Silas back to his side as the final documents were signed.

"Judge Lang," Jennifer said quietly, when the papers were given to her husband, "could we talk about those terrible steps at the front of the courthouse?"

Chad watched as Jennifer laid their son in his cradle and lovingly stroked the baby's cheek.

"Now that you have Judge Lang's promise of a ramp for the courthouse, what will be your next target?" he teased.

"Every building in this town that presents a problem for you will be a target," she said seriously.

Chad shook his head and smiled. It was something she wanted to do; *had* to do. And how could he be anything but proud? But he also knew that his loving wife would never raise the consciousness of a nation in her lifetime. In both their lifetimes added together, for that matter. There would be benefits to many because of her efforts, and there would be disappointments for Jen. "Jen, you'll never manage."

"Watch me," she said succinctly as she drew a small blanket over her son. "I'm determined," she added.

*That* was something he knew and knew well.

She turned toward him then, and the smile she had for him was secretive, seductive, as she slowly walked across the room to him. "Now it's just you and me, Mr. Moran."

He grinned as he pulled her onto his lap. "It seems there is never enough of 'just you and me,'" he said.

"Well, we have two sons now," she reminded him. "But I'm confident we can work something out. For example," she whispered against his ear, "now is the time for you to take me to bed."

Chad needed no second request.

He settled himself in their large bed as Jennifer tended to the fire. When he looked across the room, she had turned to face him, and his heart began to thunder in his chest as he stared at her in anticipation. "I love you beyond the meager trappings of this earth and this body," he said raggedly. "I hope you understand . . . it would be humanly impossible for anyone to love as deeply and as fiercely as I do."

With a slow smile Jennifer shrugged her white cotton nightdress from her shoulders, and it pooled at her feet. "Oh, yes, my darling. It is entirely possible."

## ROMANCE FROM THE HEART OF AMERICA

### Diamond Homespun Romance

*Homespun novels are touching, captivating romances from the heartland of America that combine the laughter and tears of family life with the tender warmth of true love.*

___ WINTER SONG     1-55773-958-7/$4.99
     by Karen Lockwood

___ MOUNTAIN MAGIC 1-55773-964-1/$4.99
     by Suzanna Gray

___ WEDDING BELLS   1-55773-971-4/$4.99
     by Lydia Browne

___ ALMOST HOME     1-55773-978-1/$4.99
     by Debra S. Cowan

___ SWEET LULLABY   1-55773-987-0/$4.99
     by Lorraine Heath

___ YOURS TRULY      0-7865-0001-8/$4.99
     by Sharon Harlow

___ SUMMER'S GIFT    0-7865-0006-9/$4.99
     by Deborah Wood

___ FAMILY REUNION  0-7865-0011-5/$4.99
     by Jill Metcalf

___ PICKETT'S FENCE  0-7865-0017-4/$4.99
     by Linda Shertzer (July)

# FREE Romance

*(a $4.50 value)*

## Send in the Coupon Below

To get your FREE historical romance and start saving, fill out the coupon below and mail it today. As soon as we receive it we'll send you your FREE Book along with your first month's selections.

---